W9-AZM-527

EMMA
IN THE
NIGHT

Also by Wendy Walker

All Is Not Forgotten

EMMA
IN THE
NIGHT

Wendy Walker

St. Martin's Press
New York

EMMA IN THE NIGHT. Copyright © 2017 by Wendy Walker. All rights reserved. Printed in the United States of America. For information address St. Martin's Press, 175 Fifth Avenue, New York, N.Y. 10010.

ISBN 978-1-68331-632-9

For my sisters and brother–
Becky, Cheryl, Jennifer, and Grant

EMMA
IN THE
NIGHT

According to the Greek myth, Narcissus was a hunter who was exceptionally beautiful and proud. He was so proud, in fact, that he rejected anyone who tried to love him. Nemesis, the goddess of revenge, decided to punish Narcissus. She lured him to a pool of water where he was able to see his own reflection. He fell madly in love with himself and stared at his reflection until he died.

ONE

Cassandra Tanner—Day One of My Return

We believe what we want to believe. We believe what we need to believe. Maybe there's no difference between wanting and needing. I don't know. What I do know is that the truth can evade us, hiding behind our blind spots, our preconceptions, our hungry hearts that long for quiet. Still, it is always there if we open our eyes and try to see it. If we really try to see.

When my sister and I disappeared three years ago, there was nothing but blindness.

They found Emma's car at the beach. They found her purse inside, on the driver's seat. They found the keys in the purse. They found her shoes in the surf. Some people believed she had gone there to find a party or meet a friend who never showed. They believed that she'd gone for a swim. They believed that she'd drowned. Maybe by accident. Maybe a suicide.

Everyone believed Emma was dead.

As for me, well—it was not as simple as that.

I was fifteen when I disappeared. Emma would never have taken me to the beach with her when I was fifteen. She was a senior in high school and I was a nuisance. My purse was in the kitchen.

Nothing of mine was found at the beach. None of my clothes were even missing from the house, according to my mother. And mothers know things like that. Don't they?

But they found my hair in Emma's car and some people clung to this, even though I had been in her car countless times. They clung to it anyway because if I had not gone to the beach with Emma, if I had not drowned in the ocean that night, maybe running in to save her, then where was I? Some people needed to believe I was dead because it was too hard to wonder.

Others were not so sure. Their minds were open to the possibility of a bizarre coincidence. One sister drowned at the beach. One sister run away, or perhaps abducted. But then . . . runaways usually pack a bag. She must have been abducted. But then . . . bad things like that didn't happen to people like us.

It had not been an ordinary night, and this fueled the coincidence theories. My mother told them the story in a way that captivated audiences and gathered enough sympathy to quench her thirst for attention. I could see it in her eyes as I watched her on the news channels and talk shows. She described the fight between me and Emma, the shrill screaming and crying of teenage girls. Then the silence. Then the car leaving the property after curfew. She'd seen the headlights from her bedroom window. Tears were shed as she told the story, a collective sigh echoing throughout the studio audience.

Our lives were pulled apart in search of answers. Social media, friends, text messages and diaries. Everything was scrutinized. She told them how we had been fighting about a necklace. *I bought it for Emma for the start of school. Her senior year! That's such a special time. Cass was jealous. She was always so jealous of her sister.*

This was followed by more tears.

The beach faces the Long Island Sound. There is not much of

a current. At low tide, you have to walk a long while to get in over your knees. At high tide, the water rolls so gently, you can hardly feel its pull against your ankles, and your feet don't sink into the sand with every wave the way they do at the beaches up the coast that face the Atlantic. It is not easy to drown at our beach.

I remember watching my mother on the TV, words coming out of her mouth, tears coming out of her eyes. She had bought new clothes for the occasion, a tailored suit, dark gray, and shoes by an Italian designer who she told us was *the best* and *a statement of our status in the world*. I could tell by the shape of the toe. She had taught us a lot about shoes. I don't think it was because of the shoes that everyone wanted to believe her. But they did. I could feel it coming through the television.

Perhaps we crumbled under the pressure at our private school. Maybe it was some kind of suicide pact. Maybe we'd filled our pockets with rocks and walked slowly into our watery graves like Virginia Woolf.

But then, where were our bodies?

It took six weeks and four days for the story to stop leading the news shows. My celebrity mother went back to being plain old Judy Martin—or Mrs. Jonathan Martin, as she preferred to be called—formerly Mrs. Owen Tanner, formerly Judith Luanne York. It's not as complicated as it sounds. York was her maiden name before she took the names of her two husbands. Two husbands are not a lot of husbands these days.

Emma and I came from the first one—Owen Tanner. Emma was named after my father's mother, who died of a bad heart when he was seventeen. My name, Cassandra (Cass for short), came from a baby book my mother had. She said it sounded like the name of someone important. Someone people admired. Someone people envied. I don't know about any of that. But I remember her brushing my long hair in front of her bathroom mirror, admiring me with a satisfied smile.

Look at you, Cassandra! You should never be without a mirror to remind yourself how beautiful you are.

Our mother never told Emma she was beautiful. They were too much alike for words of affection to pass between them. Praising someone who looks the same or acts the same or is wearing the same clothes is like praising yourself and yet it doesn't feel that way. Instead it feels diminishing, like that other person has stolen praise that should have come your way. Our mother would never allow Emma to steal something as valuable as praise.

But she said it to me. She said I had the best of both gene pools. She was very knowledgeable about these things—things like how children got blue eyes or brown eyes or math brains or music brains.

By the time you have children, Cassandra, you might be able to choose nearly every trait! Can you imagine? Oh, how different my life could have been if those scientists had worked a little faster! [sigh].

I didn't know what she meant then. I was only seven. But when she brushed my hair like that, when she shared her secret thoughts, I listened with great interest because it would fill me with joy from my toes to my eyebrows and I never wanted it to end.

But it always did. Our mother knew how to keep us hungry for her.

When we were young like that, she would ask us if she was pretty, the prettiest girl we'd ever seen, and if she was smart, the smartest woman we'd ever known, and then, of course—

Am I a good mother? The best mother you could ever want?

She always smiled big and wide eyed when she asked. And when we were young, Emma and I, we would tell her yes in our most sincere voices. She would gasp, shake her head and finally squeeze us so hard, like the excitement at being so wonderful was too much to contain, like she had to wring it from her body with some kind of physical exertion. After the squeezing came a long sigh to exhale the excitement she'd freed from her bones. The excitement would exit her body on hot breath and fill the entire room, leaving her quietly satisfied.

Other times, when she was sad or angry at the world for being cruel to her, for not seeing how special she was, we would be the ones to say it, knowing it would bring her back from her dark place.

You're the best mother in the whole wide world!

And we believed it, Emma and I, when we were young like that.

I remember these moments in bits and pieces that won't fit together anymore, like sections of shattered glass that have been weathered, their edges smoothed. Strong arms squeezing hard. The smell of her skin. She wore Chanel No. 5, which she told us was very expensive. We were not allowed to touch the bottle, but sometimes she would hold it for us while we inhaled the fragrance from the top of the sprayer.

Other fragments contain the sound of her voice as she screamed and thrashed around on her bed, tears wetting the sheets. Me hiding behind Emma. Emma staring quietly, studying her, making calculations. Waking up to our mother's elation. Waking up to her despair. I remember, too, this feeling I would have. It is not attached to any particular moment. It's just a memory of a feeling. Opening my eyes each morning, fearful because I had no idea what awaited us that day. If she would hug us. If she would brush my hair. Or if she would cry into her sheets. It was like trying to pick your clothes without even knowing what season it was, winter or summer.

When Emma was ten and I was eight, our mother's spell started to fade in the bright light of the outside world—the real world, where she was not that pretty, or that smart, or that good a mother. Emma had begun to notice things about her and she would tell me when she felt like it.

She was wrong, you know. It didn't matter what followed, whether it was some opinion our mother had about another mother from our school, or a fact about George Washington, or what kind of dog had just crossed the road. What mattered was that she was wrong, and every time she was wrong, our voices grew less sincere when we answered her.

Aren't I a good mother? The best mother you could ever want?

We never stopped saying the word. *Yes.* But when I was eight and Emma was ten, she knew we were lying.

We were in the kitchen that day. She was mad at our father. I can't remember why.

He has no idea how lucky he is! I could have any man I want. You girls know that! My girls know.

She busied herself with some dishes. Faucet on. Faucet off. The dish towel fell to the floor. She picked it up. Emma stood on the other side of a giant island. I stood beside her, my shoulder tucked in next to hers, and I leaned toward her so I could disappear behind her body if I needed to. Emma felt so strong to me then, as we waited to see which season it would be. Whether it would be summer or winter.

Our mother started to cry. She turned to look at us.

What did you say?

Yes. We answered as we always did when she asked us if she was the best mother.

We walked to her side, waiting for our hug and the smile and the sigh. But none of that came. Instead, she pushed us both away, one hand on my chest and one hand on Emma's. She studied our faces incredulously. Then she gasped, breath going in, not out.

Go to your rooms. Right now!

We did as we were told. We went to our rooms. I tried to talk to Emma, I remember asking her as we walked upstairs, Emma storming and me scurrying, *What did we do?* But Emma talked about our mother only when she wanted to—when she had something to say. The story of our mother would be written by her, and her alone. She pushed my hand from her arm and told me to shut up.

We did not get any dinner. Or any hugs. Or any kisses good night. The price for these things, for our mother's affection, went up that night and in the years that followed. The things we had to say and do to convince her of our admiration inflated the more we said and did them—inflated and also changed so that her love became scarce.

A few years later, when I was eleven, I looked up my name, *Cassandra*, when I saw it in a book about myths. It actually comes from Greek mythology, the daughter of King Priam and Queen Hecuba of Troy: "Cassandra had the gift of prophecy but the curse that her prophecies would never be believed." I stared at my computer screen for a long time. My mind had run away. Suddenly, the entire Universe made sense and it was all centered around me, how my mother had given me this name, but really it must have been fate. Fate, or God, or whatever—he had entered my mother's mind and put this name in her head. He knew what was coming. He knew that I would predict the future and that no one would believe me. Children have a way of believing in fantasies. I now know that my mother naming me Cassandra and what happened to us was nothing more than a random concurrence of events. But at the time, when I was eleven, I felt responsible for all that would happen.

That was the year of my parents' divorce. That was the year I told them what I knew—that I could see what was going to happen. I told them that Emma and I should not live with our mother and her new boyfriend, Mr. Martin, and his only child—a son named Hunter.

My parents' divorce was not a surprise to me. Emma said she wasn't surprised either, but I didn't believe her. She cried too much for that to be true. Everyone thought Emma was tough, that nothing bothered her. People were always wrong about Emma because she could react to upsetting things with an unsettling hardness. She had dark hair, like our mother, and her skin was very soft and pale. When she was a teenager, she discovered bright red lip gloss and dark black eye shadow, and how she could hide behind them like paint covering a wall. She would wear short skirts and tight sweaters, mostly black turtlenecks. I don't have just one word to describe how I saw her. She was beautiful, severe, tortured, vulnerable, desperate, ruthless. And I admired her and envied her and drank in every moment she would give any piece of herself to me.

Most of the pieces were small. Many of them were meant to hurt me or exclude me or win points with our mother. But sometimes, when our mother was asleep and the house was quiet, Emma would come to my room and crawl into my bed. She would get under the covers and lie very close to me, and, sometimes, she would wrap her arms around me and press her cheek into my shoulder. It was then that she would tell me things that fed me and kept me warm and made me feel safe even when I woke up to our mother's winter mood. *Someday it will just be the two of us,*

Cass. You and me and no one else. I can remember her smell, the warmth of her breath, the strength of her arms. *We'll go wherever we want and we'll never let her in. We won't even care anymore.* I can still hear her voice, my sister whispering to me in the night. *I love you, Cass.* When she said these things to me, I thought nothing could ever touch us.

I let Emma convince me to betray our mother during the divorce. She could see the next move of every player on the board. She could change their course by changing her own. She was responsive, adaptable. And she was never committed to any particular outcome except her own self-preservation.

Cass, we need to live with Daddy. Don't you see? He will be so sad without us. Mom has Mr. Martin. Dad only has us. Do you understand? We have to do something and do it now! Or it will be too late!

Emma didn't have to tell me this. I understood all of it. Our mother's boyfriend, Mr. Martin, moved into our father's house the second our father moved out. His son, Hunter, went to boarding school, but he lived with us when he came home for vacations and weekends, and he came home a lot. Mr. Martin's ex-wife had moved to California a long time before we ever knew them. Mr. Martin was "semiretired," which meant he'd made a lot of money and now played a lot of golf.

I could see that our mother never loved our father, Owen Tanner. She ignored him so glaringly and with such indifference that it became difficult just to look at him, to look at the pain that radiated from his body. So, yes, our father was sad.

I told Emma that I could see our father's sadness. What I didn't tell Emma was that I could see other things as well. I could see the way Mr. Martin's son looked at Emma when he came home from school, and the way Mr. Martin looked at his son looking at Emma, and the way our mother looked at Mr. Martin when he was looking at them. And I could see that this was going to result in a bad future.

But seeing the future is a worthless gift if you don't have the power to change it.

And so when the woman from the court asked me, I said I wanted to live with my father. I said that I thought things would be bad in our house with Mr. Martin and his son. I think Emma was surprised by my courage, or perhaps taken aback at what she perceived to be her influence over me. In any case, when I made this move on the board, she adjusted her course and sided with our mother, sealing forever her position as the most favored child. I never saw it coming. Everyone believed her and no one believed me because I was only eleven and Emma was thirteen. And because Emma was Emma and I was me.

Our mother was irate because the people I had told this to could have made it so that we didn't have to live with her. How could she be the best mother in the world if she didn't have any children left? When she finally won, I found out just how angry she was.

After everything I've done for you! I knew you never loved me!

She was wrong about that. I did love her. But she never brushed my hair again.

And don't ever call me Mother again! To you, I'm Mrs. Martin!

After the dust had settled from the divorce, Emma and our mother would dance together in the kitchen as they baked chocolate cake. They would laugh hysterically at YouTube videos of cats playing the piano or toddlers walking into walls by mistake. They went shopping for shoes on Saturdays, watched *Real Housewives* on Sundays. And they fought almost every day, loud, screaming, swearing fighting—the kind of fighting that seemed to me, even after years of watching them, to be terminal. But the next day, sometimes the same day, they would again be laughing as if nothing had happened. No apologies were made. No discussions about how they could get along better. No boundaries for the future. They would just carry on.

It took me a long time to understand their relationship. I was always willing to pay the price for her love, whatever price she decided to set. But Emma knew something I didn't. She knew that our mother needed our love as much as we needed hers, maybe even more. And she knew that if she threatened to take it away, to raise the price on her affection, our mother would be willing to negotiate. Back and forth, they made their trades, resetting the terms almost daily. And always looking for ways to improve their power at the bargaining table.

I became the outsider. I may have been beautiful, as my mother said, but I was beautiful like a doll, like a lifeless thing people look at once before moving on. Emma and our mother had something else, something that drew people in. And so they were fierce competitors in their secret club, for each other's love, for the love of everyone around them. And all I could do was watch from a distance, one short enough that I could see the escalation. Two nation-states in a constant battle for power and control. It was unsustainable. And so it continued, this war between my mother and my sister, until the night we were gone.

I remember the feeling I had the day I returned. Having made my way to Mrs. Martin's house—to my house, I guess (though it did not feel like my house after being away for so long)—on a Sunday morning in July, I stood frozen outside in the woods. I had thought about my return relentlessly for three years. Memories had filled my dreams at night. Lavender soap and fresh mint in cold iced tea. Chanel No. 5. Mr. Martin's cigars. Cut grass, fall leaves. The feel of my father's arms around me. Fear had run away with my thoughts during the day. They would all want to know where I'd been, and how I came to be missing. And they would want to know about Emma.

The night we disappeared haunted me. Every detail played over and over and over. Regret lived inside my body, eating me alive. I had thought about how to tell them, how to explain it. There had been time, too much time, to construct the story in a way they would be able to comprehend. I had thought it through, then unraveled it, then thought it through again, self-doubt and self-loathing erasing and rewriting the script. A story is more than the recounting of events. The events are the sketch, the outline, but it is the colors and the landscape and the medium and the artist's hand that make it what it is in the end.

I had to be a good artist. I had to find talent where none existed and tell this story in a way they would believe. I had to set aside my own feelings about the past. About my mother and Emma. Mrs. Martin and Mr. Martin. Me and Emma. I loved my mother and my sister in spite of my selfish, petty feelings. But people don't understand any of that. I had to not be selfish and foolish. I had to be the person they wanted me to be. I had nothing with me but the clothes on my body. I had no evidence. No credibility except for the fact of my own existence.

I stood frozen in the woods, filled with terror that I would fail. And there was so much at stake. They had to believe my story. They had to find Emma. And to find Emma, they had to look for her. It was all on me, finding my sister.

They had to believe me that Emma was still alive.

TWO

Dr. Abigail Winter, Forensic Psychologist, Federal Bureau of Investigation

Abby lay in bed, staring at the ceiling, contemplating the extent of her defeat. It was six o'clock on a Sunday morning, mid-July. The sun was up, pouring light into her room through sheer curtains. Her clothes were strewn across the floor, shed in an effort to find comfort in the thick summer heat. The air conditioner had begun clanking again, and she'd chosen quiet over cool. But now even the sheets felt like a burden against her skin.

Her head pounded. Her mouth was dry. The smell of scotch from an empty glass turned her stomach. Two drinks at midnight had overpowered her restless mind and brought her a few hours of relief. And a hangover, apparently.

At the foot of the bed, a dog moaned and raised his head.

"Don't look at me like that," she said. "It was worth it."

Three hours would get her through a day of catching up on paperwork. She had reports due on two cases and corrections to a deposition she'd given back in February—as if she would have any memory of what she'd said that long ago about anything.

Still, this was no victory over her mind—the mind that controlled her body, and sometimes seemed intent on destroying it.

The contemplation was interrupted by her phone ringing on the nightstand.

Her body ached as she reached for it beside the empty glass. She didn't recognize the number.

"This is Abby." She sat up and tugged on a twisted sheet to cover her body.

"Hey, kiddo—it's Leo."

"Leo?" She sat up straighter. Pulled the sheet higher. Only one person called her "kiddo" at age thirty-two, and that was Special Agent Leo Strauss. They hadn't worked together for over a year. Not since he'd transferred to New York to be closer to his grand-children. Still, his voice reached into her very core. He had been like family.

"Listen. Just listen," he said. "I know it's been a while."

"What's going on?" Abby's face drew tight.

"Cassandra Tanner came home."

Abby was on her feet, searching for clean clothes. "When?"

"Half an hour, maybe less. Showed up this morning."

Phone pressed between shoulder and ear, Abby pulled on a shirt, then jeans. "Where?"

"The Martin house."

"She went to her mother?"

"She did, not sure what that means . . ."

"Emma?"

"She was alone."

Abby buttoned her shirt, stumbled to the bathroom. She felt the surge of adrenaline, her knees buckling. "I'm heading to the car . . . Christ . . ."

A long silence made her stop. She took the phone in her hand, braced herself on the bathroom sink.

"Leo?"

Abby had not forgotten the Tanner sisters. Not for one minute of one day. The facts of the investigation into their disappearance had lain dormant in the shadowed corners of her mind. But that was not the same as forgetting. They were with her, even after a year of being off the case. They were in her bones. In her flesh. She breathed them in and out with every breath. The missing girls. And the theory of the case that no one else would believe. One call and the dam was broken. All of it was flooding in, sweeping her off her feet.

"Leo? You still there?"

"I'm here."

"They pulled you in from New York?"

"Yeah. You'll get a call from New Haven with the assignment. I wanted to make sure you were okay with it first."

Abby looked up into the mirror as she considered what to say. Things had not ended well when the case got cold.

"I'm working this case, Leo. . . ."

"Okay . . . I just didn't know where you were at. They said you had some counseling. . . ."

Shit. Abby hung her head. It was still there, the anger or maybe frustration, or disappointment. Whatever it was, she could feel it stirred by the concern in his voice.

The Bureau had offered her counseling and she had taken it. "It's normal to feel this way," they told her. *Yes,* Abby had thought at the time. She knew it was normal. *Some cases get under the skin.*

Everyone agreed this case had been maddening. No one knew what to call it at the time. Murder, kidnapping, accident. They'd had an eye on the disappearance from the runaway angle as well— sexual predators, terrorist recruiters, Internet stalkers. Everything was in play. The car at the beach, the shoes of just one of the sisters left by the shore. They'd found nothing to suggest the younger one had been with her except Cass's hair—which could have been left there on any number of occasions. There was nothing to suggest they had planned to run away together. And nothing to suggest foul play, either murder or abduction, of either one. There were no bodies, no suspects, no motives, no strangers on their social media sites or phone logs or text messages or e-mails. Nothing obvious had changed in recent years. The truth is, they might as well have brought in NASA and called it an alien abduction.

But this was not the reason Abby had seen the shrink. She had been doing this work since she finished her PhD nearly eight years ago. There had been other difficult cases. She could see them all when she summoned them. The brutal beating of a prostitute. The execution of a neighborhood drug dealer. The hanging of a dog on the branch of a tree. The list went on and on—cases that were never solved, or never prosecuted, the victims' families, and sometimes the survivors, left choking on the injustice.

There had been relief in talking to another professional. Though Abby had never been a practicing therapist—"I don't have the patience for patients," she used to joke—that did not mean she wasn't a believer. Talking could bring perspective. Talking could dull the edges of the blade. But even after a year of talking and talking, the *endless* talking, the Tanner investigation remained with her. That it cut less deep did not help wrestle the demons it summoned in the dark of night.

And now her sessions with the shrink were coming back to bite her.

"I'm working the case, Leo. . . ."

"Okay, okay . . ."

"What do we know? Has she said anything? . . ."

Abby heard a short sigh as she turned away from the mirror and headed back into the bedroom to find her shoes.

"Nothing, kiddo. She took a shower. Had some food. Now she's resting until we can get there."

"A shower? How did that happen?"

"It was her mother. She wasn't thinking. She almost started the wash—"

"With Cass's clothes? Before forensics? Christ!"

"I know . . . just get moving. Call me from the car."

The phone went quiet again, but this time he was gone.

Shit! Heart racing now, she pulled on a pair of boots, called out to the dog, who followed her through the small ranch house to the kitchen. She poured some food into a bowl. Rubbed his neck. Opened the back door so he could go out.

"Keys, keys . . ." she said out loud, back in the living room, searching. She was frantic to get to the door. To get to her car. To get to Cassandra Tanner.

Her head felt light, her vision starting to blur. Chronic sleep deprivation had its side effects. She stopped and braced herself on the back of a chair.

No one had believed her theory three years ago, not even Leo, and he had been like a father to her. It was one thing to have a cold case. It was another thing to leave stones unturned.

The company shrink listened, but she did not hear. She said things like "I can understand how you feel that way." Classic feeling validation. They taught that in undergraduate psych classes. She would ask what had not been done. She would let Abby ramble on and on about the family, the mother, Judy Martin, the divorce, the new father, Jonathan Martin. And the stepbrother, Hunter. Together, they had deconstructed every piece of the investigation and in a way that was meant to lead Abby to a place of comfort.

The shrink—"You did everything you could."

Abby could still hear the conviction in her voice. She could see the sincerity on her face, even now as Abby closed her eyes to stop the spinning in her head. She took a long breath and exhaled hard, her hand clenched on the wood back of the chair.

Their analysis of the investigation had become Abby's Bible, the verses giving her rambling, desperate thoughts a path to salvation.

Verse number one. The normalcy reported by the outsiders— friends, teachers, the school counselor. Cass envied her older sister. Emma was annoyed by Cass. Cass was quiet but determined. Emma was more free-spirited. Some used the word "undisciplined." But she had been looking at colleges, filling out applications. Everything indicated that she was just biding her time until she could get out of that house.

The shrink—"All of that sounds pretty normal, Abby. They were on time for school. A very prestigious private school. The Soundview Academy. They spent summers at expensive camps, some in Europe. They did sports. Had friends . . ."

Abby had grown impatient with her.

Verse number two. Abby explained that whatever happened to them, they had been vulnerable to it. And that vulnerability had started at home. It always did. In spite of how these stories were depicted in the news, it was not a mystery what lured teenagers from their homes. An acute traumatic event. Chronic neglect, abuse, instability, dysfunction. The dark void of unfulfilled need. The vulnerability to sexual predators, terrorist groups, religious fanatics, antigovernment extremists. The perpetrator found a way to satisfy that need, to give it what it craved. The predator became a drug. The teenager, an addict.

So when the initial frenzy died down, when they realized the girls were long gone and that finding them would require a slow and methodical unraveling of their lives, Abby had turned back to the family.

When she opened her eyes, the room was still. Her keys were there, on the table next to the chair, and she took them in her hand. She walked to the door and let in the harsh sunlight and a burst of hot, oppressive air from the outside.

No one had objected then. In fact, the entire investigation turned inward, on the family, and on the Martin home in particular. Physical forensics were done at the house. Bank accounts, credit cards, phone records were collected and analyzed. Friends and neighbors were interviewed.

Abby could recall the conversations then, at the start of the investigation. "Yes, yes, this is all good information. All good." Teenage girls had gone missing. Where there's smoke, there must be fire—so they looked for the embers close to home.

The girls' father, Owen Tanner, had been happily married to his first wife before they were born. He and his wife had a little boy, Witt. They had a nice house, family money. Owen worked in New York City at an import firm his family owned. They specialized in gourmet foods, which were his passion. He had a healthy trust and didn't need the income, but his wife thought it was good for him to work. Ironically, that's where he'd met Judy York, the sexy brunette with large breasts and a magnetic personality. Owen had hired her to manage the office.

After the affair, his divorce and the new marriage, Judy and Owen had the two girls in four years. According to Owen, Judy had not been an ideal caregiver to her young daughters. She was capable, he'd insisted. But she was not willing. Owen said that she slept twelve hours every night, then watched reality television and shopped for clothes all day. She would open a bottle of wine at five o'clock and finish it by ten when she went to bed, words slurring, that magnetic personality suddenly repulsive. She told him, allegedly, that she had done her part by giving birth.

This had been the first alarm bell.

With her Bible now open, the verses spilling out, Abby bounded to her car as if she could somehow outrun them. None of this would matter now. Because Cassandra Tanner was home. Because soon she would know the truth and whether she'd been right or wrong. Because soon she would know if she could have saved them from whatever it was that had happened.

Agent Leo Strauss had been the lead on the investigation. It had not been their first time working together, so there had been a rapport. He had been her mentor, in work and in life. His family had included her in holiday dinners. His wife, Susan, baked her cakes on her birthday. There had been a bond between them that made it difficult for Abby to hide what she was thinking. How Judy had seduced Owen Tanner. Neglected her children. Had an affair with a man from the country club. About the bitter custody fight. And about the toxic home Judy made for her daughters with Jonathan Martin and his son, Hunter.

Abby had thought the investigation would barrel down this freeway once they had the divorce file and, in particular, the report of the attorney who had been appointed to represent the children. The guardian ad litem, or GAL, as they're called in Connecticut. It was right there in an independent record—the voice of Cassandra Tanner four years before she disappeared. Telling them all that something was not right in that house. Something with Emma and Jonathan Martin and Hunter. To Abby's ear, it was a ghost from the past telling them where to look.

That report had been the second alarm bell. But the forensics had not supported her theory.

Verse number three.

The shrink—"What did you think they would do with this report from the divorce file? After all the forensic evidence came up clean? The house, the phones, the money? All they found was one broken picture frame—isn't that right? Which the mother said resulted from the girls' fight over a necklace?"

She thought they would order psychiatric evaluations. She thought they would conduct more coercive interviews. She thought they would see what she could see.

The shrink—"The woman who wrote that report during the divorce—the GAL—she dismissed Cass's concerns about the Martins, didn't she?"

Yes, she did. But she was an incompetent hack. She dismissed the fears of an eleven-year-old girl, believing her mother instead—believing that girl was lying to help her father.

The shrink—"Because the father, Owen, was so devastated by the affair and the divorce, right? Parents do that in custody fights. Use the children . . ."

Yes, they do. But Owen agreed to settle, to spare the children. Anyone who's worked in that field knows that the person who cares more about the children usually loses. And Owen lost. There was nothing to indicate he had told his daughter to lie.

Then there was the story about the necklace.

Verse number four.

The shrink—"This is when you decided to push for the psychiatric evaluations? When you found out about the necklace?"

Judy Martin told the story to the press. How she bought the necklace, a flying-angel medallion on a silver chain, for Emma and how Cass was bitterly jealous—and how they'd been fighting about it the night they disappeared.

Only that wasn't the truth. Leo interviewed the woman at the store who sold Judy that necklace—a twenty-dollar trinket. The woman was the store's owner, a small shop that catered to teenage girls with overpriced jeans, short miniskirts and trendy throw-away jewelry. She knew the girls and their mother. They'd been shopping there for years, and the mother never failed to express her disdain for the merchandise in a whispered voice that would carry throughout the store.

The woman recalled two encounters with Judy Martin and the necklace. In the first, Judy, Cass and Emma stopped to browse while shopping for school clothes. The younger girl, Cass, picked up the necklace and sighed. She asked her mother to buy it for her. Judy Martin took it from her hands, told her it was "cheap garbage" and that she should learn to have better taste. The girl asked again, telling her mother how much she loved it. The angel reminded her of Tinker Bell from *Peter Pan*—and that had been her favorite book when she was little. Apparently, her father had read it to her every night. *Peter Pan.* This did not help her cause. Judy Martin admonished her even more harshly, and then started walking away. Both girls followed. The older one, Emma, bumped shoulders with her sister, making her trip. She held up her hand to her forehead in the shape of an L. *Loser.*

The next day, Judy Martin returned and bought the necklace. The woman remembered smiling because she thought the mother was buying the necklace for the girl who'd asked for it—the younger one. Leo asked her, holding two pictures in his hands— "Are you certain it was this girl, Cass Tanner, and not this girl, Emma Tanner, who picked out the necklace?"

The owner was certain. "When I saw that interview, the one with the mother, Judy, I couldn't believe it. She was saying how she'd bought the necklace for the older daughter, Emma. And I guess she did—right? Gave the necklace to Emma and not to the other sister, who wanted it?"

Emma had worn the necklace every day. Friends confirmed it. Her father confirmed it. The school confirmed it. There was no doubt that Judy Martin had gone back to the store and bought the necklace for Emma. Not Cass.

The shrink weighed in. "Maybe the clerk was mistaken, Abby."

That's what Leo had thought. And that's what the department had said when they dismissed her theory about the family after the evidence came up with nothing solid—and after the family had started to push back with lawyers and tears in front of cameras.

But Abby knew the truth. This is what they do, people like Judy Martin. They are masterful in their deception. They are relentless in their manipulation. Abby had not only studied these things; she had lived them, too.

Verse number five.

The shrink—"Was she ever diagnosed? Your mother?"

No. Never. And Abby had been the only member of the family to know there was something that needed to be diagnosed. Not her father. Not her stepmother. And not even her sister, Meg, who to this day still thought of their mother as "overindulgent" and "free-spirited."

The shrink—"Do you think that's why you went into this field? Why you wrote your thesis on the cycle of narcissism in families?"

And what did that prove? It had not been a conscious decision, studying psychology. But when Abby had first read about narcissism and narcissistic personality disorder, the adrenaline had rushed in so hard and fast, it sent her to her knees. Right there in the library at Yale. Right there in front of her roommate, who thought she'd had a stroke. Abby had wanted to curl up on the floor and swim in it—the understanding that was seeping from the words in that textbook.

It was an illness that everyone thought they understood, assigning the label "narcissist" to every girl who looked twice in a mirror and every guy who never called. Books and films labeled every selfish character a "narcissist," but then there would be redemption, reconciliation, seeing the light. Few people really knew what this illness was. What it really looked like. There was never redemption. Or reconciliation. There was no light to be seen. It was the combination of these things—misperception and overuse—that made this illness so dangerous.

Verse number six.

The shrink—"Let's play it out. Let's say they did push harder—went to court to get orders for psych evals, battled the local media, which was squarely behind the grieving parents. Let's say they found that Judy had some kind of personality disorder. And maybe Owen Tanner had depression. And maybe Jonathan Martin was an alcoholic and his son ADHD. On and on—let's just say they found the mother lode of psychiatric conditions. That does not mean they would have found the girls."

And there it was—the lifeboat. Abby had climbed into it, and it had saved her. Anytime she fell out, when she thought about that necklace, the third alarm bell that had convinced her beyond doubt that the family was involved in the girls' disappearance—she would climb back into that boat and keep herself from drowning.

"It may not have saved them."

It may not have saved them.

This verse, this lifeboat, had saved *her*. But it had not brought her one moment of peace.

As she peeled out of her driveway, the sun's light piercing her eyes, she turned to the last page of the Bible, the one verse that had been left blank. The one that called out for words. For answers. And she couldn't stop herself from hoping that now, finally, it would be written.

THREE

Cass

I lay in the bed with my mother's arms around me. My hair was wet and I could feel water bleed into the pillowcase and turn cold against my cheek. She was crying. Sobbing.

"Oh, Cassandra! My baby! My baby!"

I have already said that I had imagined this moment for three years. And after all the time I had to prepare, I was, still, shockingly unprepared.

Her body felt frail to me, and I tried to remember the last time I'd felt it. She had withdrawn much of her physical affection after the custody fight, but not all of it. There were hugs on special occasions, her birthday and Mother's Day especially because our father gave us money to buy her gifts. I did not remember it feeling like this. Hard bones.

"My baby! Thank you, God! Thank you!"

What I had not been prepared for, and what I had not imagined even one time during my years of imagining the moment of my return, was the expression on her face when she first saw me again on her front porch less than an hour before.

I had stood there for ninety seconds before ringing the door-bell. I was counting them in my head, which is something I have done for as long as I can remember. I can count seconds perfectly, and from there, minutes and even hours. I had to ring the bell four times before I heard feet bounding down the hard wood stairs from the second floor. It is an above-average-sized house where we live, but where we live, the average house costs over a million dollars. It was built in the 1950s, a traditional white colonial, with three additions, including the porch, and multiple renovations. Mrs. Martin did more work after we were gone. I could see a sun-room and study where there had once been a small garden. We also have nearly five acres of property, a pool house, a tennis court and lots of woods to get lost in. Land is very expensive here. So while the house was small enough that I could hear my mother coming down the stairs, she was coming down stairs of a very costly estate. She would want me to make that clear.

As I heard the lock turn, I felt the ground give way beneath my feet. I had been through the same door thousands of times, behind Emma, looking for Emma, calling for Emma. Every face my sister ever wore, changed by mood and growth and the weath-ering of time, came before my eyes as though they were warning me while the door slowly opened. I almost said her name. I could feel it in my mouth. *Emma.* I wanted to fall to my knees, bury my eyes into my hands and hide behind my sister as I had done as a child. I did not feel capable of doing what had to be done with-out her.

But then I saw the first strand of my mother's hair from behind that door, and the faces of my sister vanished and I became calm.

Mrs. Martin was wrapped in a silk robe. Her hair was tangled from restless sleep, and a thick line of eye makeup was caked under her lower lashes.

"Can I help you?" She asked the question with a sprinkle of politeness on top of a mountain of annoyance. It was six in the morning on a Sunday.

She was looking at me, studying my face, my eyes, my body. I did not think I had changed much. I wore the same size clothing. The same size pants and shirts, even the same for my bra. My hair was still light brown and long past my shoulders. My face was still angular, my eyebrows thick with big arches. When I looked in the mirror, I still saw me. But I guess that's the thing—we all change so gradually, a little every day, that we don't notice it. Like the frog that stays in the water until the water is boiling and the frog is dead.

The moment I had not been prepared for—the one thing I had not ever imagined in all those years—was that my mother would not recognize me.

"It's me," I said. "It's Cass."

She said nothing, but her head jolted back as though my words had just punched her in the face.

"Cass?"

She looked harder, her eyes now bulging and moving frantically from place to place, head to toe. Her right hand covered her mouth. Her left hand grabbed hold of the doorframe, catching her body as she stumbled toward me.

"Cass!"

I had to force my feet to stand still as she lunged at me, hands, arms, face, all touching me, pawing at me.

A guttural moan left her body. "Uhhhhhh!"

Then she started screaming for Mr. Martin.

I had prepared for this part and I did what I thought I would do, which was to let her feel what she was feeling and just stand there and do nothing. Say nothing. You probably think she was ecstatic, elated, filled with joy. But Mrs. Martin had reinvented herself as the grieving mother with the missing daughters, so adjusting to my return would involve a painful unraveling.

"Jon! Jon!"

The tears started then as more footsteps sounded from the second floor.

Mr. Martin called out. "What the hell is going on?"

My mother didn't answer him. Instead, she grabbed my face with her hands, pressed her nose right up against mine and said my name with that same guttural sound. *"Caaaaaaass!"*

Mr. Martin was in his pajamas. He had put on weight since I saw him last and he looked even older than I remembered. I should have expected that. But when you're young, you see people over a certain age as just old, and there does not seem a need to imagine them any older. He was very tall and very dark—hair, skin, eyes. I had never been able to read him well. He was adept at hiding his feelings. Or maybe he just didn't have many of them. Few things made him angry. Fewer things made him laugh. On this day, though, I saw something I had not seen before on his face—utter bewilderment.

"Cass? Cassandra? Is that you?"

There were more hugs. Mr. Martin called the police. He called my father next, but there was no answer. I heard him leave a message, saying only that it was important and he should call back right away. I thought that was very considerate of him, not giving my father the details of this shocking news in a voice mail. It made me wonder if he had changed.

They asked me the questions you would expect. Where had I been? What had happened to me? When I didn't answer them, I heard them whisper to each other. They concluded that I was traumatized. Mr. Martin said they should keep asking questions until I answered. My mother agreed.

"Cass—tell us what happened!"

I did not answer them. "We need the police!" I cried instead. "They have to find Emma! They have to find her!"

Time froze for what seemed like forever, but was only eight seconds. Mr. Martin shot a look at my mother. My mother calmed down and started to stroke my hair as though I were a fragile doll she didn't want to break—and that she didn't want to move or speak.

"Okay, sweetheart. Just calm down."

She stopped asking me questions but my hands were shaking. I told her I was cold and she let me take a hot shower. I told her I was hungry and she made me some food. I told her I was tired and she let me lie down. My mother stayed by my side and I pretended to sleep while I secretly soaked in the Chanel No. 5 that lingered on her neck.

When the cars started to appear, Mr. Martin went downstairs. He did not come back up. I could see each car as it entered the property because the window from my mother's room has a view of the top part of the driveway. First came the state police in three marked SUVs. Next were the paramedics in an ambulance. It took another forty minutes for the specialists to arrive in all sorts of cars. The FBI agents would be among them. And some kind of evidence evaluator. And, of course, a psychologist.

Some people took samples from my nails and skin. They combed through my hair. They drew some blood. They checked my heart and pulse and they asked me questions to make sure I wasn't insane. Then we waited again, for the people who would ask me the questions about where I'd been, and where Emma was.

I had not been in my mother's bed since I was a little girl, since well before the divorce. We were not forbidden. It was just not a place either of us, Emma or I, wanted to be after we learned about sex. Our parents' bed was the place they "did it," and we found that disgusting. We used to talk about it when we played with our Barbie dolls.

They get naked and Daddy puts his dick inside her.

Emma would say things like that with complete nonchalance, as if it didn't faze her at all. But I could sense her anger from the words she chose and because I knew her so well.

She took off Ken's clothes and Barbie's clothes and mashed their androgynous crotches together. Ken was on top. Emma made oohs and aahs.

That's what they do in their bed. I'm never going in there again.

Emma had learned the truth about sex from our half brother, Witt Tanner. Emma was eleven. I was nine. Witt was sixteen. Emma had come home from school upset. We usually took the bus because our mother didn't like to interrupt her nap. Sometimes we walked. We attended a private school, so we were on the same campus no matter what grades we were in, and Emma always let me walk with her even though I was annoying. It was on these walks she would tell me things she had come to know, usually about boys. On this day, though, she had been quiet the whole way, telling me to "shut the hell up" every time I tried to talk to her. When we got to the house, she ran to her room and slammed the door.

Witt lived with us every other weekend before the divorce of our father and mother. He spent the rest of his time at his mother's house. That added up to 96 hours out of 672 hours each month. It was not a lot. It was not enough.

But the day Emma learned about sex was a Friday that Witt

was at our house. He was playing a video game in our family room when we came inside.

What's wrong with her?

I went into the family room and sat down as close to Witt as possible without being in his lap. He leaned into me, bumping shoulders. He didn't say anything except to ask about Emma and why she'd run upstairs. Usually on every other Friday, we both would find Witt and cling to him like plastic wrap until he went back to his mother Sunday night. He was soft-spoken and easy to be around. But he was also strong and he always knew what to say and how to say it.

I used to think that Witt was a gift our father had given us to make up for the mother he had given us. I know that's stupid, because we wouldn't be here if she wasn't our mother and because Witt was born before we were, before our father had even met our mother. And anyone looking at Emma could see Mrs. Martin—in her eyes, her jaw, the way she spoke. Still, that's what I used to think.

Witt finished the round of his game. He cursed at having been killed or out of lives or coins or whatever. He looked me in the eye and asked me how my week had been. He kissed my forehead and messed up my hair, and I smiled so hard, I could feel water in my eyes. Then he said he was going to check on Emma, which he did. She let him in her room and he came out soon after, shaking his head and laughing. No one told me anything then. But when we were playing with our Barbies a few days later, Emma couldn't resist shattering my ignorance. She was over the shock of it, and this thing that men did to women was now part of the fabric of her.

That day I was upset, do you remember it? And Witt came in to talk to me, do you remember? Well . . . I was upset because some jerk told me that sex is when a boy pees on a girl and then she has a baby.

I remember wanting to cry myself when she said this. I remember thinking that life could not possibly be that humiliating. And I remember thinking that I would never, ever let a boy pee on me even if it meant I could not have babies. The moment didn't last long, but still—I remember the reaction I had and that I understood why it had made my sister run to her room and slam the door shut.

Witt told me what really happens. Boys don't pee on you.

Emma explained about penises and vaginas and sperm. Then she took off the clothes of our Barbie dolls.

I suppose it's strange that our brother was the one to tell us about sex. But that wasn't the only parental duty he took on.

Our mother didn't like being our mother. She said she wanted to be our friend. She said she was waiting for us to grow up so we could all do fun things together like shopping and going to get our nails done. She used to tell us about her plans to take us on vacations where we would get spa treatments and sit on the beach reading magazines and sipping drinks that tasted like coconut and had little umbrellas. She made them for us sometimes during the summer. She said when we were older, we could have ones that tasted even better and made you feel relaxed and happy. I would fall asleep dreaming that dream our mother put in our heads, the dream where we were all three like sisters.

There were lots of dreams back then, before our mother started her affair with Mr. Martin. Witt talked of college and wanting to be a lawyer like his mother. He sometimes had girlfriends and they would kiss in the basement. He learned to drive and got his own car. It was like he was paving the path for us to become grown-ups, and he did it with such glee that he made it seem like something worth doing.

This place feels big now, like it's the whole world, like what happens here matters. But it's not. And it doesn't.

Witt said things like that after he went to Europe one summer.

This place is small. Very small. And you can leave here one day. You can become something else. Anything you want. And when you come back, this place won't feel big anymore. It will appear the way it really is, which is very little and small. Almost nothing.

This gave me comfort, this thought of our home, our family, our mother being very small. So small that maybe the bad things I thought would happen would not happen after all.

I did not see my father's car enter the driveway. It turned out that he had slept through the phone ringing. My father could sleep through an earthquake. They eventually sent a squad car to tell him his daughter was alive.

My father suffered, and I found his suffering unbearable to witness. I have had a lot of time to reflect on our story inside this house. And I've been through things that have shattered the prism through which I see our story, through which I now see everything, so very differently. He kept a nice house for us. It had four bedrooms so Witt could always be there when we were, even after he went to college. And it was close to town so we could come and go to meet our friends. Emma liked that because she had a lot of friends. For me, it was always a reminder that I did not.

Our father's house after the divorce was bright with sunshine but dark with sadness. His sadness. He told us that ever since the divorce, he struggled to remind himself that happiness is a state of mind. *The glass is half empty. The glass is half full. It's pouring rain.*

The flowers will grow. I am going to die one day. I am alive on this day. He said that after the divorce and losing *my girls,* he could see that everything he had, everything he loved, everything that made his life feel like a life could disappear at any moment. He said we, his three children, felt like drops of water in his hands, moving toward the cracks between his fingers, where we could slip through and leave him, one at a time or all at once until his hands were empty and his life became an empty space, an empty heart, I think he said until his life was nothing more than air going in and out of his lungs. These were the things he would talk about at dinner, and it was dreadful.

Sometimes Witt would get mad at him, tell him he should find some friends to tell this stuff to, not us, because we were his children and not his friends. He would tell him to see a shrink, and that all his bad moods were not because of the divorce. Our father would say he didn't need a shrink. Then Witt would say, *Fine, then why don't you just shake it off?* But our father said he couldn't shake off the problem of knowing that the more you have, the more you have to lose.

And then we were gone, proving him right.

A woman with short blond hair walked from her car toward the house until she was out of my view. After seventy-four seconds, I heard the door open and close in the foyer, then the sound of feet coming up the stairs.

I closed my eyes and pretended to sleep again. My mother slipped her arm out from under my neck and quietly crept from the bed to answer the knock at her door. She pulled a blanket up around my shoulders so gently, it made me shudder. This was what had plagued my father. In spite of everything she did that she shouldn't have done, and everything she didn't do that she should have, something that felt like love was in her and she would take it out at times like this and show it to us and make us hunger for more. All of us, each in our own way.

Emma would sometimes dress Barbie in an evening gown. Ken, still buck naked, would chase after her.

Please, Barbie, please . . . let me put my dick inside you. Please, I'll do anything!

Her voice was derisive and full of anger. We were young, but we still understood why our father was driven mad by our mother's indifference, and how his madness had taken over every part of his brain and his heart so there was nothing left for us.

One day Emma took Barbie and threw her against the wall. She said nothing. We both sat on the floor, silently, looking at the doll. She had landed on her back, her dress flowing around her, white teeth shining through smiling red lips. This memory was now before my eyes—so vivid, my heart was pounding in my ears. Emma was the one brave enough to throw a doll against a wall while I gasped and then covered my mouth. She was the one brave enough to bargain for our mother's love, even though she risked losing it every time. She was the one brave enough to challenge our mother's beauty by wearing red lipstick and short skirts. Every day of our lives here, Emma fought for what she wanted, for what we should have had, while I hid in the shadows she was willing to cast for me.

Emma shielded me from our mother's storm, and whether she did it for my benefit or just because that was who she was and that was what she needed to do, it served the same purpose. She kept me safe.

Doubt filled me up top to bottom when I thought about those storms. Why had I come back here? I was free! I could have gone anywhere! Then I told myself why. For Emma. For Emma! And to make all the wrong things done to us right again. It was my turn now, to be the lightning rod. Still, conviction is not the same thing as strength, and I was terrified.

I heard some whispering at the door. My mother sighed with disapproval but ultimately relinquished her control over me. Three sets of feet walked across the carpet to the edge of the bed. My mother sat down beside me and stroked my hair.

"Cass? Cass—these people are from the FBI. They want to talk to you. Cass?"

I let my sister enter my mind. I let her push aside the vision of that indestructible doll, taunting us from the floor. I opened my eyes and sat up. The woman with the short blond hair was standing by the edge of the bed, and I knew this was the gatekeeper to finding my sister.

"Cassandra? My name is Dr. Abigail Winter. I'm a psychologist with the Federal Bureau of Investigation. The man with me is Special Agent Leo Strauss. We're here to see how you are, and maybe just talk a little bit if you feel up to it."

I nodded my head. The words were in my mouth—words that I had carefully crafted and rehearsed. But they were trampled by a stampede of emotions.

I started to sob. My mother pulled me close and rocked me back and forth.

On the other side of my mother was the woman with the short blond hair. Dr. Abigail Winter. Through my watery eyes and the breath that was heaving in and out of me, I could still see her clearly, and how she was looking at my mother.

I fixed my sight on her and her alone, over and in spite of my mother's body that was enveloping me.

"Find Emma!" I said through my gasping and crying.

My mother let me go and pulled back far enough to see my face. "She said that before . . ." She was still looking at me as she spoke to them. "But she doesn't say anything else. I think something's wrong with her!"

Agent Strauss spoke then, his voice calm. "Cassandra . . . where is Emma? Where can we find her?"

The words I said were not the words I had rehearsed.

I was not being a very good artist to my story.

FOUR

Dr. Winter

F ind Emma!"

Everything stopped when Abby heard those words. Heart, lungs, limbs, all still. Frozen. She could not take her eyes from the young woman on the bed, the woman who had been just a girl when she disappeared. Abby had studied her face from every stage of her life. Photos, home movies, social media posts—not only the features but the expressions as well had been painted onto a canvas that became the Cassandra Tanner Abby believed she knew.

Her hair was darker. It was longer as well, with waves that had not been there before. It fell around her shoulders, the silk bathrobe and the pillow that was tucked behind her head. The features of her face were sharper, cheekbones and brow bones. Hazel eyes set deeper beneath full brows. Abby could not look away, mesmerized by the figure before her and the one piece of the puzzle that had just been revealed. *Emma was alive.*

"Cassandra . . . where is Emma? Where can we find her?" Leo asked.

"She's still there!" Cass cried out, frantic now.

"Where, Cass? Where is Emma?" Leo repeated. His voice was calm and it drew Cass in. She looked at him cautiously while she forced a long breath in and out. Then she told them about Emma.

"The island," she said. "She's still on the island."

"What island?" Leo asked.

Cass looked at her mother. Judy Martin had probably changed a great deal, but all Abby could see was everything she had seen before. She was a woman consumed by her appearance. Even now, there was fresh makeup and the smell of hair spray. She let the thought come and go. But she filed it away.

Cass looked to Abby then, which was strange since Leo had asked the question.

"What island, Cass? Do you know where it is?" he asked again.

Cass shook her head and started to cry.

Judy removed her hand from her daughter's hair and pulled her body away so they were no longer touching.

"You have to find it! Please! Find the island. Find my sister!"

Leo looked at Abby then, then back to Cass, cautiously. "Is Emma in danger? Is she being held against her will?"

Cass nodded. "They wouldn't let us come home. For three years. I had to leave her behind. It was the only way, but now you have to save her!"

"Get forensics back," Abby said. She wanted to hear the story—from start to finish—but if Emma was in danger, they needed to run it from every angle. Leo agreed and texted his colleagues to return from the first floor.

Cass went on to tell them about an island, and a man named Bill who lived there. She told them, too, about his wife, Lucy, and how they had both "taken us in" and "given us a home" and how everything had been "really good until it turned bad." Without hearing the story in order, it was impossible to understand how it came to be that their refuge "became a prison," and how only Cass was able to escape. And how "Emma is still a prisoner there." And why she didn't know exactly where it was or how to find it "because of how I got there and how I left." And *why* she left. *God,* how Abby wanted the answer to that question.

But she sat calmly even as the urgency pushed against the thin walls of her patience.

Judy Martin kept asking questions. She was standing now, and pacing the room. "What do you mean Emma is there, on this island? What are you talking about? This is crazy! How do you not know where it is? How can you not tell them? None of this makes sense, Cass! Dr. Winter, don't you see how crazy this is? Is she well? Maybe she's not well? You need to examine her!"

"I do know things!" Cass yelled into the room. "It's in Maine! It's north of Portland!"

The forensics team was back in the room, and they wanted to get the physical description so they could start to run an analysis.

They asked Cass about the seasons there. The foliage. They spoke to each other about the soil in her shoes. The pollen and mold and dust on her clothing. Other people's hair on that clothing, maybe on her body. There could be DNA evidence that they could try to match in their system. Then there were the less tangible things, like what she had smelled in the air and the kind of food she ate. People who came and went, what they sounded like. Their accents and the words they chose.

Cass worked with them for nearly an hour. She tried to explain why it had been impossible to leave.

"The water was very cold, even in the summer. Lucy was always warning us about hypothermia. We only saw one person other than Bill and Lucy. His name was Rick and he drove a boat to and from the island to deliver groceries and gas for the generator.

There were no lines to the island. No cables, like for a phone or television or electricity. But we had a satellite dish. I could see other land from three sides of the island. It was miles away. The fourth side faced the ocean, like we were at the very edge of some kind of inlet or harbor, but it was enormously wide. You couldn't see houses or people or anything like that on the other land, and it was very hard to get to our dock. There were rocks underneath the water, and you could only see them during low tide."

Her voice grew steady. Her composure sound.

She told them about the current, and how strong it was on that one side that had the dock, the south side, and how it pulled everything to the west. She described the storms that rolled in, and how severe they were. How she could see them for miles and miles before they reached the island, like a wall of wind and water pouring from the sky, creeping toward her. There would be a few seconds of sprinkles, shooting sideways on the wind, before the downpour would arrive.

She told them about the sky and how seeing it like that, unbroken, from left to right was like being inside "one of those glass snow globes."

"That was how it felt to be there under such big, open skies, but unable to leave." Her description was almost poetic. She sounded educated far beyond her one year of high school.

Then she told them about the trees, and how they were the same as in Connecticut, except there were more that stayed green during the winter.

"Conifers?" they asked.

"I don't know."

"Pine trees, Christmas trees . . ."

"Yes, like that. Like Christmas trees. But taller and thin at the bottom . . ."

Bill and Lucy's last name was Pratt. She did not know any-thing about where they were from and she never met any friends or relatives. They sometimes spoke of a mother or father but never a sister or brother. She did not know what they did for money or work. They tended to the island, to their garden and the house. She did not know where they went when they left the island on the boat with Rick. Lucy did not leave more than once a month. Bill left a few times a week, but only for half a day, at most.

They were in their early forties, she thought, but as she said, "I'm not a good judge of age." Lucy was "sort of round at the cen-ter" and had long gray hair down to her waist, which she wore hanging all around her face, never in a ponytail or bun. Cass said she could tell Lucy thought it was special, having such long hair, even though it was "gray and frizzy and not something you would ever want to touch." She had a lot of wrinkles around her mouth and eyes, and a slight gray mustache above her upper lip.

"All of these things are disgusting to me now, so maybe I'm exaggerating them. When I first met her, I found them endearing."

Bill was very tall and he had brown hair but he used dye. Gre-cian Formula. She'd seen the boxes in the groceries when they came from the mainland, so she thought he was probably gray on his head.

"What about the groceries? Any receipts, store names on the bags?"

"No. Not that I can recall."

"And what about brands of food? Anything different, local farms, fresh baked goods, things like that?"

"Yes, there was fresh bread but no names. They came in brown paper bags. The milk brand was Horizon. We had all kinds of brands. Land O Lakes butter. Thomas' English muffins . . ."

"How about fruit, fish?"

"Yes, but I don't remember any names. Just green boxes with berries, blueberries in the summer. Small ones. And lots of fish. Wrapped in white paper. Emma hates fish. Even lobster and shrimp. But there was a lot of fish."

"White fish?"

"Yes. It was white. Like in fish and chips. Only they didn't like to fry things, Bill and Lucy. They said it wasn't healthy."

Abby sat in a chair, her hands clasped together tightly. This was all useful to locating the island, but it was moving them away from the story, from the answer she'd been waiting for, to the question that had tortured her.

They asked Cass about bills, mail, boats that went past. Did she remember any of their names? "No," she answered. Boats never got that close to them, because of the rocks and the current, and many of them were small fishing boats. The boat that came to the island was called *Lucky Lady*. They ran the name. There was a *Lucky Lady* in nearly every harbor. But the fishing boats . . .

"What did they look like, these fishing boats?" They showed her pictures from the Internet.

She identified lobster boats, which supported her belief that the island was in Maine.

She told them, too, how the island smelled of gasoline some-times because of the generator, and they told her this was helpful.

Judy Martin kept interrupting and asking the same questions. "But how did you make it there three years ago and then make it home now without knowing where you were? It doesn't make sense, Cass! How did you not leave for three years? You're all ask-ing the wrong questions! Trees and goddamn blueberries!"

One of the forensics pulled out her phone. "Did any of them sound like this?"

She played a recording. She said it was a Maine accent. She explained about the added *r* and the long *a* and *e,* which sounded like "ah" and "eh." And Cass told them the boatman talked like that.

"Emma used to say he sounded like a hick, which was not very nice, but Rick was not very nice. That's part of the story. Rick is how I escaped."

"Yes, yes! The escape. Let's talk about that." Mrs. Martin threw her hands into air.

Cass told them that she escaped in the *Lucky Lady.*

"It wasn't easy. Rick depended on the Pratts for everything, and they did not want us to leave. . . ."

"Go back to the boat . . . how far did it take you before you reached land?" they asked.

She told them how the boatman brought her to a dock inside a harbor. She didn't keep track of the time it took to get there, but it felt like a while. It was pitch-black and hard to tell which way they were going. Then a friend of his let her ride in the back of his truck.

"How long did you ride in the truck? Did you notice the time, the roads, the direction? Street signs, highway names, anything?"

She told them that she stayed under a blanket until they got to Portland so no one would see her. They stopped for gas and she saw a sign. It said Rockland. They stopped one other time for gas and another time on the side of the highway so she could go to the bathroom in the woods.

"It took three hours and fifteen minutes to get to Portland. The roads were slow and curving. We were going south. I saw that sign! Isn't that enough?" Cass's voice was shaky again.

"Maine has over thirty-five hundred miles of coastland and close to five thousand islands, and off the coast near Rockland there are hundreds," one of the forensics explained. "So anything else you give us would be helpful."

Judy jumped in, impatience seeping from every pore. "Why, Cass, did you wait all night to get back here? Why didn't you go straight to the police from the shore so they could find this island?"

"I don't know. I didn't think about it. I didn't think it would be so hard to find it. The driver of that truck asked me where I wanted to go and I said the first thing I thought of which was here. Home."

She started to cry again.

"I just wanted to come home."

Abby heard footsteps bounding up the stairs; then the door opened. She was sitting in a chair by the bed when Owen Tanner burst in like a tornado. He didn't greet her, though Abby doubted he'd forgotten who she was. He was simply overwrought. He ran to the bed, hugged his daughter. He was crying, moaning like he was in pain. He was thin and gaunt, as though he'd been slowly disappearing these past three years. She hadn't noticed it during the investigation, because she had seen him frequently, even after they had concluded their interviews. He would come once a week or more to the field office in New Haven, demanding updates, requesting access to their reports and the list of calls to the hotline. She thought then that his pain had been a parasite, feeding on him all this time. And nothing could bring back the parts of him that had been eaten away. That was what she could hear in his cries as he held his child.

Owen pulled away, his face wet and contorted with despair. He began his own inquiry about Emma, to know where she was. He had a million questions and he shot them out as if no one else in the room had thought of them before he arrived and "My

God!" Emma was at the end of one of them and why couldn't Cass just tell them where to go and get her?

When he had finally exhausted his questions on that front and came to accept that finding Emma was not going to happen that moment, he sat down on the edge of the bed, almost on top of his daughter, blocking Judy from her sight. It was then he asked Cass the other question, which Abby knew had tortured him the most since the night he lost his daughters.

"Why? Why did you and Emma leave with these people?"

Owen had told Abby during the first investigation that she was wrong to look at the family history. He told her that he understood why teenagers left to join jihads and cults and got lured by perverts. He said in one of his interviews with her, "Those kids were not normal kids. I've seen them on the news. Maybe no one saw it before it happened, but after it was all perfectly clear why they'd left. Right? There's nothing like that with my girls. I'm not sitting here thinking that this all makes perfect sense because of this thing or that thing. Do you understand? There is nothing to find here. Nothing at all!"

"Why did you leave with these strangers?" Owen asked again, looking for confirmation.

Cass finally answered him, a hint of anger in her voice that surprised Abby. But it was her answer that surprised them all.

"We left because Emma was pregnant."

FIVE

Cass

My father squeezed the breath from my body when he first saw me again. He barreled past Dr. Winter, Special Agent Strauss and Mrs. Martin and fell into me, sobbing. I did not have a chance to even look at him, to absorb the deep lines that grief had carved into his forehead and the grayness that now covered his skin. That would come twelve seconds later. In that moment, those first twelve seconds, he needed to take from me all that was lost over those three years, and he was not deterred by the impossibility of this task. I indulged him because I love my father very much and feeling his arms around me again had me crying also and saying his name over and over.

Daddy . . . Daddy . . .

I cried for him many times on the island, even though I knew each time, in my heart, what I knew again on my mother's bed as he held me that morning. No matter how many times I cried his name, the cries a plea for him to help me somehow even if only to give me the strength to help myself, my father had nothing like this to give me.

I let myself cry and I tried to give him the things he needed. I had expected him to need things from me when I returned home. Still, I was also shocked by the resentment I felt. I wanted to scream at him. *I need things, too! I need to tell my story before it explodes right out of my chest!* No one seemed to care about my things.

When I said the words, when I told them we left because Emma was pregnant, my father's eyes grew wide and frantic, like he was lost in a storm. "I don't understand! Did she have a baby? Is there a child? My God!"

I answered the second question first.

"She had a little girl. But they took her. Bill and Lucy took her from Emma and made her their own. It started out like they were just helping take care of her. They kept her in their room at night. They said it was just for a few days so Emma could rest. Emma didn't want them to, but they did anyway. Then they just never stopped."

"And they wouldn't let you leave? They held you prisoner? I don't understand, Cass!" My father demanded an answer.

"We asked to leave. And when they kept saying not yet, not now, things like that, we made a plan to leave, only we couldn't see how to do it when they always had Emma's baby with them. So we decided that I should leave and then bring back help. And I tried, but failed. I've been trying to tell you . . . and when I found another way years later, Emma said she couldn't leave without her daughter. I tried to make her come with me. You have to believe me, that I tried!"

I felt a surge of panic like the shock you get when your finger brushes a light socket. The thought of baby feet and baby hair and baby smiles, and the pain when they would take her from my arms, and Emma—I suddenly missed her like I would miss my

own heart if it were torn from my body—and all of this was just
too strong to hold in.

"Find them!" I yelled into the room.

I wanted Emma. I wanted revenge. I wanted that sweet little
girl. I wanted justice.

"Find them and make them pay for what they've done!"

My father covered his face with his hands. I think it was at
this moment he started to understand the kind of place I was trying to tell him about, trying to tell all of them. There was just so
much and I didn't want to forget anything so I kept trying to go
back to the beginning. Maybe I should have started with the first
time I tried to escape and what they did when I got caught. Or
the things I had to do to finally make it home. In so many ways,
I still felt like a child, afraid I would be in trouble. Afraid no one
would believe me.

My father stood up. "We need more agents! We need to do
something! Right now! My daughter and granddaughter are being held prisoner by these people! My God!"

Behind my father, I could see Mrs. Martin looking at me like
I was crazy. She'd been doing that all morning and I wanted to
scream at her *Maybe you're the one who's crazy!* and then watch her
break into pieces.

Agent Strauss tried to reassure him. "We have a team of agents
ready to begin the search. We will find this island."

My father hung his head and held it firmly between his palms.
He started to nod then, and I could read his thoughts—*Yes, of
course. That's why a girl leaves home. That's what was so compelling,
she would leave everything behind.*

He turned to look at my mother for some kind of solidarity. His
shoulders lifted slightly, his palms now stretched out and open to
the sky and tears streaming down his face.

"We couldn't have known, Judy. We couldn't."

He was trying to be kind, but Mrs. Martin didn't want his kindness.

My father used to make comments about the relationship between Emma and our mother, about how Mrs. Martin looked at Emma like a younger version of herself. He said she liked it when Emma got attention as a little girl. She would tell him that people did the same thing when she was little—turn their heads and ooh and ahh. She and Emma were cut from the same cloth. They were the same. What my father didn't understand was that after Emma got older, Mrs. Martin didn't talk about her likeness to Emma, because of pride. It was her way of stealing back the attention Emma got—attention that used to be hers.

I knew what my father was thinking as he tried to comfort her. That this ignorance of such an important fact about Emma might be a blow to her pride, to her ego. If she and Emma were so alike, how did she not know Emma was pregnant?

I was never able to sit still when this thing was happening between them—my mother silently brooding and my father prancing around like a circus clown trying to cheer her up. It made me feel rage inside because he couldn't see anything. He couldn't see that she still knew how to reach inside him and twist him up even after she broke his heart and stole his house and his children. Even then.

I was not surprised when this was Mrs. Martin's response after he tried to comfort her on the day I returned.

"Of course I couldn't have known! You drove a wedge between us so she never talked to me about these things. You did that! And look what happened!"

Dr. Winter did not seem surprised either that my father tried to comfort my mother, or that my mother used his kindness to whack him in the head. That was when I knew she had been involved before, when we disappeared. I imagine she had learned a lot about our family when they were trying to find us. But it was the lack of surprise she had in this moment that made me think she could *see* our family.

Agent Strauss stepped in. "I think we need to hear what happened—from the beginning. Please . . . let's get things to the lab and let's hear the story, Cass. If you're up to it."

Dr. Winter smiled at me and nodded. The people from the forensic team left. Everyone sat back down, my father on the end of the bed, my mother back next to me. Dr. Winter sat in a chair with a small notepad flipped open and a pen in her hand. Agent Strauss was standing beside her.

"We should speak to Cass alone," he said to my parents. They looked at each other, then at me. They didn't move.

"No . . ." I said. "I need them here. Please . . ."

My breath was choppy from the attack of emotions and I tried hard to steady my voice. I could not tell my story without my mother with me to hear it.

Agent Strauss sighed. "For now," he said. He glanced at Dr. Winter, who nodded in agreement.

I asked if I should start from the very first night and Agent Strauss said yes. I let out two long breaths, like long sighs, and I started to calm down. Then I went back to that night in our house. The night we disappeared.

"The night we left, Emma and I were fighting. Do you remember that?"

Mrs. Martin answered. "Yes. Over that necklace."

I had never forgotten the first time I heard her say this in an interview. I remembered everything she said about it, about the necklace. And about that night.

"I loved that necklace, so Emma wore it every day because she knew it upset me to see it on her neck. That day, at school, we were walking home together and Emma was nervous about something. I could tell. She was distracted. We walked in silence the whole way. When we got home, she went to her room and closed her door. She didn't come down for dinner, remember?"

Mrs. Martin shook her head and stared at me like she was losing her patience. It made me want to ramble on and on.

"I don't know, Cass. I don't remember about dinner," she said.

"I tried to talk to her but she wouldn't let me in her room. I pounded on the door until she opened it. She was afraid you would hear and she didn't want to draw attention to what she was doing. I walked into her room and saw some clothes laid out on her bed. She had just taken a shower. So I asked her if she was going out, and where and why on a school night. I was trying to make her mad because she had been so weird all day. But she seemed different. Less interested somehow, like this was all beneath her. She started organizing her purse. She put on her clothes. Then she turned toward the bathroom door and just pushed me out of the way. 'Come back here!' I screamed at her. . . . Do you remember all of that?"

Dr. Winter answered. "I remember your mother telling us about that. How she heard you fighting and then she saw the car pull out of the driveway."

My mother had this story down perfectly. And so did I.

"I knew she was leaving because she'd put her car keys in her purse. The necklace was on the bed next to the clothes and I snatched it up before she came back for it. I put it around my neck. 'I have the necklace!' I said. 'You can't have it back until you tell me where you're going!' She came storming out of the bathroom, yelling at me to give it back. She tried to grab it off my neck and I pushed her away. Then she finally got her hand on it and she ripped it off me. It broke the chain. But she didn't care. She put it on her neck and tied the chain like a rope, in a knot, so it would stay. She looked in the mirror and adjusted the angel. Then she just turned and went back into the bathroom.

"I was so furious! I went out to her car and got in the way back. She keeps blankets in there for when they go to the beach to drink and I hid under them. I thought, 'I'm gonna go where she goes and get pictures of her doing things she's not supposed to be doing and then I'm gonna get her in trouble.' It's all so stupid, isn't it?"

Dr. Winter looked at me sympathetically. "No, Cass. You were fifteen. It sounds very normal."

Mrs. Martin copied her. She was very good at taking cues when she didn't want anyone to see what was in her mind. Or her heart.

"Yes, sweetheart." Her words were nice but her tone was laced with frustration.

"I waited there for a long time before the driver's-side door opened and closed and then we started to move. I remember feeling nervous about my plan to get her in trouble. The car stopped at the beach, in a spot in the very back of the lot. I heard Emma sigh really hard and long, like she was nervous, too. But then she got out of the car, left her purse, and the keys, and walked to the shore. I waited a few seconds and then got out, slowly and quietly. I followed her and I know she didn't see me, because she kept going toward the water without looking back. When she got there, she took off her shoes and waded into the water. I stood behind the changing room, peeking out from the side. I could see her in the moonlight, and I thought maybe she was going to swim with all her clothes on. But she didn't move. She just stood there looking at the water and splashing it with her toes.

"And then there were headlights coming from behind me. They shined onto her and she seemed startled but then she started walking toward the car, away from the water. I know she was startled because she forgot her shoes. She walked right past the changing rooms where I was hiding and watching. The lights went off. Then the engine. A door opened and a man got out. There was also a woman in the car but she stayed inside.

"Emma started to walk toward the car, toward this man, and I felt this horrible fear that she was leaving forever. I ran toward the car and screamed her name. 'Emma!' I started to see him more clearly. He was older. He had brown hair and a kind smile and he folded Emma into his arms in a big hug.

"They both stopped when they heard me call out for her. The man looked at Emma, and his smile went away. Emma stormed over to me. She was so angry. She was desperate. She knew I had just spoiled her plan. She grabbed my arms and told me she was leaving, that she couldn't take it anymore. I started crying, grabbing at her. I was so upset. I couldn't imagine life without Emma. She was my sister and I had never been without her.

"She pulled away and walked toward the car. She said to the man, 'Let's just go.' But he shook his head. They spoke in whispers. Then she shook her head and he grabbed her shoulders and looked at her sternly. She came back to me and she said 'Now you have to come with us.' I was scared. I didn't know where they were going. We saw headlights coming down the beach. It was the sand groomer. It always comes at night. There was no time to think. Emma grabbed my arm and pulled me toward the car. I don't know if I tried to break free. I honestly don't know. My feet were moving and they walked me to the car. We all got in and we drove away."

I stopped there and looked around the room. Dr. Winter, Agent Strauss, Mrs. Martin—they were all staring at me now, mesmerized by the story.

It was Agent Strauss who broke the spell. "Do you remember anything else that this man said? Either on the beach or in the car? Did they introduce themselves, explain what was happening?"

I shook my head. "No one said anything. It was creepy. We just drove until we got to the boat."

"Do you remember how long you drove? What time you left and what time the car finally stopped?"

"I wish I could. I know that would be helpful because we went right from the beach to the boat, and then to the island. I fell asleep for a while. We stopped for food and to use the bathroom. We stopped for gas another time and it was still dark out and much colder than it had been at the beach. It was still dark when we got to a dock. It smelled like pine trees. I'm sorry. I usually keep good track of the time."

"That's okay, Cass. Just continue the story. What happened next?" Agent Strauss said.

"I remember thinking that maybe I didn't know my own sister at all. I mean, I had not known about Bill. I had not known about her plan to leave home. I had not even known she was pregnant. I thought she was going out to meet a guy. I was so stupid! It made me scared and I wanted to leave and run home as fast as I could. But then I thought I would be in so much trouble if I left without knowing where Emma was going, and for leaving in the first place and for hiding in Emma's car. It's so clear what I would do now, being older, and knowing what could happen to us. But then, in my mind, and not knowing, I felt like I had to stay with her until I knew where she was going. I made a plan to do that, and then to find my way home. I remember feeling better having this plan and I lay my head down against the window. The woman, Lucy, had given me a blanket and I pulled it over my head, over my whole face and everything.

"I woke up to the sound of music playing and the wind on my forehead. Emma had rolled her window all the way down. Her head was hanging far enough out so the wind could catch her hair and blow it hard away from her face. She was humming and Bill and Lucy were smiling. It was an Adele song. Do you remember how much she loved Adele?"

Emma didn't like to drive me places. But sometimes, when something bad enough had happened in our house, she'd get very drunk and then she would take me in her car and she would make me drive, even though I was not old enough. We would go down North Ave because it was straight and we could go very fast. She would roll down the window, stick her head out just enough for the wind to catch her hair. And she would sing so loud and so hard, she would start to cry. Sometimes she would smoke a cigarette. But mostly she would sing until she cried and I would just drive and watch her from the corner of my eye and be frozen by the sight of her. It was like watching a tornado. Beautiful. Terrifying. Sometimes I wished I could be like that, and feel things like that. But Emma felt enough for two people, and I was mostly grateful that she had her role and I had mine.

I think there are two types of people. Ones who have a scream inside them and ones who don't. People who have a scream are too angry or too sad or laugh too hard, swear too much, use drugs or never sit still. Sometimes they sing at the top of their lungs with the windows rolled down. I don't think people are born with it. I think other people put it inside you with the things they do to you, and say to you, or the things you see them do or say to other people. And I don't think you can get rid of it. If you don't have a scream, you can't understand.

As I watched Dr. Winter that first day, I got the sense that she had a scream. She was not a normal person. It takes one to know one, I guess, and I could just tell. She was beautiful—blond hair, very fit, big pouty lips and high cheekbones. Her eyes were pale blue but suspended in a perpetual state of anxiety, and she walked and talked and moved with strength, more like a man than a woman. Her eyes, and the way she moved, stood in such stark contrast to her otherwise feminine traits that it made her intriguing. Mysterious. I imagine men found her irresistible. And yet she did not wear a wedding ring. People like Dr. Winter, intriguing, mysterious people, always have a scream inside them.

I didn't know I had one until the night I finally escaped from the island.

No one answered my question about Emma liking that music, so I continued my story. "I can still remember exactly how I felt when we got to the dock and Bill opened the car door and the cool air came in with that smell, the Christmas tree smell, and also the smell of the water. It was nothing like the water here, or even when we went to Nantucket that summer when I was ten I think, or maybe nine. There was no fish smell, or seaweed, or you know that rotting smell that comes when it's really hot and there are all those open shells? There was none of that. Just water and Christmas, cool against my face while my body was warm under the blanket. And then, also, there was a sense of adventure and something else that I've thought about all the time since that night because it was part of what made me get out of the car and get on Rick's boat instead of running away into the woods."

Agent Strauss interrupted me to ask about the woods. "What kind of woods? Were there streets and houses, like a neighborhood or just trees and the shoreline? And what about the boat?"

I told him what I remembered—that when I woke up, I felt that cool air and then saw water on one side, with the dock and a small motorboat. And the boatman. Behind us and all around was a forest of pine trees and brush. The road was not paved. There was no parking lot or building. Just a small wooden dock and one boat and the boatman.

"So this boatman, Rick, he must have taken the boat to the dock from somewhere else? Sounds like he didn't keep the boat there, or you would have seen his car. . . ."

It went on like this for several minutes. I had already described the boatman to them, and not just his accent but that he seemed as old as Dr. Winter, and he was always tan and had a scruffy layer of light facial hair all the time—never cleanly shaven and never a full beard. He was not much taller than I was, maybe five nine with a thick, muscular build. His neck seemed larger than it needed to be, or maybe his head was small by comparison. And he had very short hair, dark brown. His eyes were brown as well. He wasn't ugly but he wasn't someone Emma would have even looked at twice. He was the kind of guy who passes in a hallway without being noticed.

I knew that the Pratts paid him to come back and forth to the island and that I thought he relied on them a lot for money because he was very loyal to them. I did not know how loyal until much later. Until the first time I tried to escape.

Dr. Winter was not a patient person. I could tell by the way she shifted her body in the chair, crossing and recrossing her legs. Fidgeting with her pen. But she let Agent Strauss go on until he was done even though she didn't seem to care much about the woods and trees and cars, or even about the boatman. When she asked me the next question, I started to believe that we would actually find my sister.

"Cass, go back to that night. Go back to that feeling you had— the one that made you get on that boat."

I took a long, deep breath and closed my eyes. This part was important and I wanted to make sure everyone knew it.

"I told you that I had a plan to go home in the morning, but that I wanted to find out what was going on and where we were and why Emma knew this man and why she had run away. When I knew all of that and I knew she was safe, I would go home. And because I had this plan that would make it impossible for anyone to blame me for anything, and then the smell of the trees and water—it just felt so clean. I felt so clean. And because I was clean, I could let myself enjoy this one night when everything was being turned upside down, when everyone would have to stop and open their eyes to see that things were not perfect for Emma because she had left this way and taken me with her. I felt alive. I felt hopeful. It's hard to describe. Something had lifted off me. Something heavy."

Dr. Winter looked at me with narrow eyes, like she was concentrating very hard. "What wasn't perfect, Cass? What did you want people to see when you left?"

The room got quiet and I realized I had said too much. Agent Strauss didn't let me answer, and I was relieved.

"It sounds like you felt powerful," he said.

"Yes! Like by going on that boat, I was going to change everything."

"So you got on the boat. Emma got on the boat. Then Bill . . ." Agent Strauss said, moving the story forward even more. Dr. Winter let him do it, but I could sense that she wanted to go back to her question, the one Agent Strauss had not made me answer.

"And then Rick untied the lines and pushed us off. I thought for a second that he was going to stay on the dock because we started to move away and he was still pushing. But then he grabbed hold of the rail and got on with us. I remembered the boats in Nantucket and how we were told not to try to do that, try to get on a boat that was moving away from the dock, because if we fell in and the water pushed the boat back toward the dock, it could crush us. Is that right, Dad? Did that happen in Nantucket?"

My father was staring at me but he didn't answer. I think he was in a state of shock, or maybe swept away by the storm inside his head. Mrs. Martin said his name sternly. She said it twice, like this. "Owen Tanner! Owen!"

I realized then that he had been listening and that he had heard my question because he answered it. "Yes. I did say that. That did happen in Nantucket."

But my father did not want to hear about the boat and the dock and how I felt powerful the night I went to the island.

"Cass," he said, "was this Bill person the father? Did this man get your sister pregnant?"

I tried to explain the best I could.

"I couldn't talk to Emma that night. We were never alone, not for a minute. We were given separate rooms. Bill and Lucy brought us into their house and got us settled. I couldn't see much. It was very dark and because the house runs on a generator, they use flashlights and candles at night after dark. Lucy gave me a sandwich and a toothbrush and she did her best to pretend she wasn't bothered by me being there, but I knew she was. I heard her speaking harshly to Bill when she thought I was brushing my teeth. But I wasn't brushing my teeth. I was standing near the bathroom door, listening. Emma was taken down another hallway. She looked back at me and smiled like she was really excited and I should be excited, too.

"So I just tried to go to sleep. The room was small. It had a twin bed and a dresser and a mirror. That was it. But it did have a window. I turned out the light and got under the covers. I was tired but my mind was racing. I don't know how long I lay there awake before I heard Emma's voice.

"I went to the window and saw that Emma was in a room across a small courtyard. I didn't know anything about the house that night, but of course I came to know it well. Every inch of it. There was a courtyard in the back and the house formed a U shape around it. So across the courtyard, I could see the bedrooms on the other side, and that night I could see Emma, Bill and Lucy in Emma's room. They were talking and then they both hugged Emma. As soon as they left, I opened my window and called out. I tried to do it in a whisper, but she couldn't hear me so I raised my voice until she did. She came to her window and leaned out the way I was. 'Where are we?' I asked. But she didn't answer. She just looked back with this knowing smile, like she knew exactly what she was doing and like she was certain that what she was doing was the best thing anyone could ever do. She rubbed the silver angel on the necklace.

"I kept thinking that night that we were in a safe place. Once Rick left, there was only a large wooden rowboat at the dock and no cars anywhere. I knew we were on an island because the boat approached from the back and docked on the side, and from the front, where the house faced, you could see it was just water forever and ever. I was excited about this new place, but I barely slept because I was so worried about how I would get a ride home or find a phone to call you to come and get me. I went over the things I would say to Emma and Bill or maybe Lucy. I was already feeling bad because we had traveled far and getting home would be difficult. I knew Emma would be furious with me. I didn't know then that she was pregnant.

"The next day was when she told me. I asked her who the father was and she said she couldn't tell me that. She said Bill and Lucy were going to help her have the baby and start a new life. You have to believe me. I did plan to come home. But all of that changed in the morning when Emma pleaded with me. She said if I went home, you would make me tell you where she was and that she wouldn't be able to have her baby, so I promised her I would stay. I'm so sorry! I know I caused a lot of problems. But I had to choose my sister."

I looked at my mother then, and said it one more time so there would be no doubt.

"I had to choose Emma."

SIX

Dr. Winter

They interviewed Cass Tanner for two hours after the forensics team left. She had given them more than enough to begin the search for the island where she and her sister had been held captive for nearly three years. She was physically and emotionally drained and had once again asked to rest.

Leo wanted her to go to the hospital for a thorough physical examination. Abby wanted to give her a comprehensive psychological examination. She had refused both, and because she confirmed there had been no sexual or physical abuse, because she had shown no signs of cognitive impairment, they let it go. For now.

Her parents had stood behind her on this and had already begun fighting over whose house she should be resting in. Abby and the agents agreed to return in a few hours so Cass could continue her story and work with a sketch artist on drawings of the Pratts, of the boatman, Rick, and of the man with the truck. It would take that long to get someone in from the city on a Sunday morning anyway. Still, a few hours would not pass quickly.

"It's going to be in the details. In something she doesn't even know is important," Leo said.

They had retreated to his car to escape the swarm of agents and local cops—not to mention the Martins and Owen Tanner. A press conference was being planned, and after that, the house would be a circus.

The field offices in New Haven and Maine had already run searches through the FBI's National Crime Information Center, or NCIC, and the DMV, turning up nothing on Bill and Lucy Pratt. No land records, deeds, birth certificates, tax filings. No social security numbers. They would move on to utilities, credit cards, cell phone carriers—but this road was narrowing fast.

"They're off the grid. Or Pratt isn't their real name. Maybe both."

Abby looked at the house from the passenger-seat window. "Fits the story. If these people were taking in runaway teens, it makes sense they wouldn't use their real names."

Leo turned the ignition so he could roll down the windows. "Do you mind? It's so damn hot. And I'm so damn old. Can't stand the summers anymore."

Abby didn't answer him.

"What are you thinking?" he asked.

She turned her gaze from the house to the dashboard. "We need to go back through the file. There's no way this happened without a trace of anything—no calls or e-mails or text messages. Maybe there was some kind of code when she was making this plan. Maybe she told the father, whoever he is, and he was pressuring her. Maybe we'll see it—now that we know what to look for."

Leo shrugged. "I don't know, Abigail. Or we could just spin wheels again."

The story of the night the Tanner sisters disappeared had been shocking to hear. It explained everything—the shoes at the beach, the car. Why Cass left with nothing but also why nothing of hers was found at the beach or in the car with Emma's. It explained the fight over the necklace and the car leaving late at night. And it explained why neither girl returned.

Still, the complete absence of any evidence of Emma's pregnancy or her plan to leave home to have the baby was unsettling.

Cass had gone on from the story of that first night to explain why she didn't try to leave, and why she didn't know who the father was. Abby had hung on her every word, desperate to fill in the missing pieces after so many years of wondering. Everything had made sense while she was telling the story, but it had left Abby hungry for more.

"So Emma wouldn't tell Cass who the father was or how she found the Pratts?" Leo asked, though the question was rhetorical. "That seems strange if they were so close."

"It fits their relationship," Abby answered. "Emma keeping secrets like ammunition. Cass treating Emma like an authority figure, like a mother. Not asking questions. Doing what she was told. Not demanding answers."

She started to say more about this. How there is always the "chosen" child in families like this one, the one who becomes the target of the sick parent, leaving the other neglected sibling to turn to that chosen child for needs that should have been met by a grown caregiver. But all of this was tied to the theory of the case Abby had not been able to let go of—that Judy Martin was a narcissist, that her illness was somehow related to the girls' disappearance. It was the theory that had caused the Martins to retreat and hide three years before. And the theory that had driven a wedge between Abby and Leo. None of that would be productive now. Still, Abby added it to her file.

Leo pulled out his phone. He had a sheepish look on his face. "I may have accidentally recorded the interview," he said. It was against Bureau policy to record interviews with witnesses without their consent.

Abby smiled and pulled out hers. "I may have made the same mistake."

Leo searched the recording of their session on his phone.

"Here it is," he said, pressing play.

"She said if I ever left, I would tell the police who had helped her. And if she told me about the father, I would tell that, too, and then he would take the baby. She was scared. This wasn't about her keeping secrets from me just to be mean, which she did a lot. And she was also right. If I had left the island, I would have told everything and anything I could to help find her and save her. And to punish the wicked people who wouldn't let us leave. I'm doing that now. I'm telling you everything I can think of and I don't care who gets in trouble."

Leo stopped the recording. "She says later that she thinks the father was a boy Emma met in Paris that summer—at her summer program. The timing of that fits."

"She had the baby in March. She was in Paris June and July. It does fit. But what about this mysterious person who links her to the Pratts?"

Leo found another piece of the interview to play.

"She just said it was someone she trusted. She said when she told this person she was pregnant and needed to leave home to have her baby, this person found the Pratts. Emma said it took nearly two weeks. That it had something to do with runaway teenagers. Emma said that the Pratts were not going to adopt the baby but were just going to help her take care of it until she could figure out what to do. I can't even tell you how strange it was when we both saw Lucy get crazy, keeping the baby for herself, keeping Emma away from her own child, there was like this panic that grew so slowly, a little every day, from little moments that were just not right, but then what did we know

about what was right? We had never raised a baby. We had never had a child. Maybe this is what people do when they help you like that."

"That's when she looked right at you, Abby? Remember?"

Abby nodded, her eyes fixed on Leo's phone and the voice of Cass Tanner.

"When you don't know something like that—like how to take care of a baby—but then the people who have taken care of you and pretended to love you are doing something that seems wrong, it can make you feel crazy. Like your thoughts about them being wrong are crazy because they're saying all these things that sound right. And because there are these moments when it seems as though the love is real."

Leo stopped the recording again. "Do you think she was trying to tell you something? Something she wasn't able to say?"

"Maybe. Or maybe she thought I was the person in the room most likely to understand it because of my training."

"Was she right?"

"Yeah. She was right."

Cass did not have to explain any of this to Abby. The girls had been isolated with two parental figures—people whom they had reached out to for help. They had not been drugged and thrown in a trunk. They had not been abducted at gunpoint or brainwashed. They had sought refuge, from what exactly was still unclear, but they had been offered something truly generous. And then there had been many months of what appeared to be genuine affection coupled with family activities like board games, TV, and the daily tasks of making food, collecting wood for the fire, tending to the house and the laundry in conditions that were antiquated at best.

Cass was also given ballet lessons, something her mother had refused her.

"I told Lucy that I had always wanted to dance. Remember?"

Judy Martin had not remembered. Or maybe she just pretended not to remember. This was the first Abby had heard of it, so if Cass had wanted to dance, she did not tell anyone who had been willing to admit it three years ago, when every detail of Cass's life was being investigated.

"She bought me two pairs of shoes and six leotards and Bill installed a barre in the living room. Lucy didn't know about dancing, but we got a video and some books and I practiced every day for forty-seven minutes because that was how long the video was. And you know what else? After Emma had her baby, she started to join me and we danced together, sometimes to music that wasn't very balletlike. And then we would laugh and Lucy would laugh with us. And in between times like that, Emma would cry to hold her baby and Lucy would scold her and tell her to go to her room."

Lucy had homeschooled them. There were textbooks that came in the mail and were delivered by the boatman. They studied every day, took tests and wrote papers. Lucy appeared to be highly educated and she had deep conversations about novels and history. All these things help forge a strong bond between the Pratts and the Tanner sisters. Of course there would be confusion when their interests became adversarial and the Pratts started to turn on them.

Abby remembered a small, insignificant piece of the story, which now felt more important. "She said something else—find the part where she talks about the books they read. . . ."

"Here . . ."

"My favorite book we read was The French Lieutenant's Woman. *It was so tragic. Lucy explained to us why Sarah Woodruff had lied about her life as the Lieutenant's lover. How she knew that people be-*

lieve what they want to believe. She explained everything so well and we both thought she was really smart and insightful."

"People believe what they want to believe." Leo repeated Cass's words.

"So what is it we all want to believe?"

"I don't know, kiddo. But this person who helped Emma find Bill Pratt—it had to be an adult. We can look for people who might have crossed paths with Emma back then—and who had affiliations with groups like that, or maybe worked with troubled teens. That narrows things down. Maybe we can go back through the file for that," Leo said.

He kept talking when Abby didn't answer.

"We'll have the sketches of the Pratts and the boatman later today. He might be the key to this whole thing—the boatman. He shops and gets gas and lives on the mainland. We find him, he brings us to the island. Or we find where he lived, where he kept the boat, and we narrow the search to a few dozen of them. That's all we need."

Leo had already said this. Abby had already thought it. They all had. Cass had given them so much information yet so little to help narrow the search. They'd asked about the shape of the island, the size. The curvature of the land masses she could see in the distance. Marine life. Plant life. Animal life. She had seen many landmarks, lighthouses and topography, but nothing unique for coastal Maine.

And it was not like California, where everyone traveled everywhere up and down the coast. These towns that were nestled in the jagged inlets and harbors were isolated and insular. People traveled between them mostly by boat because there were few bridges connecting them, and the drive back to the thoroughfares was long and slowgoing. The locals kept their heads down and worked hard making a living from fishing and vacationers. The tourists came and went with the summer months, usually returning to the same place year after year. Many of the properties along the coast were second homes to people who wouldn't know one town from the next. Reaching them with national media would be a challenge as well, and this would make the sketches less useful than everyone wanted to believe.

There was a chance someone from the Pratts' former life would recognize them. A family member, neighbor, schoolmate. They were in their forties, so it was unlikely they'd been on that island and off the grid for more than a decade. They had to have worked, gone to school, accumulated the resources that now afforded them the luxury of hiding.

And there was also the story of the boatman.

"Go back to him," Abby said. "Go back to the part about the boatman."

Leo found the story of Rick and his time in Alaska.

"I think Bill told us Rick's stories because it made him and Lucy feel like they had saved his life and they wanted us to think that they were good people. I didn't know how much about it to believe. They said he was abused by his parents, physically with beatings and stuff, and that's why he used drugs and was violent with them. He left home and went to Alaska because you can get good jobs on fishing boats there and they don't care how old you are. You can make around fifty thousand dollars in a few months, and you get to live on the boat and get free food so all that money you can just save and then live off of it for a while. But Bill said some of the men on those boats were bad men. Evil and violent and without any consciences or morals. They used to catch seagulls with their fishing hooks and then torture them to death on the deck. They had

contests to see which one could cause the most screaming by the birds because birds can make a scream when they are in pain. Bill said it was from being out at sea for so long. He said it wasn't normal and it destroyed their minds. But I thought, after hearing the story, that it probably had more to do with type of people who end up there. Don't you think?

"Rick felt this way—like he was damaged. He told Bill that he started to think he was one of them. He felt like he belonged there because they were all living on the outside looking in at normal life, at love and families. None of them had that. Rick tortured the birds. He caught the fish. He ate the nasty food and drank a lot of cheap whiskey. But then something really bad happened. A woman from the state fishing office came on the boat for a week to monitor their catch and practices because I guess that has to be done for the law in Alaska and she just happened to have that job. She was in her forties, married with kids. Kind of ugly, and I guess very hard-looking from working with all these psycho fishermen. But she didn't like what they were doing to the birds and so she told them to stop or she would report them to the police when they got back to shore. They didn't like that. So one night, they went into her room and pulled her out of bed and up the stairs to the deck, where they took off her clothes, tied her up in fishing net and took turns having sex with her. Rick said the men who did this went into every fisherman's bunk and made them come to the deck to watch or take a turn. He said more than seven men had a turn before they cut the net and let her go back to her room. Rick said he was not one of the seven but he was made to watch. He said he was afraid of what they would do if he refused. When it was over, he went back to his bunk and threw up all night."

Cass went on with the story. She said the woman was trapped on the boat for nine days. She did not leave her room, not even for food. There was no way to get off the boat until the helicopter came on the day it was scheduled. They would not allow her to use the radio to call for help sooner. She reported that she feared for her life. That she heard them sometimes through the walls, debating whether she would report the attack and if it would just be better to kill her and say it was an accident. There were a lot of ways to die on one of those boats. When the boat got back to port two months later, all the men were questioned about the incident. But they were not fired, and none of them was prosecuted. They stuck together with their story that she made it all up because she tried to have sex with one of the fishermen and was turned down. No one believed her.

"Rick came to Maine to work as a driver of a delivery boat. He started using heroin. When the Pratts hired him for a job and then got to know him and saw his addiction, they took him in, helped him get clean. Helped him make amends by telling the authorities what had happened on that boat. By then, the woman didn't want to be involved. But the story was reported in the paper, and all of the men who had participated in the incident were named there."

Leo stopped the recording.

"Cass said the boatman helped her escape, but she didn't say how this story plays into any of that," Abby said.

"We can ask her when we go back in. But I think we have enough to find this guy. How many gang rapes on a fishing boat in Alaska could be in the papers? We find the article, the reporter maybe, and we'll know the town he lived in. That should be enough."

Abby was quiet, thinking about this story.

"I know that expression, Abigail. Even after all this time. There's nothing you could have done. We worked every lead we could find."

Abby hesitated before telling him the truth. But then she did. "It was hard to be in the room with her."

"Cass?"

"No—that felt like a miracle. To see her alive, even after what she's been through. My God, compared to the things I've imagined. The things that have snuck into dreams . . ."

"I've never stopped seeing her face. Or Emma's," Leo said. "So it was seeing Judy that was hard? Even now? Even knowing she had nothing to do with their disappearance? I thought you'd be relieved."

Abby looked away.

But Leo was not deterred. "Do you want to talk about it?"

"About what?" Abby asked.

"About the fact that I didn't push back hard enough against the Martins. That I didn't bring it to the Assistant U.S. Attorney to get a warrant. That I thought the case was hitting close to home for you. Too close, maybe. We haven't seen you all year. Susan missed baking a cake for you."

Abby closed her eyes hard. She felt guilty about that. But she also felt betrayed, and that was hard to shake. "I know what that woman is, Leo. And it hit way beyond my home. She makes my mother look like Mother Teresa."

"And that had to push buttons. I'm an old man and I've been at this a long time. Buttons get pushed and we start to mold things to make them fit. I couldn't watch you go to war over a hunch that seemed driven by something other than the facts."

Abby finally looked at him. He had said all of this before. It wasn't that she didn't believe him. He had been trying to protect her from herself. That's what he'd said. But he was wrong then. And he was wrong now. Even if Judy Martin had not been involved in her daughters' disappearance.

"I've missed all of you. And I missed Susan's cake this year. I'm sorry about that."

Leo smiled and patted her on the knee.

Abby reached for the door. "I might go back in. Talk to Judy. Talk to Jonathan. See if I can get something more out of Owen on this person who might have helped Emma. I just—"

"Need to do something. I know. I'll check in with New Haven. I got the sense from the forensic team that we may have to sell this a little."

"I know. Emma's a grown woman now. We're going on Cass's word that she couldn't leave the way Cass did. Do what you can to get the bodies on this."

"I will."

Abby got out and closed the door behind her. As she walked toward the house, she sensed something familiar, something visceral like the creaking of floorboards in an old familiar hallway. Abby heard them—these echoes from the past, which had been here the very first time she met Judy Martin.

When she was in graduate school, she'd written her dissertation on narcissism, which was the colloquial name for narcissistic personality disorder. Her advisor was aware of her family history but agreed that this very history could benefit the work if she could remain objective. For two years, she read studies, interviewed doctors and compiled her own set of data from sources around the world. The disorder was relatively rare, affecting only 6 percent of the population. The majority of that 6 percent were men, so the data became increasingly limited as she focused on the issue that resulted in the paper—"Daughters of Mothers with Narcissism: Can the Cycle Be Broken?"

The paper was enormously successful. She received high grades from the examiners, but more important, the work was widely published and became the cornerstone of several Web sites seeking to help women impacted by the disorder. There were so many misperceptions. So much ignorance. Abby had broken with the formalities of her profession and written something that could be understood by anyone willing to take the time. In plain words, she described the symptoms: grandiose sense of self-importance; fantasies of unlimited success, power, beauty, brilliance; requiring excessive admiration; elevated sense of entitlement; takes advantage of others to achieve their own ends; lacks empathy; unwilling to recognize or identify needs and feelings of others.

She went beyond that to explain the pathology, and the cause. Contrary to our cultural perceptions, these people were not arrogant and self-centered. They did not truly believe they were exceptional to their peers. It was the exact opposite. They were so profoundly insecure, so fearful of being injured because of their perceived inferiority, that their minds had created an alter ego to protect them. This alter ego of perfection shielded them from their fear of being harmed, of being powerless, of being victimized. It was a fear so profound, it was unbearable. Unsustainable. And so the mind did something about it.

But it was not easy to support a fake alter ego. Narcissists had to become master manipulators. They surrounded themselves with people they could control and dominate—and they developed an eye for them. They learned how to be charming and appear confident so people would find them attractive, drawing near enough to be pulled into the trap. For men, it began with his wife and extended to subordinates in the workforce. Cult leaders were invariably pathological narcissists. For women, it often centered around her children.

Men chose submissive, codependent spouses. Women sometimes chose insecure men to dominate, but other times they sought out powerful men who were drawn to women for sexual promiscuity and deviance. Narcissistic women learned how to be enticing that way, and so they could lasso these powerful men and feed off their significance in the world.

She went on to address the most crucial question—how did these people get so profoundly insecure in the first place?

It began in early childhood.

She had tried to explain this to Leo: "It's like a bone, self-esteem, self-confidence. We take it for granted, but it's like anything else that develops after we're born. There's a time that it has to happen—in the first three years. From that first breath, a baby starts to learn that when she cries, someone feeds her, and when she smiles, someone smiles back, and when she babbles, someone replies. And she learns that she has power to get the things she needs to live—food, shelter, love. That's the bone, that's where it starts. And if that doesn't happen, if the bone doesn't develop, it never will. Everything done to remedy the defect is just a splint."

Leo had pushed back. The Tanner sisters were not left to cry all day, or to starve. There was no evidence of abuse or neglect. "Those are the easy lines to draw," Abby had responded. "But there're not the only ones."

Imagine the infant who one day cries and gets fed, and the next day cries and goes hungry. One day smiles and is kissed and hugged. The next day smiles and is ignored. This is what psychologists called "preoccupied or unresolved attachment" with the primary caregiver—usually the mother. There was love one minute and disdain the next. Affection that was given in abundance for no reason and then taken away without cause. The child has no ability to predict or influence the behavior of the parent. The narcissist loves a child only as an extension of herself at first, and then as a loyal subject. So she will tend to the child only when it makes her feel good.

Without that bone, there was no way for that child to develop confidence within any other relationship, no foundation to build on when that child grew up. Without that inner confidence, love, friendship, intimacy—the things we can't live without—that person always felt vulnerable. Only absolute dominance and control of other people could alleviate this perception. That was how the narcissist was created.

Abby had concluded from her research that these primary caregivers in the early years—again, almost always mothers—who were incapable of sustaining a healthy attachment to their children were often narcissists themselves. She matched the indicators of narcissism with the indicators of preoccupied or unresolved attachment—they fit like a lock and key. These were the cases that lived in the shadows. On the outside, these mothers appeared normal, exceptional even. Because the children were seen as an extension of the narcissist mother, they were not physically abused. They were not starved. They were, to the untrained eye, loved, adored, well cared for. But the narcissist does not experience real love or empathy, and desperately needs to keep the child in line—admiring the parent, worshipping the parent so that parent can feed her alter ego. So begins the unpredictable roller coaster for the child. Any deviation from this total admiration and love of the parent results in punishment—from the withdrawing of love and affection to acts of outright violence.

This was the final blow. The child of the narcissist becomes subjected to the same treatment that created her deeply flawed mother, ensuring the creation of another damaged soul.

No one sought treatment without some kind of threat—divorce, detachment from a loved one, unemployment. The thought of giving up the alter ego was too terrifying and, in many cases, had become so much a part of the fabric of that person, it was impossible to even disentangle it from the rest. It was almost always missed by marriage counselors and court shrinks. It could be hidden on a routine psychological profile. Even experienced therapists could miss it and be lured in by the often charismatic personalities of their patients. Some thought it was entirely untreatable.

"Don't you see!" Abby had pleaded with Leo. "All the signs are there . . . the way she slept all day, expected Owen to take care of them . . . how she forced Cass to call her Mrs. Martin after the custody fight . . . and the story of that necklace . . ."

Leo had not seen any of this and had begged her not to push the issue. The Bureau had listened to her arguments, but there was nothing to suggest the Tanner girls had been impacted by some rare personality disorder their mother may or may not have.

"They would have ruined you, Abigail. They have money and lawyers, and you have what, a story about a necklace? What does that story even mean?"

Abby had tried to explain what was so obvious to her. "It's classic behavior for a narcissistic parent. She has to keep all the children loyal and devoted solely to her, so she drives a wedge between the siblings, favors the stronger one, who's more likely to turn on her. She is ruthless about this because her alter ego is fed primarily by the complete submission of her children."

Leo had argued back and forth about how these distinctions would label every parent a "narcissist" or a "borderline" or something equally onerous. Maybe Judy Martin was just a shitty mother, or a selfish bitch. That was how they managed to hide from the world. Exactly like that. But he would not be swayed. And without the backup from the lead investigator, the theory had been dismissed.

But she was not wrong.

She heard the echoes now as she entered the Martin house. She was certain of it. A story had unfolded here—a story about

Cass, a story about Emma. Judy Martin had a starring role. And maybe Jonathan Martin. Maybe his son, Hunter. And it was more than a little troubling that this story was not among those being told—not by Cass or Judy or even Owen. Cass kept insisting that her mother be present for her interviews. It was as if she didn't want to talk about the past, to tell the one story that most needed to be told.

Yes. Abby was certain.

The only question that remained in her mind—what did this mean for finding Emma?

SEVEN

Cass

I have always liked the expression "rude awakening." It's one of those perfect expressions that says everything about something in very few words.

The first time I heard it was during my parents' divorce. The woman who talked to us about where we should live said it to me during one of our meetings. I had already told her that I thought we should live with my father, and why I thought that, and she kind of smiled and leaned back in her chair.

She asked me if my father had told me to say those things about Mr. Martin and his son, about how I felt weird around them and about how Hunter looked at Emma. And she asked whether he told me to say things about my mother that were unmotherly. I told her no, and that I had not said these things to my father, ever, so how could he have told me to repeat them? But I could see she didn't believe me. She told me how it was very common for parents to coach their children during a custody fight and how she *sees it all the time*. She said it was hard for her to believe me because Mr. Martin was very genuine in his desires to make a nice family for us and because my mother had devoted her entire life to raising us, giving up her career and her life in New York to be a stay-at-home mother.

Mrs. Martin cleaned up very well for the custody fight. She stopped sleeping late and napping and began driving us to school every day. She made us hot food for breakfast and sometimes even did our laundry herself. She came to every event at the school, cheering like a crazy fan, and she made us do our homework the minute we walked in the door. Our house was spotless and orderly. And she and Mr. Martin stopped drinking before five o'clock and going into their bedroom during the day.

I suppose I should have been grateful for this. Our mother was finally acting like the kind of mother we saw when we went to our friends' houses and the kind of mother our half brother, Witt, had, which is why Witt is one of those people who does not have a scream inside him.

It was hard to imagine Witt having this other, normal life because we never saw him in that life. Before our father and mother got divorced, we saw Witt those ninety-six hours a month when he came to stay with our father for his visitation, and after the divorce, we saw him for ninety-six hours at our father's new house when we went to visit him. The rest of the time, he was with his mother and we were not a part of that life. But he described it in a way that made sense of things, and it was that sense of things that made it impossible for me to be grateful for our mother's sudden turnabout during the divorce.

This isn't normal, Cass, Witt said to me one night when he had come for a weekend visit. It was before the divorce, and our mother had dragged our father out to the club for dinner. *The way you and Emma take care of yourselves—it's not normal. Most kids wake up to breakfast and a ride to school. They come home to dinner and clean clothes and someone hassling them about their homework and turning off the TV or getting off their video games. It's not like it makes you happy all the time. But here, I always have one eye open. When I go home, I close both eyes at night.*

I used to have to imagine what that would be like, to have someone watching over me. To close both eyes at night. When the custody battle happened, and our mother did start doing all those things for us, I still kept one eye open. And that was when I understood what Witt was trying to tell me. It wasn't about the things he described. I know there are a lot of kids whose parents work all the time and have to do the things Emma and I did for ourselves. But they still close both eyes. It's not the many things. It's the one thing that's behind the many things. I don't even know what to call it. It didn't matter that Mrs. Martin started doing our laundry and checking our homework, because she was only doing it for herself, for the case. It was not for us—that was the one thing that was still missing.

Emma didn't seem bothered by this the way I was. She started wearing three outfits a day and throwing them on the floor of the laundry room. She wasted food so we ran out of things before the housekeeper was coming. One time she even poured out an entire gallon of milk, right down the drain. And she created stuff to do that required rides and waiting around. She joined the cast of a school play. She started playing field hockey again. She started a study group that met at the library.

She came to me one night the way she used to do, after our mother was asleep. She crawled into my bed, under the covers, and pressed her cheek against my cheek. I could feel her heart beating fast like she was excited, and I could feel her face smiling against my skin.

Did you see the look on her face when I told her I needed a ride to rehearsal at six and then a ride home at eight? Wait until she has to come to the show on both a Friday and Saturday night. She'll miss the whole weekend at the club. And I signed her up to help with costumes!

Emma was making her pay, and it made her happy.

When it stops and she stops taking care of you, Cass, I'll do it. You know that, right? I'll always take care of you.

I felt my own heart beating faster then because even though I didn't know if she actually would take care of me, if she would be able to even if she tried, she meant it with her whole heart.

I closed both my eyes that night.

Our father was not happy. He nearly went insane watching all this unfold. He would pace back and forth, his face bright red, talking to his lawyer on the phone, trying to explain that everything our mother was doing was a charade. *He* had driven us to school every morning. *He* had gone to the events, and gone alone. *He* had supervised our homework, coached our sports teams, watched movies with us on Saturday nights. He had moved out only to prevent fighting in front of us, and now he never got to see us. This woman from the court was coming into our lives, looking at one picture, a snapshot, and deciding our fate based on a façade, a lie. She couldn't, or didn't want to, see all the other pictures taken on all the other days when Mrs. Martin hadn't prettied us all up for the lens.

My mother used to hire a professional photographer every fall to take our portraits. He came all the way in from the city and charged not only for his time, but also for the black-and-white prints that would come to hang in white wooden frames on the walls of our hallway upstairs.

The hallway has a balcony on the other side, which opens to the foyer below. My mother liked that people could see from the foyer to the wooden railing that lined the balcony and then just above it to the wall of portraits. There were over thirty of them by the time Emma and I disappeared, starting from when we were born to that last fall when Emma was seventeen and I was fifteen.

I used to wonder what people thought when they saw those photos from the foyer, people who didn't know us well enough to come upstairs, but could see our photos from the foyer as they were greeted by Mrs. Martin at the front door. The photos were so expensive and so beautiful—our faces always looked peaceful and angelic. Some of the worst fights between Emma and our mother came on the days of the photos. Every time the photographer came, Emma would refuse to wear what she was told or to put her hair back or to smile. You could not know that from just looking at them from below. And you would think that the person who went to all this trouble to pay for these pictures and frame them just right and hang them just so must cherish their subjects more than life itself.

That's how I felt about the woman from the court. How she was seeing only the pictures that my mother had hung on the wall and drawing conclusions from them that were not even close to the truth. Just like the guests who caught glimpses of us from the foyer.

My father eventually conceded, settling the case and making us live with Mr. Martin and Hunter. The woman had recommended this to the court, and fighting her would mean another year in a legal battle, making me and Emma talk to more people and take all kinds of psychological tests. Our father said he would have to call witnesses at a trial, including friends and relatives, and try to get them to say bad things about Mrs. Martin and how the woman had told him that all of that would be very harmful to me and Emma. He said he was settling to save us from more pain. When he told me this, I wanted to scream at him, *No! I want to fight! Lead me into battle and let me get bloody!* He was our general and we were his soldiers and I, for one, was willing to die for the cause.

I would not learn until years later, after combing through my past with Witt, that what my father was really afraid of had nothing to do with me and Emma. He had become so upset about the affair and the divorce that he had started smoking pot again the way he did in high school. My mother had no proof, but she knew my father very well and she was very clever. Her lawyer threatened to file a motion to force my father to take a drug test. He surrendered the next week. Looking back, I think it would have led me to the same conclusion about my father, and that is that as much as I loved him, he was a weak man. I don't think it matters that his weakness made him smoke pot to ease his pain rather than the fact that he was just weak. The result was the same for me and Emma.

The woman said to me, *It can be a rude awakening to see the truth about your parents during a divorce. People will stoop to low levels just to punish their spouse for leaving them.* I knew what she was implying—that our father was making up all these bad things about Mrs. Martin and these good things about himself because he wanted her to pay for cheating on him and leaving him. But because I knew the truth, because I knew what all the other pictures looked like—the ones that didn't make it to the wall in our hallway, the ones that were never even taken at all—the rude awakening was not what she had said, but instead the realization that grown-ups can be wrong, they can be stupid and inept and lazy at their jobs, and that they won't always believe you even when you are telling the truth. And when they have power over you, these stupid, inept people who can't see what's right in front of them, when they don't believe you when you tell them, bad things can happen.

This never left me. In the three years I was away and as I walked back through my mother's door, this fact about stupid people not believing the truth was as much a part of me as my lungs and my heart.

Dr. Winter and Agent Strauss stayed until the late morning, when my mother asked them all to leave so I could rest for a while. I was an adult woman and I had committed no crime, so they could not make me go to the hospital or the police station or do anything I didn't want to do. I told them more things about the island that might help them find it. I gave them descriptions of the people they thought they might be able to find in their systems, like Bill and Lucy and the boatman. They asked a lot of questions about why Emma had not come with me, and I told them over and over it was because of the baby. I told them how the Pratts looked after her like their own child and how she slept in their room. It was one thing for me to slip out undetected and get to the boat. But a two-year-old? Who was sleeping in the same room with our captors?

I had thought about killing them. I did not say this to Dr. Winter or Agent Strauss. I had thought about how I could kill one without waking the other. I did not have a gun. It seemed like the simple thing—if you set aside the fact that killing is a sin. Just go in at night and kill them in their sleep. Take the baby and leave. Burn the house down. What would the boatman do then? Would he make us stay on that island? I did not make a plan to do this. But it is only natural when you are imprisoned to think about how to escape, and killing them was an obvious way to do that. It was more difficult than you might think. Without a gun, there was a risk of killing just one, and they were both equally capable of killing me right back.

I had to cut myself off then, as they pressed for details about

these two people I had lived with for three years. I could detect
their concerns about Emma from the questions they were asking
me. There could be no ambiguity about my imprisonment there,
no wondering whether or not there should be a furious search for
my sister. And yet, I had not been in a cage or locked in a room. I
had not been chained to a radiator or bound in any way. I sat with
them at dinner every night. I let them teach me things. I smiled
and laughed and talked about my observations, my childhood,
my life as it was evolving. Anyone looking in from the outside
would never know how desperate I was to leave after the confusion about what was happening cleared, or how many times I
thought about leaving after that and about doing terrible things
to make that possible. What they would see would be two kind
people taking care of me, loving me, believing in what they were
doing. They would see what they wanted to see, like that woman
from the court. Even like my father.

People could be stupid and not believe the truth.

Agent Strauss was a good man. He was old like my father and
he wore a gold wedding ring. He was not very tall, but he seemed
strong because his shoulders were broad and he had a thick gray
beard that started to show by the early afternoon.

Something about that, about all of him made me think of him
as strong and manly. I did not know anything about him that
could justify my holding this opinion about him also being a good
man. But I just knew. It was in his eyes and the expression his
face held when he watched Dr. Winter speak. And it was in the
concern he held for me and for finding Emma even when some of
the other agents seemed skeptical. I decided I would like Agent
Strauss.

He returned with Dr. Winter two hours and thirty-nine minutes later. The sketch artist was not available until the following

morning, which seemed very strange to me, and which again raised alarms inside my head that the search for Emma was not going to be given top priority. We agreed I would see a doctor in the morning and let Dr. Winter conduct a psychological exam. This would satisfy my mother. She said I didn't seem right in my head. I heard her say it to Mr. Martin when he finally came back upstairs. And I'm sure she said it to anyone else who would listen. She had stopped crying and started making the calls to friends and relatives, and the publicist she had used three years ago. The shock of my return was transforming into her new reality.

The focus when they came back in was on my final escape. They wanted every detail because, as Agent Strauss said, there could be something in the details that I didn't even realize was important. I doubted that was true because I had given so much thought to them.

"Just tell us from start to finish," he said.

So I did.

"The boatman, Rick, waited for me on the west side of the island, not on the dock. The west side was all rocks, like huge slabs of gray rock, not stones, and they just disappeared into the waves. In high tide, you couldn't really see the rocks at all. The water came and crashed right up to the tree line. But in low tide, you could walk a long way out on the rocks. Bill liked to walk out there and fish. He would wear high rubber boots and take nothing with him but a box of fishing stuff, a rod and a six-pack of beer. They were cans of beer. They had blue writing on them. Is that helpful? . . . One time I followed him. This was before Emma had her baby. It was when I still looked at Bill and Lucy like they were good people who loved us.

"I started to walk on the rocks to catch up to him. I had this stupid idea that he would teach me how to fish and that we would be, I don't know, maybe like father and daughter because I was missing my father so much. I remember wanting that so badly as I walked on the rocks, you know, like that feeling when you get an idea to do something that might make someone love you? I used to get that same feeling when we made Mother's Day cards in school and I would always write on mine 'Number One Mom!' or 'Best Mom in the World' and I would get that feeling, thinking that it might make you happy, Mom . . . do you remember?"

"Yes, of course, sweetheart," Mrs. Martin said. "I always loved your cards."

"But the rocks were so slippery. You couldn't see it, this film of slippery stuff covering the rocks. Bill told me back at the house that day that the rocks are covered with diatoms, which are like algae. He told me after he'd stopped yelling at me because I fell on those rocks trying to catch up to him and I slid down a large one and into the surf. Even though it was low tide, once you go to the water's edge, it got very deep very quickly, which is why you can fish there because the fish like to hide in the deep pockets between the places where the rocks stick out. I fell in and went under quickly. The current was so strong. I had no idea. You could not swim from any point off the island, so I had never been swimming and had never felt it before. When a wave came in, I got slammed against one of the rocks, and then when it went out, it pulled me with it and my head went under. And it was so cold because it was just early spring and the water never gets warm there anyway.

"Bill had to jump in to save me. I thought I was going to drown. The rock was too slippery for me to grab hold, so I just got slammed up and then pulled under like a rag doll. It was horrible. And then I felt his hand grab my arm. Bill had waded in from the other side, where he could stay standing, and he held on to this little tree that was trying to grow between the rocks, and then he grabbed me with the other hand. He held me while the water tried to pull me back under, and then when the wave came back in and pushed me, he used that force to bring me to his side and then up onto the rock. I lay there crying and gasping for air. Bill sat there staring at me, shaking his head with disapproval, but then he scooped me up and held me so I would stay warm.

"I don't know why I told that whole story. The only important thing is to know that Bill would never have suspected I would make my escape there, by those rocks. And that made it the perfect place to meet Rick in his boat. We did it at high tide. He threw me a life jacket with a rope tied to it, and I put it on and got in that water, even though I could still remember almost dying there. I just closed my eyes and then let him pull me to the boat. He grabbed the top of the jacket and hauled me up until I was on the deck, shivering. He had dry clothes for me and a hat and a blanket. He drove the boat along the side you couldn't see from the house and then he dropped me off up the coast, not inland where the harbor was, but definitely on the shore. His friend was waiting with the truck. I got in, and that was that. I think I told you the rest this morning."

This story made my father cry because of the part about wanting Bill to be my father and it made my mother unnerved because she still could not understand how I did not know where this island was. She said we should wait until the examinations were complete before any more stories were told. She said this as if I were not in the room, but then she stroked my hair and kissed my forehead and told me, *"Everything will be all right, sweetheart."*

My parents fought that day about where I should stay. My mother won. In spite of the excitement and stress that my homecoming had provoked, the irony of this did not escape me. I slept the first night in the guest room. My mother had turned our rooms into a study and a den. She said it had been too painful to see my things every day, so she put them all in the attic for a while and then finally gave them away to charities.

As I walked down the hallway, whose walls were now adorned with modern art, I remembered the second rude awakening I had in this house.

It happened the third weekend in April when Hunter was home from boarding school. He'd brought a friend whose name was Joe, and he was a junior like Hunter. Emma was a freshman. She had just turned fifteen.

On Fridays when it was Mrs. Martin's weekend, Emma and I would try to make plans with our friends, even if we had to invite ourselves to the friend's house. Sometimes Emma would let me sit on her bed and watch her pluck her eyebrows or put on makeup before she went out. And sometimes she would tell me things about her life because she had no one else to tell them to who wouldn't gossip about her or judge her or try to steal her plan. On this Friday, we were staying home because Emma had a plan to make Joe her boyfriend.

I'm having Natasha Friar over because Hunter said she was hot and that will keep him busy. And while he's busy with Nat, I'll be busy with Joe.

Our mother and Mr. Martin had already left to go to the club for golf and dinner with their friends. They told us to *be good* and not to leave the house. Emma leaned into the mirror to finish putting on her mascara. I was sitting on the edge of the bathtub, thinking about her plan, and how clever she was, and how beautiful she looked when she put on her tight clothes and red lip gloss. I must have been too quiet, or maybe I stared so long that she started to feel my eyes burning a hole in her skin.

She stopped what she was doing and turned to look at me, one hand gripping the mascara wand and the other waving a finger at me. *Stay out of the way, Cass. I mean it! You can have one drink with us but that's it. If you mess things up for me, or Hunter, one of us will kill you!*

Hunter and his friends arrived in a car service at 9:12. Nat had been at our house since 7:14 and was already drunk on Mr. Martin's apricot brandy. Emma was too nervous to be drunk, though she'd made us both a fuzzy navel. I went upstairs to my room.

I don't know what time it was when I came out of my room, because I had fallen asleep but then woken up. I felt unnerved, like I couldn't get back to sleep until I knew if our mother and Mr. Martin had come home, and whether anyone else was asleep, and where they were all sleeping, and also what had happened with Emma's plan. It's strange to fall asleep after drinking and then to wake up and not know what's going on outside your own door, in your own house. And so I went out, not with the intention of ruining Emma's plan with Joe or Hunter's plan with Nat, but just to get my bearings so I could go back to sleep.

From outside my room, I could see down the hall to the master bedroom. The door was closed and there was no light coming from the crack at the bottom. Hunter's door was open and his room was dark, which meant he was downstairs in the TV room, probably, maybe with Nat. But across the hall, in the guest room, the door was closed and a light was flickering at the bottom.

I could tell you that I thought maybe someone had left it on and I needed to check. I could tell you that I was worried about Nat and thought she was in there, passed out with the light still on. I could tell you I thought the same about Joe, or the other couple Hunter had brought home. But none of that would be true. The truth is that I knew Emma was in that room, and although

I had no need to open that door, I had an unstoppable desire to do it.

I will never forget what I saw in that room that night. Yes, Emma was having sex with Joe. She was on the bed and he was on top of her, between her legs, his face buried in the nape of her neck. And, yes, it was the first time I had ever seen people having sex, so it was shocking. But that image faded over the years. What lingered and became indelible was my sister's face when she turned and looked at me. It was that expression, the one I tried to describe to my father and Mrs. Martin and the agents when I told them about how she looked at me from that window across the courtyard, like she was certain that what she was doing was the best thing anyone could ever do and that she was exactly where she was supposed to be, doing what she was supposed to be doing. That night, as I closed the door and went back to my room, where I waited for my nerves to settle, I was still a believer in Emma's certainty. I remember thinking that she was always right—she said she would make Joe her boyfriend, and she had done just that.

But the next time Hunter came home for a weekend, he did not bring Joe. Emma tried to hide her disappointment. We went outside to smoke and get away from our mother and Mr. Martin. We were out by the pool house. Hunter told Emma she had made a fool of herself calling and e-mailing Joe when he never re-sponded and obviously had just used her for the weekend. Emma called him an *asshole*. Hunter called her a *whore*. Emma told him Nat had said he didn't know how to kiss. Hunter said Nat was a *skank*. It went on like this for the entire cigarette until finally Hunter told her Joe had a girlfriend. Emma went quiet. Her face quivered but she did not cry—not then, anyway. Hunter was smiling as he put the cigarette out with his shoe. He seemed satisfied, as if he had just won a battle. Emma ran back to the house ahead of us, and as I walked back with Hunter, I could see his satisfaction fade. A war had begun in our home, and it would not end until the night we disappeared. Hunter had not wanted to defeat Emma, because defeat meant the war was over. And Hunter never wanted anything with Emma to be over.

Still—Emma had been defeated in that one battle. That knowing look on her face that night when Joe was on top of her did not mean she was right. In fact, she turned out to be very, very wrong about him and her plan to make him her boyfriend. That was the second rude awakening—the moment when I saw Emma defeated, when I realized that she could be defeated. I did not like knowing this. Not one bit.

A light from down the hall pulled me back from the image of Emma on that bed with Joe. My mother had come from her room. She seemed startled to find me still in the hall and not tucked away and sound asleep.

"Are you all right, sweetheart?"

She walked toward me, and I let her. She put her arms around me, and I let her. She smelled of face products and Chanel No. 5, and I will admit to feeling a warm current rush through my body. It was the same current I had felt that morning, only it had grown stronger. Loving our mothers never goes away, and I was surprised to learn this at that moment when I was having this memory of Emma and her defeat.

"Sweetheart, I think you're confused about that night when you left. No more stories about Emma and that island until we get you checked out, okay? I think you might be having dreams or fantasies, and if you tell them something that's wrong, then it could make things worse. Do you understand? You were in your room that night, Cass. After you and Emma had your fight. You were in your room when Emma left the house, not in the back of Emma's car. Don't you remember?"

Mrs. Martin was stronger than I had ever imagined, and now she was turning the tables on me, on my story, and I felt desperate because that meant we might never find Emma. The agents were already questioning why she had not escaped with me.

Still, even through my desperation and rage, I was that same victim I'd been as a child, the one who gave in to her extortion, who paid whatever price was set for her love and who let Emma draw fire so I could run for cover. I thought I'd built walls these past three years to protect myself from Mrs. Martin, but if I had built them, they were made of sand and they crumbled in her arms.

"The things you're saying can't be true, Cass. I'm so scared that something is wrong with your mind."

I wanted to hate her for saying these things to me. But I couldn't. I still needed to love her.

And so when she whispered one last thing in my ear, "I love you," and when she tried to hug me tighter, I allowed this third rude awakening in, and I let her.

EIGHT

Dr. Winter

It was not easy to leave the house, to leave Cass. Abby was haunted by the fear that she would disappear all over again.

The fear was irrational. The state police had agreed to leave a patrol car at the top of the driveway, day and night, until the Pratts were found. Judy and Jonathan Martin would be there, and her father would be ten minutes down the road. But more than anything else, Cass had no reason to leave and every reason to stay. She was desperate to find her sister.

Still, on the rare occasions when optimistic thoughts had beaten their way into Abby's consciousness, when she had allowed herself to imagine this moment when the Tanner sisters were found, this was not how it played.

They interviewed Cass for three more hours before Judy finally asked them to leave for the night.

"She's not well. I know it!" Judy had spoken about Cass as if she had not been right beside her. "I would have known if Emma was pregnant. And if she was, I would have helped her. She knew that. You know how close we were. You did all those interviews. None of this sounds like my daughter!"

She had insisted that Cass have some rest, and she won out over and above the objections of Abby and Leo. Abby agreed to do a formal psychological examination the following day, and Judy agreed to take Cass to the doctor first thing in the morning with one of the forensic agents.

And that was that. The excitement had quieted with the mundane tasks of assignments and logistics. Field agents in New Haven, Maine and Alaska had begun their work. Leo went back to the city to get some sleep. And Abby went home.

She walked into her house the same way she did at the end of every day, dropping her keys in a small ceramic bowl shaped like a hippopotamus that sat on a table next to the sofa. Her niece had made it in kindergarten and sent it in the mail last Christmas, neatly folded into plastic Bubble Wrap. Her dog was soon upon her, his entire body wagging with anticipation of food and attention. She reached down and rubbed his ears.

Her house, the dog, the reminders of her family—they had all been here, waiting for her to return from this miraculous day. But all of it seemed indifferent, unchanged by the momentous event of Cass Tanner's coming home.

Maybe because there were still so many questions. As much as Abby hated to admit it, Judy Martin was not wrong. Emma was not the kind of girl to let anyone tell her what to do, especially not with something this important, this intimate. Owen would have supported whatever decision she made, and Judy would have matched his generosity with something even grander just to prove she was the better parent. They were far more likely to fight over Emma's child than make her get rid of it.

Maybe that's what Emma feared—another fight that would never end.

Leo had pushed hard on every front to get something, *any-*

thing, that would help them find this one island in the thousands of islands off the coast of Maine. In all the conversations with the Pratts and the boatman, the groceries and packages he delivered, the lobster boats and sailboats and motorboats all off in the distance—was there not one name of a harbor or a yacht club? Cass said she had tried to find out where they were. She'd asked questions; she'd sifted through garbage. The Pratts were very careful. And all she could recount from the boats were names she could see on the larger sails, Hood and Doyle and Hobie Cat. Abby could see her face as she said the words over and over: "I tried! Every minute of every day, I tried!" She said the island felt enormous to her, like everyone saw it and knew it, only they were never close enough to see her, or hear her. It had felt unique to her, this prison, and so she always imagined it would be easily found. She knew the town where she got in the truck. She had counted the minutes to Portland. Abby's impression was that she was telling the truth.

Cass had also insisted that the story of that first year and her first attempt to escape were important, and so they had let her tell it. She said it explained how she came to understand how difficult it would be to leave, and why it took so long. She said it explained how she came to know that the boatman would eventually help her find her way home, but that it would take time. And planning. But the story would not be finished before Judy made them leave, so Abby arrived home with more questions than answers.

She went to the kitchen and fed the dog. Then she opened the fridge. She took out some leftover pasta and put it in the microwave. She felt sick and was hoping it was from hunger. She hadn't been able to eat all day.

At a small table in the corner, she set down the plate and a glass of water. Then she pulled out her phone. There were three texts from Meg, which she'd answered dismissively throughout the day. She removed her sister from her thoughts and played the recording she'd made of the interview with Cass.

She started it where Cass had left off in the morning.

"I wanted to leave the morning after we arrived. I only slept for three hours and twenty minutes that first night and when I did, it was short, like an hour at a time, and then I would wake up in a panic. I heard the lobster boats—though I didn't know what kind of boats they were at the time—they were trolling some time after the sun came up. It sounded like a faraway hum. I got up and looked out the window. I could see Emma in her room and I started to cry. She rushed out of her room and came to mine and sat on my bed. 'I want to go home!' I told her. That was when she told me she was pregnant, and that we couldn't go home, at least not right away. She said Bill would take care of us and that we would have a good life there. I got very angry with her, I yelled at her and she yelled back, telling me she wouldn't let me mess up her plan to have her baby.

"I already told you that in my mind I had to choose between Emma and home. And so I chose Emma."

Judy barged into her story then. *"But three years, Cass? You chose to stay for three years? Tell us why you couldn't leave. You still haven't explained it."*

Cass continued.

"It's hard to explain. I think there are two reasons we stayed. First, while the days went by slowly sometimes, the years went by fast. There is something about living that close to the ocean, surrounded by the water, that changes time. Hours can pass just staring at the waves and feeling the wind on your face. And there is so much work to deal with the wind and the water, to keep it from ruining a house, especially without regular electricity.

"Second, there were the good things I've been trying to explain.

Emma talked to me more and more. We became friends and I didn't want that to end. Not ever. Sometimes I thought about how much I wanted to be home. But then there were these other things, like being close to Emma and how nice Lucy and Bill were to us. So there were these good things and the time passing so fast . . . but then the bad things started to come, after Emma had her baby.

"They wouldn't let me near her when it was happening. She went to them first, in the middle of the night, because she was still very close to them and she trusted them. I didn't even wake up until I heard Emma screaming. I could also hear Bill yelling at Lucy and Lucy yelling back like they were both scared and angry at the other for not making it easier. I thought she was going to die. I really did. There was so much screaming—and it was screaming from pain that was coming out of Emma. Like she was being tortured. And in between the screaming from pain, there was crying and sobbing from desperation because she knew it wasn't over. And I couldn't help her! I tried to go to her, but Bill pushed me out of the room, with both hands and this red face that looked like it was on fire. Emma yelled at me, too. She told me to leave because I would only make it worse. It went on for most of the night until finally it just stopped. I sobbed into my pillow because it was so terrible. Not being able to help her. Not being wanted for my help. And not knowing if she was even going to be okay.

"And then I heard the baby cry. And I heard Bill and Lucy laughing and crying like they were happy now. I went to the hallway so I could hear more, but I didn't hear anything from Emma. Not that whole night or the next morning. Nothing until the next afternoon.

"That's when they took Emma back to her room. She tried to sleep, but her breasts got huge and swollen. She asked if she should breast-feed and they said not to bother. Lucy said it wasn't that good for babies anyway, and Emma didn't know any better.

"I stayed outside her door so I could get her whatever she needed.

'*Cass,*' *she would whisper,* '*it hurts so much!*' *I brought her ice packs every few hours to keep on her chest, and after a few days the milk just stopped coming.*

"*From that first cry, Lucy had that baby all day and all night. When Emma tried to hold her, Lucy said not to bother. She said Emma should rest and study because she had her whole life ahead of her. She said,* '*That's what we're here for, my love!*'

"'*Cass,*' *Emma would whisper,* '*have you seen her today? Is she bigger?*'

"*Emma cried for hours and hours, missing her baby.* '*I need to hold her! Please! Just for a few minutes!*' *she would beg. Lucy always had an excuse. The baby was sleeping. The baby was sick. The baby was getting used to her bed. Emma would hear her cry and she would stand outside their locked bedroom door and yell at them.* '*Please! I hear her now. I know she's awake! Bring her to me!*'

"*Emma pleaded with me then.* '*Cass, you have to find out what's going on. Why they won't let me see her!*'

"*So one day, I started a conversation with Lucy.* '*You're so good with babies, Lucy. How do you know so much?*'

"*We knew they didn't have children, because they told us and because there was no sign of any children anywhere. No pictures or baby things. Lucy kissed the baby's forehead. She smiled and said,* '*God wanted me to have babies when he was making my soul, but then he made a mistake when he was making my body. It's my cross to bear in this life, Cassandra. Not able to do what I was born to do.*'

"*Then she bounced Emma's baby in her arms, and her smile turned happy.* '*Until now, right, my little peanut? My precious angel? My sweet Julia.*'

"*I told Emma what she said. I told Emma I thought she might be crazy, that she had been mothering us, but now she had a baby and that baby had ignited something inside her. Emma's eyes got very wide.*

'That stupid bitch named my baby? She gave her the name Julia?' Emma said she would hate that name for the rest of her life and would never let it leave her lips.

"We were both shaking then. I had confirmed what we both suspected. Lucy had gone crazy, and Bill didn't know what to do about it. You know how sometimes you have two parts of yourself—one part that wants you to do something crazy and the other part that sees how crazy it is but doesn't do anything, because it doesn't want to upset the crazy part? You don't want to cut yourself in half. . . . That's what they were like. They were like one person with two parts. And the Lucy part was stronger.

"That happened in the fall, one year after we left home. By then we both knew something was wrong. The baby was six months old, and she was getting bigger and easier to handle. But still, they would not let Emma take care of her. Lucy held that baby like it was her own. Something just snapped in Emma. She went to their door and pounded on it with her fists. 'Give me my baby right now!'

"Bill got very mad at her. He yelled from the other side of the door, 'Go back to your room, young lady, or there will be dire consequences!'

"'Give me my baby!' Emma yelled, and pounded again on the door. I was standing beside her, frozen with fear because the situation was escalating and I knew it wouldn't end well. Emma had fire in her veins but no power. I think the fire made her feel powerful and stopped her brain from working. We heard loud footsteps and then the door opening. Bill was there and he had this look on his face that was beyond angry—he looked like he needed for this to stop or he would lose his mind. I think on the other side of the door, Lucy was pleading with him to get us under control, to make Emma stop asking for her baby, and I think he had no idea what to do about any of this. He couldn't make his wife stop, so he turned his rage to Emma and he slapped her clear across the face. She stared at him in shock. So did I. And he stared right back, just as surprised as we were by what he had done.

"'I told you to leave! Why didn't you listen to me?' He said this in a pitiful, whiny voice and he even had a tear in his eye. Emma said nothing. She turned and left and I followed Emma back to her room. We sat on her bed. She took my hands in hers and she said, 'You have to get out of here and bring back someone to help us.'

"We came up with a plan. I told her I would find a way to leave. I told her to start fighting with me and make it look like I left because of her and that I wanted no part of her, so that way when I left, they wouldn't fear that I would return with help. And that was the plan. That I would come back for Emma and the baby. Emma agreed.

"From September to February, I watched three things: First, I watched the boats. I watched the hours of the day when they passed through different channels safely. Second, I watched when the boatman came and left. Third, I watched the hours when the baby slept during the night and when she needed to be fed.

"Bill kept a small rowboat at the dock. There were oars on the boat, and I thought I could use the boat and oars to leave. I was very stupid.

"The night I tried to escape, I waited until the baby had been fed and they were all asleep. I went down to the dock and got on that boat and untied it from the post. It was dead quiet and freezing cold. All I could hear was the sound of the water splashing against the sides and my heart beating fast. I was scared and excited and again, had that feeling of being powerful because I was taking charge of my life and getting away from these crazy people and saving my sister and her baby. It was also so hard to leave Emma, to leave the baby, like I was leaving a piece of me behind. So I just kept thinking about how I would return, maybe even that same night if I got lucky, with help. With someone who would save us.

"I grabbed the oars and started to use them to steer the boat. I had watched Bill do it sometimes when he didn't want to wait for Rick. He would make it through that part of the current that pulled things back to *the island, and then all the way into the harbor until he disappeared from my sight. But it was so much harder than I thought. I didn't know to sit backwards. I didn't know how to put the oars in the rings, and they were so heavy and the current was so strong against them. One got pulled right out of my hand and fell into the water and was carried away. Then the whole boat started to drift alongside the island toward the west, where those rocks were. The boat was totally out of my control. I went from side to side, pushing the water, pulling on it with the one oar that was left. The boat would spin a bit, then just keep on going with the current. I felt this panic like my head was going to explode. I knew if we headed toward the west end of the island, I would get stuck in the rocks. And that's just what happened. The boat got lodged between two rocks. I pushed with the oar. I got out and tried to shove myself from the rock with my hands. My feet kept slipping. I don't know how long I tried before I heard the motor, and saw the lights of another boat. Then I saw the face of the boatman. I saw Rick and his stone-cold stare.*

"He didn't say anything to me. He tied a rope around the boat and started to drive away with it, his boat pulling Bill's. I screamed at him to help me. 'They won't let us leave!' I yelled as loud as I could. 'They won't let us leave!' But he just drove off, taking the boat with him. Leaving me alone on the rocks."

Abby hit pause and wrote down the time of this piece of the recording. Cass had started to cry then. Abby asked her what she was feeling and she said she was remembering the despair, the feeling of self-loathing at her stupidity, her immaturity. She said she also felt rage, and that she had learned that rage is powerful and it can make you do stupid things. Listening to it now, some time gone by and Cass not right in front of her clouding her mind with the wonder of her return, it felt out of place with the story. Cass hadn't done anything worthy of self-loathing. She had risked her life trying to escape and save her sister.

She pressed play again.

"I'm so sorry! God, I'm so stupid! I wanted to believe that I could save us! I wasn't thinking!"

That was when Owen rushed to her side to hold her. *"No, Cass. No! It's not your fault. You were so young!"*

"I thought I could bring us home!"

Abby remembered the rest of it. When Cass calmed herself down, she finished the story of that night. How she watched the rowboat get pulled back to the dock. How she watched the *Lucky Lady* disappear back into the harbor. How she sat there for a long time, given the cold—twenty-two minutes, she said—shivering and thinking through her options, even through the tears and the despair and the disbelief. She said she thought to herself that the land was right there, and how far could it be, really? A few miles? She said she almost jumped in. *"Maybe I would make it. Maybe I wouldn't drown or get hypothermia."*

Then she considered hiding in the woods, making a fire, trying to signal a boat by yelling and screaming. She thought about making words with rocks or grass that someone could see from a helicopter. But she said she had only a few hours and she did not have a saw or matches. And although she was strong, she said, she was not that strong.

Her third option was to go back to the house. Climb into bed. And see who the boatman really was, inside his heart or inside his conscience. If he said nothing, she would make a new plan. If he told them what she'd tried to do, she knew she would be punished. In the end, she got too cold to stay outside any longer, so this was what she decided to do.

They got sidetracked then, with details about the birth, the baby, the rowboat and currents. She gave more descriptions of lobster boats, their markings, their sizes, the color of the buoys they collected the lobsters from. Abby couldn't refute the importance of any of that. Finding the island was the priority, period.

Still, she had gotten up then and began pacing the Martins' bedroom. She had so many questions of her own. Obvious questions like what happened after that first attempt to escape? And how did it help Cass understand the boatman and know he would help her eventually?

Other questions were more subtle, entering her mind in faint whispers. The description of Lucy and Bill, the analogy to the fractured self, the crazy and the sane parts battling for dominance—it was sophisticated, beyond Cass's years, wasn't it? Or maybe the trauma had forced her to learn about the psychology, to deconstruct her captors.

And why had she insisted that her mother stay with her during the interviews? She was not a minor, and it went against the Bureau's practices. She kept saying she couldn't tell the story without Judy in the room.

And what about her odd demeanor, the way she told her story with such precision, adding in depictions of her emotions like she was sprinkling salt on a plate of food?

And why was she always counting the time and numbering things? Every story had been broken down into distinct parts, and moments had been clocked to the minute in her head, by counting to herself. She did not have a watch or a phone. It was as if she needed to keep everything organized in her mind.

A memory was before her. Two girls playing with a tea set in a yard. A gingham tablecloth lay across the grass. The tea set was still in a basket.

It was Abby's sister, Meg, there with Abby. Meg was three years older and she was explaining why she needed to play with Abby's tea set. "There are four reasons," Meg said. Abby tried but couldn't remember them now, the reasons. She wasn't even certain this memory was real. They couldn't have been more than six and nine. Were they even younger? It didn't matter what the reasons were. It was about the numbering. *There are four reasons.*

Abby got up from the table and poured a scotch, drinking it as she leaned against the kitchen counter.

Meg had done that all through childhood. She was remembering it now. *There are two reasons for this. . . . There are six things I like about that. . . . There are three things I eat for breakfast.* When had she stopped doing that?

Abby downed the scotch and poured another. She needed sleep tonight.

How did she not know this about Meg, her sister, her only sibling and now the only family she had left in the world? Did she still count and number things? Abby had been there a few months ago. Meg, her two daughters, her husband, two dogs—had a seemingly normal life (although far too rural for Abby's taste) in Colorado. She tried to remember the things they had done together. The hot, buggy hike in the mountains. Shopping for school clothes for her nieces. They'd gone to a movie. Abby could see that Meg was a good mother, that her daughters were loved. That was not her concern.

One evening they went out alone, as they always did on this annual reunion. During the rest of the year, there were phone calls and e-mails, Christmas and birthday cards and Facebook posts with cute photos and heart-shaped emojis. But those were not moments to open the door to the past.

The conversation always began with the benign updates. "How's work? How are the girls?" And before their father died— "Have you spoken to Dad?" He spent his final years in Florida with his second wife, playing golf and tending to her rather substantial needs.

But it never took long for the path to wind into the trees, where the questions became more intimate and the answers harder to find. This last visit had focused on Abby. "Are you seeing anyone? When are you going to give someone a chance?"

From there, the path continued into the woods until it disappeared entirely, leaving them lost in the darkness of the past. "You know too much, Abby. That's the problem." Meg was convinced that Abby's research and, arguably, her obsession with their mother and her theories on narcissism were preventing her from just living—from falling in love with someone, from trusting someone. "You have to move forward. Don't let her ruin your life from the grave."

Abby always listened, nodding occasionally, looking sincere. It wasn't about whether Meg was right or wrong. The only thing that mattered was the impossibility of her prescription.

Had there still been counting? Abby couldn't remember. The last time she'd thought about this thing with her sister was when she was writing her dissertation.

She set the glass down on the counter.

There was a case study she'd read while doing her research. The daughter of a mother with severe pathological narcissism had developed a coping mechanism, called an "affectation," to create order in a world that was disordered. She had found a way to manage the radical and unpredictable affections of her mother that included a methodical organizing of everything in her life. She kept track of things with numbers. "Three reasons for liking the piano. . . . Two ways I like to wear my hair."

She also assigned a gender to everything—colors, numbers,

letters of the alphabet. *A* was female, *B* was male. There was no sequential sense to the assignments—they were unique to her imagination. *D, E, F, G* and *H* were all male, for example. But then *X, Y* and *Z* were all female. Red and orange were female. Blue and green male. On and on it went, the ordering of static, benign objects and concepts to calm the storm that was stirred inside her from the faulty attachment to her primary caregiver—in that case, the mother.

The girl had not developed a personality disorder, and had gone on to have a healthy family of her own. The research concluded that she had escaped the cycle, and it posed the query as to whether this affectation had been the reason.

Abby's thoughts shifted back to her sister, Meg. She had not escaped their mother's wrath entirely. There had been years of drug use and men and debilitating anxiety. But she had found her way out.

It was the aspect of her research that had most fascinated her—the cycle of the illness and how children escaped it. It was as if the human soul within them was fighting to the bitter end to survive, to find a way to hold on to this instinct to love and be loved—because that was the very thing that got lost with this illness. Some developed OCD traits like Meg, controlling other aspects of their lives to replace the chaos with the parent.

Others sought out adult relationships that were codependent—the spouse they knew would never leave them, or serial relationships where they could conquer and move on, proving to themselves over and over that they had the power to get what they needed from other people. The serial monogamist, the playboy, the "slut" (though Abby so hated that word). Meg had done all of these, the counting of things, then the cycling through men when she was younger, then settling down with a man who worshipped her.

And what had Abby done to escape? Meg would say she rejected things that were too feminine, things that represented
their mother. Makeup, short skirts, high heels. She would say
that Abby lived behind an invisible shield—that she didn't let
anyone in who could hurt her or disappoint her.

But Abby had a rule against self-diagnosis, so she let these
thoughts pass through her as she always did.

She felt tired. The dog was at her feet, and she joined him on
the floor. Glass in hand, the dog now in her lap, she closed her
eyes and let her mind continue to wander, back now to Cass and
her counting of things. Was that how she escaped her mother?
That, and attaching to Emma as if Emma were her mother? It
wasn't perfect—Emma had been cruel at times, indifferent at other
times. But it had been something.

And what about Emma? What if Emma had not escaped?
What if the things Abby knew about Judy Martin were the tip of
the iceberg? What if escaping the cycle had been impossible for
Emma, the "chosen" child who took the biggest emotional blows?

God, was she tired—tired, and now buzzed from the scotch.
She could hear Leo's voice as they wrapped up the day: "We'll find
her, kiddo. We will find Emma." But what if they couldn't? What
if they went round and round again, not seeing the truth?

Something didn't feel right about Cass's story—the one she
was telling and the one she wasn't.

Leo's voice faded. She was now wishing he were sitting beside
her, his arm around her shoulders, his voice so calm, whispering
that everything was going to be okay, that this would not be like
last time, that they would find Emma—even though she wouldn't
believe him. She could pretend to. For one night. For a few hours
of peace. She could pretend.

She let her head fall back against the wall and closed her eyes.

NINE

Cass—Day Two of My Return

I slept for just four hours and twenty minutes the first night after my return. I awoke from a disturbing dream and was unsettled, and from then on my mind would not rest. It made me angry because I knew what I had to face on the second day.

In the dream, Bill was holding the baby over the edge of the dock. She was crying, her voice like a knife cutting into me. He let go and I watched her disappear into the cold, black water. That sweet, precious baby with the curly blond hair and big blue eyes. That innocent child. Her crying had stopped as fear turned to terror, paralyzing her little body. The moment her skin felt that water, she froze—from her eyes to her feet—nothing moved. She couldn't even reach out with her arms to take hold of Bill as he pulled away, leaving her to die.

I awoke to a rage so powerful, I thought it would explode from my chest and incinerate us all. Burn the house to ground with everyone in it. Me. Mrs. Martin. Mr. Martin.

I took a pillow and pressed my face into it as hard as I could and I screamed things I would not want anyone to hear. Hateful, violent things. And I knew then that I would never stop looking for Bill and Lucy Pratt even if the FBI did. I would find them and I would make them pay.

But then I lay still, the pillow in my arms, and I made myself remember about how Emma would hold me just like I was holding this pillow. I tried to hear her voice. *We'll go wherever we want and we'll never let her in. We won't even care anymore.* I felt myself begin to calm, even though I knew none of that could be true anymore. I could not leave this house until they found Emma.

Mrs. Martin knocked on my door at eight o'clock. I said I was awake and would be down after I had a shower. She told me she had found some clothes that might fit me and she would leave them in the bathroom. She made sure to tell me that they were her clothes from a few years back when she'd put on some weight from all the stress of losing her daughters. She'd found an old pair of Hunter's sneakers that looked like my size. Her feet were smaller than mine, so the sneakers would have to do until she could take me shopping.

We went to the doctor at nine o'clock. His name was Dr. Nichols, and he had been my pediatrician for my whole life before I disappeared. My mother thought I would be comfortable with him, and she was not wrong about that, except that I was a woman now and so I would not let him examine me below the waist or touch my breasts. Because an agent came with us who wanted all kinds of tests done, I let them draw blood. I promised to find a gynecologist and let her examine me, but I was not ready for that now. I told the doctor about my cycles to reassure him that everything was in order, and he was satisfied and willing to give me a clean bill of health pending all the blood test results. He gave me some shots that I needed and then we were done. The agent was not satisfied, but I was a grown-up now and they couldn't make me do anything I didn't want to do.

We went back to Mrs. Martin's house right after the doctor. My father was waiting there. So were Dr. Winter, Agent Strauss, and the woman who was supposed to draw the sketches of Bill and Lucy and the boatman.

None of this happened as mundanely as I have described. By morning, the entire world knew I had returned, and media trucks lined our quiet street for half a mile past our driveway. The story was as big as when they found Elizabeth Smart, or those three women who'd been held as sex slaves for ten years in Cleveland. They took pictures of Mr. Martin's car as he drove us to the doctor, and some of them followed us and got pictures of me walking into the office. Inside Dr. Nichols's office, everyone hugged me and a few of the nurses cried, even the new ones who had never met me before. Dr. Nichols gave me a big hug. Then he shook his head like he couldn't believe I was standing in front of him and he said something like *It's a miracle!* I didn't mind any of this. I smiled at everyone, not a big happy smile, but a polite, grateful smile. It was genuine. I was not happy, because I did not have Emma with me and because I did not want to be where I was. But I was grateful. With all the media would come a bright spotlight on the search for Emma. I would have dressed up like Shirley Temple and sung them a song and danced them a dance if it would have kept them interested in our story.

Everyone wanted to spin theories about what went on with Bill and Emma and me and wonder if we had been made his sex slaves and did Lucy watch. I didn't care and I didn't blame them. That was the only part of the Elizabeth Smart story I remembered and I don't consider myself a bad person, and so I did not judge anyone for the things they wanted to think about.

There were also conversations, endless stories about the events in everyone's lives since I'd been gone. My father spoke mostly of

Witt, how he'd gotten married to a nice woman named Amie. He lived in Westchester and had just started working as a lawyer, like his mother. He told me about how much everyone had missed me and Emma, how devastated they all were and how they couldn't wait to see me when I was ready. Everyone wanted to see me, of course—Witt, aunts, uncles, grandparents. Mrs. Martin said the same thing to me, about the people who wanted to see me, now that the news had spread. She was very chatty about her charity work and gossip about my friends from high school and their mothers and their affairs and divorces and financial troubles. But mostly she talked about Hunter and his girlfriend and how much she hated her, how *that girl* had kept Hunter from seeing them and how she only cared about the money he was making as an investment banker.

All this information left their mouths electrified by the nervous energy my return had generated. And when it reached me, every single piece, I felt the shock as it entered my brain. I don't know how else to describe it. I wanted to cover my ears and not let any of it enter. I knew they wanted to zap me into their world, magically transform me into the daughter I would have been if I had never left, the young woman who held their history the way family does, living every mundane moment together. But I could not absorb it the way they needed me to. I felt detached, like a stranger eavesdropping on the train. I did not want to be in the present with them—not without Emma, not without justice. Until I had those things, I would not let them distract me with their stories from their normal lives.

I helped them with the sketches of the Pratts and the boatman. They also wanted to know about the man who drove the truck, so I gave my description of him as well. Agent Strauss told me that the sketches I helped make of them would be all over the news as well. It made me nervous that whatever I told the artist would become images in people's minds and that they would search for those images as they walked down the street or in line at the grocery store or in the faces of their friends and neighbors. What if I got them wrong?

It was a long morning. First the doctor, then the sketches, then more stories from the island. Dr. Winter spent some time alone with me. That's what investigators do when they're trying to build trust with you—and also when they want to see how you behave when you're around some people but not others.

I told everyone the story of how I was punished for trying to leave that first time, when the rowboat got pulled back into the island and the boatman left me on the rocks. After all of that, there was no time for the psychological examination Dr. Winter wanted me to have and which Mrs. Martin was now asking about incessantly. I was tired and I needed to rest. Hunter was coming to visit that afternoon.

I know what people said about me after my return—that I seemed flat and unemotional. They were fascinated by my demeanor, and when we were alone, Dr. Winter told me this was because very few people have things like this happen to them, and so everyone watches very carefully to see what it does to you. She said it was like meeting a space alien. And when people watch someone carefully and then don't see what they expect to see or what they want to see, they exaggerate the disparity.

I don't think I was flat. I had cried, and for long periods of time. I was so upset that Dr. Nichols gave me some pills to calm my nerves. I have never been able to show my feelings like Emma, on the outside. But that does not mean they are not stirring inside me. By the time I finally escaped, I think my feelings eclipsed anything Emma had ever felt. I could feel the scream inside me. I had felt it that morning when I had to cover my mouth with a pillow so no one would hear it. I contained it only out of fear for what it might do if I let it out. I did my best to think calmly and choose calm words.

After I told the story of the first time I tried to escape, I had to leave the room. I lied and told them I needed some water, but really I needed to let the rage finish what it was doing and leave my body. I didn't want them to see it.

Hunter came to the house in the late afternoon. I was in the bed in the guest room when the car came down the driveway. I was not asleep. I could not sleep. But I was exhausted. It's one thing to imagine doing something, like a marathon or doing one hundred sit-ups. But when you're actually in it, trying to do it, it's then you realize that you had no idea how hard it would be. And that maybe it wasn't possible at all.

That was how I felt that second afternoon in the guest room as I waited for Hunter and his girlfriend to arrive.

My father had wanted me to see Witt and his wife that same day. But my mother made the arrangements with Hunter and I had agreed. I needed to see him, even though I was dreading it. I needed to see him with my own eyes.

"Cass!" I heard my mother call from the bottom of the stairs. "They're here! Come down, sweetheart!"

I lay still and listened to the sound of her fake excited voice as it trailed up the stairs from the living room. I could no longer make out the words, but I knew what she was saying because she was using the tone she always used when she was thinking mean things but saying nice things. I felt myself judging her, but it was not satisfying the way it had been when I was younger and free of the guilt that now made me a hypocrite. I would get out of this bed and brush my hair and gargle with mouthwash and put Mrs. Martin's fat clothes back on my body. I would go downstairs and give him a big hug and shake his girlfriend's hand and have some tea. I would smile as I thought my own mean things and said my own nice things. I had been thinking mean things for many years. They surely would not leave me just to ease my conscience.

Hunter looked different from how I remembered him. His face had become more angular, nose, cheekbones, brow all more pronounced. His hairline had receded a bit. And he was muscular, strong. My mother told me he had started lifting weights at his fancy sports club. She said it was probably a cover story he used so he could cheat on his girlfriend, but I could see from the size of his arms that some of his story must be true. Mrs. Martin had to believe this because this woman was very beautiful and very young. She had long, luscious blond hair and chiseled cheekbones and deeply set eyes and a big pouty mouth. Mrs. Martin was not the most beautiful woman in the world when Hunter's woman was around. So she had to concoct her theory about Hunter cheating on her. She had to believe that Hunter didn't *really* love her.

Hunter walked to me from across the room. His head was tilted slightly and his face was scrunched up like he was about to cry. It was the face people make when their child loses the spelling bee, or falls off a horse, or scrapes a knee on the sidewalk.

"Cass! My God!" he said.

I did not move. I took a long breath and held it firm as he wrapped his new strong arms around me and rocked my body back and forth.

His girlfriend pounced upon us, and I could see in an instant why my mother hated her.

"I'm Brenda." She said this while Hunter was still hugging me. She said it so he would stop.

I pulled out of his embrace to greet her, and when I did I felt the hesitation. He did not want to let me go, which I found strange. He had never once hugged me like that.

"It's so horrible, Cass, what happened to you and Emma. And Emma's still there! It's just too terrible to even think."

I repeated just some of the story while we sat in the living room drinking tea. I knew Mrs. Martin had told Mr. Martin, and Mr. Martin had told Hunter most of what I had told them in my interviews. Hunter kept shaking his head like he didn't believe this had happened and like it was the most horrible thing he had ever heard.

I had gone over in my mind what it would be like when I saw Hunter again, the same way I had done for my mother and my father. For everyone. I had a lot of time to think about my reunions. None of them would be the way I expected them to be. I suppose that's normal. First kisses. Graduations. Weddings. Sports victories. They never feel the way we think they will, and they never go quite the way we dream about them. Still, I was just as shocked by Hunter's reaction as I was when Mrs. Martin didn't recognize me on her doorstep.

Hunter had been obsessed with Emma right from the start. But because our families had become related, it was forbidden, and that made it unbearable for him.

I was not the only one who could see it lurking in his eyes. Witt had seen it as well, though he and I never discussed it. I just knew by the way his back got straighter when he was around Hunter; the way his light disposition disappeared along with his sense of humor. They did not have occasion to be together often. Sometimes our father would send Witt to pick us up at our mother's house when it was our weekend with him. And sometimes Hunter would be there on those weekends. Other times Hunter would pick us up from our father's house, especially in the summers, and he would see Witt when he did.

The summer after Emma had sex with that boy, Joe, from Hunter's school—when I was thirteen, Emma was fifteen, Hunter was seventeen, and Witt was a junior in college—we were all home for the last two weeks of August. Hunter was working as a caddy at our club. Witt was volunteering for a political campaign for some local senator and living with our father. Emma and I were back from summer camp in Europe and getting ready for school. Emma had started dating a boy from our country club, and Hunter was relentless in his ridicule of him. I think what happened with Joe the spring before had not helped. Hunter's jealousy grew like the weeds in Mrs. Martin's garden.

He and Emma fought almost every day, but then they would get drunk together and watch movies in the finished part of the basement. Sometimes they would sit very close, and Emma would rest her head in his lap. One night, Mr. Martin came downstairs very quietly. I was sitting on the floor on some pillows. Emma and Hunter were on the couch together, with her head in his lap and his hand stroking her hair. We were watching *The Shining*, which we had seen countless times but which still held our attention. Mr. Martin stood there looking at them for a long time. They didn't see him but I did, and I waited to see what he would do, to see if what they were doing was wrong enough for Mr. Martin to put a stop to it. But he didn't stop it. He just watched it, and then he left without them even noticing.

I remember thinking that maybe I was the one who was crazy. Maybe it was normal what they were doing, and the worst possible thought—maybe I was jealous that Hunter loved Emma more than he loved me. Maybe it was just like with our mother. I didn't even like Hunter. Still, maybe I was just a petty little sister who had to want everything her sister had. I ran upstairs and smoked one of Emma's cigarettes out my window and hated myself. Then I cried in my bed and hated myself more until I fell asleep.

The next week, there was a huge fight between my father and Mrs. Martin. One of the mothers from our school had called them both to tell them that there were pictures of Emma on the Internet. It was some new Web site all the kids were using because it wasn't owned by a large company that had to be careful about stuff like naked pictures and swearing. Kids were using it to say mean things about other kids, and about teachers also. The school told us we were forbidden to visit that site, but they never checked our phones or laptops. The pictures of Emma showed her posing in a black dress. She was acting sexy in all of them, pretending to undress by pulling a strap off her shoulder.

Then, in one of them, the dress was at her waist and you could see her naked breasts. She looked like she was laughing in that picture.

My father asked Emma who had taken the pictures, and she said it was one of her friends and they were just fooling around. Because Emma was a minor, my father was able to get the police involved, and the people who ran the Web site gave them all the information they had. They traced the IP address. The pictures had been uploaded from a computer at Mrs. Martin's house, and they were posted before Hunter left for school.

We all knew Hunter had done it and we all knew why. My father was out of his mind with rage and he said he was going to fight for custody again. My mother told him *Good luck, asshole!* but then she called her lawyer just in case. My parents called each other almost every day while this was going on, screaming and yelling, assigning blame for this and that. It was all just noise up in the clouds.

Emma's new boyfriend dumped her. He said his mother made him do it. Emma cried for three days and refused to speak to Hunter. She said she would never forgive him and would hate him forever and *blah blah blah*. This, too, floated up to the clouds and joined my parents' *blah blah blah*.

It was Witt who stayed on the ground. He waited for Hunter in the parking lot at the club one afternoon. He made a fist and he pounded Hunter's face. He broke his nose and bruised his eye sockets. But mostly he bruised Hunter's ego. Mr. Martin paid a visit to my father. I was not there, but I have heard two versions of the same story. In one version, my mother's, Mr. Martin picked up my father by his jaw and hung him against the door. He told him he would kill him if Witt ever touched his son again. In the other version, my father's, Mr. Martin came and threatened his life, and my father told him to *Go to hell*.

It did not end there. Hunter went to my father's house late one night and slashed Witt's tires. Witt reported it to the police, and the police showed up at our house to question Hunter.

Mr. Martin lied and said Hunter had been home all night. Mrs. Martin kept quiet about the fact that they had been out to dinner around the time it happened. The police wanted no part of this family feud anyway, so they closed the investigation before it ever really got started.

My father was, again, beside himself with rage but without any plan to seek revenge. Witt, on the other hand, just got himself some new tires. It didn't matter that Hunter had not been punished. Even after his nose healed, and his skin returned to its normal color, the bruise to his ego would remain forever. And that was enough for my brother. My *real* brother.

After that incident, I was left with a clearer understanding about the depths of Hunter's feelings for Emma. Love, obsession, whatever it was behind those feelings, they were so big that he would sooner destroy her than see her with someone else. And so when I returned from the island and was sitting in Mrs. Martin's living room, and when Hunter was asking me about Emma and how she was, and how she had survived, and how we were going to find her and save her—and when I could see that his concern came without any emotion, that he really didn't care about Emma anymore—I was shocked.

Then I looked at his girlfriend, at Brenda whatever. I watched how she moved and spoke and pouted. And I began to understand. She was the new Emma. It was hard then to zoom out the way Witt could. I wanted to stop everyone right there and yell, *That's it? All of it was for nothing? We went through all of that when there was a new Emma right around the corner?* I didn't know if I could stop myself. I took in air and then pushed it down into my lungs. I pushed it down until it hurt and my head started to get dizzy.

When we had exhausted the more difficult parts of my story, Hunter leaned into the sofa, his hands laced together, and pressed against the back of his head. "And you never found out who the father was? If it happened in June, I bet it was some prick she met in Paris. We should sue the camp. That's what we should do. Get their insurance to pay out."

He nodded in agreement with himself. Then he continued.

"Jesus Christ, Cass. I can't believe this happened to you. I'm so sorry. I've thought so many times that maybe I could have helped prevent whatever it was that led to your disappearing. I guess I was wrong to think that."

I shrugged. "You couldn't have done anything."

"I know. Now I know."

Mr. Martin spoke then, for the first time since we'd sat down for tea. "No one could have done anything about this. Emma had a head of steel. She did what she wanted and no one stopped her. We all loved her for that. But it got her into trouble . . . right? And more than a few times."

I wanted to break his face open with my teacup at that moment. He knew nothing about my sister except what he stole while he was spying on her in the basement with his degenerate son who was now so perfect with his fancy job and his pretty girlfriend. I wished in that moment Dr. Winter had stayed. She would have seen right through all of them!

I did not break his face with my teacup. Instead, I *used my words* . . . the way they taught us at our fancy school. "Why don't we all just keep working to find her? Then we'll know, won't we? We'll all know what could have been done to save her."

Mrs. Martin looked at Mr. Martin. She seemed unnerved. She opened her eyes wide the way people do when they're trying to send an unspoken message that someone in the room is out of line. I suppose that person was me, and it made me feel better. I wanted to be out of line. I wanted them to wonder what I would do and, for once, fear that it would be out of their control.

I excused myself and went upstairs to lie down. They were all whispering about me once I'd left the room. But I could hear the murmur.

When I cleared my head and calmed my anger, I thought about Hunter and the way he had held me and not wanted to let go. I considered the possibility that he had missed me. That he had cared for me more than I'd thought. But then the truth came rushing in and I smiled when I felt it. Knowing it felt good because it was true.

He had thought his past had vanished along with his sisters that night three years ago. And now one of us had returned. He was holding me not because he was happy I was home. He was holding me because somewhere inside his dark mind, he thought he could make me vanish all over again.

TEN

Dr. Winter

On the second day of Cass Tanner's return, the Martin house was in a state of chaos. Or maybe that was just what it felt like to Abby.

Media trucks lined the street. Patrol cars blocked the driveway. Two field agents sat at the dining room table with equipment that could trace a call from the landline if Emma called—or the Pratts, for that matter. There was always the possibility of a ransom. Unlikely—but what if they did call and nothing had been done to prepare? Just like the disappearance three years before, there was no protocol that fit this case, and to Abby, it all seemed cobbled together. Chaos inside and out.

Leo was waiting for her in the living room. He was alone. "Hey," he said. Abby could see the concern on his face.

She'd woken up on her kitchen floor, sitting upright, the dog still in her lap, not more than two hours gone by. She'd gotten up and gone through her files, but it was not good, not sleeping. And now it was starting to show on her face.

"Come and sit down, kiddo." He handed her coffee in a paper

cup poured from a paper box someone had picked up at a dough-nut shop.

Abby took the coffee and inhaled deeply near the rim. "So nothing from the physical exam? Is she on any meds?" she asked.

Leo nodded. "Small doses of Xanax. We just got the sketches done. We'll have copies in an hour. Soil analysis from Cass's shoes turned up shale and limestone. Consistent with coastal Maine."

"Where is she?"

"Upstairs with her babysitter," he answered sarcastically.

Abby smiled. "And the husband? Owen? They're not here?"

"Jonathan Martin went to the store. Owen went to see his son. Delivering the story in person, I suspect. Not the kind of thing you do on the phone."

Abby felt irritated, impatient. "Are we doing this?"

"She'll be down. I told her you were on the way," Leo said calmly.

"We need the rest of the story, Leo. Start to finish. I don't have a handle on these people yet. Or Emma, for that matter."

"Okay. I hear you."

Abby took a sip of the coffee and closed her eyes. The adrenaline was subsiding, and in its place came bone-deep exhaustion.

"What did you find in your notes?" Leo asked.

Abby sighed. Shook her head. "I don't know. I read them all again this morning, with an eye to the pregnancy and the person who might have helped her. Emma's friends her senior year. The director at the program in France where she may have met the father. The timing's right. Six weeks to discover the pregnancy and two or three more to find the Pratts and make her plan to leave—that would put her right around the time of the disap-pearance."

"Yup. And the birth in March."

"Do you remember the school counselor? She had a lot to say about Emma, about her observations of her—how she exhibited signs of arrogance but it was really insecurity."

Leo let out a soft chuckle. "Ah, yes. The pretty blonde. I believe you had some strong opinions about her. Amateur hour—right? Didn't she get her degree from some community college?"

"It was an MSW from an online university."

"Right," Leo said, leaning back into the sofa with a smile. "So, what? You think she knew Emma better than we thought? Maybe Emma was seeing her about her problems? About the pregnancy?"

Abby shook her head. "No. I don't know. She seemed very pleased with herself and how much she had observed. But no one said Emma was seeing her beyond casual passings in the hallway."

It was strange how Abby remembered all these interviews and the image of the girls that had formed from them. Yet now the details that were drawing her attention were entirely different. She was no longer seeing the information through the same lens—what had driven the girls to leave or fall victim to a predator or engage in reckless behavior? They knew where the girls had gone and the circumstances of their disappearance. The new lens had turned on the people left behind. Who would have helped her? And who would have lied about it?

"What about the half brother, Witt Tanner?"

Abby started to tell him about that interview all over again, but he had been there, in the room. He had asked the questions and listened to the same answers Abby had heard and written down meticulously.

The interview of Witt Tanner from three years ago had been the hardest to revisit. He had told them things that even his father, Owen, had not offered. Things about Judy Martin like the

story of the necklace and stories about life in the Martin home—
including some naked photos of Emma that Hunter had posted
on a Web site. That was just the beginning. Witt's affection for
his half sisters was undeniable. Their disappearance had torn him
up. And he had been sincere and forthcoming about the childhood he had witnessed from a distance. As she read her notes of
that interview, Abby had stared at three words, words Witt had
spoken and that Abby had written down on a piece of lined yellow
paper.

She is evil.

Abby had dwelled on those words and on the stories he'd told
her. Before the divorce, when Witt stayed at the house every other
weekend, there would be fights between Judy and Owen—fights
Witt and his sisters could hear without even trying. "Take care of
your fucking children!" Owen would yell. And she would yell
back, "You take care of them, asshole! You're the one who wanted
them!" And then Owen, "Really? I'm not the one who lied about
taking the pill!" Cass would fold into herself like she was trying to
disappear. Emma would stare into space with a look of concen-
trated defiance, like perhaps she was plotting revenge against both
of them for not wanting to take care of their own children, and
for making them feel so unworthy.

When they got older and Witt no longer came to the old
house, Witt said that his sisters would tell him about the fights
between Emma and her mother, unthinkable words flying from
their mouths. *Bitch! Whore! Cunt!* Emma would laugh about bor-
rowing her mother's clothes—something that made her crazy. Cass
would usually finish the story in a way that killed the laughter,
like the time Judy forced Emma to take off a dress that belonged
to her right in the kitchen, in front of Cass. Emma ran upstairs

crying, dressed only in her bra and underpants. Judy then took the dress and put it into the garbage can.

Witt had tried to explain it.

"Emma always made light of things, like nothing Judy did could touch her. But Cass, she told the stories like they were warnings about the future—like they were lessons about who Judy Martin was and what she was capable of doing."

The stories went on and on—some of them witnessed first-hand. Others that had been recounted by the girls when they saw Witt at their father's house. When Leo had heard all this during the original investigation, he had reminded her of other things. "Witt hated Hunter for slashing his tires. Witt hated Judy Martin for stealing his father and ruining his home. He was angry and violent, full of rage with a thirst for revenge."

Any story could be told to tip the scale in one direction or another. Maybe Witt had exaggerated. Maybe the facts seemed more ominous when they were filtered through Witt's dark lens, and his angry voice, and his watery eyes.

Leo's question still hung in the air. What about Witt Tanner?

"Abby?" he said when she didn't answer.

Abby shook her head and shrugged. "Nothing, really. But no way he was the one who helped Emma leave. That kid was wrecked when the girls disappeared."

There had not been anything new. That part was not a lie. But those three words, "She is evil," had been added to the file Abby was now keeping in her head.

Two sets of footsteps came from down the hall. Cass and Judy Martin entered the room, causing both Leo and Abby to stand.

"I see you got some clothes," Abby said, smiling at Cass, who sat down neatly in a small chair pulled from a desk. She folded her hands in her lap. Her knees and ankles glued together. Shoulders straight as a board.

"My mother let me borrow some. The shoes belonged to Hunter." Her voice was flat, unemotional. "He's coming to visit later."

"Years ago, I put on some weight," Judy said, not able to help herself as she found her way into a formal armchair. She was no more than a size or two smaller than her daughter, something that Abby had not even noticed until it was mentioned. But Judy could not take any chances. There could be no mistake that she was thinner than her daughter, who was now a beautiful young woman.

Abby felt her gaze pulled back to Cass, who watched intently as though willing her to see something only they could see.

"Should we continue where we left off?" Leo asked. "I think Dr. Winter has some avenues she wants to explore about the island."

Cass nodded and smiled again, politely. Her demeanor had changed drastically from the day before. There were no tears. No desperate pleas.

"Cass, you said it was that night that made you believe the boatman would eventually help you?" Abby asked her, looking down at a legal pad.

"Yes. Well, not that night but because of that night."

She looked tired, as though she hadn't slept much either.

"Because of what happened after you got back to the house—after the first time you tried to escape?"

"Yes. Should I tell the story now?"

"Yes," Abby said.

Cass took a breath, in and out, then began to speak in a slow, methodical rhythm.

"It was three days later. That night, when I got back to the house, it was dark and dead quiet, except for the generator. It came on and off when something in the house needed electricity, like heat or hot water. It was pretty loud and it was on when I got to the front door, so I went inside and up to Emma's room with no one hearing anything. 'What happened?' she asked me. I could see she was distraught that I was still there, on the island. I told her about the current and the oars and Rick taking the boat. She grabbed my arms and shook me, hard, and yelled at me through a whisper that I had ruined everything. And she was right. Six months of planning was gone. She ordered me to leave and I did. I could hear her crying as I walked down the hall.

"My room was on the other side of the upstairs, like I said, and so I had to be quiet as I walked around. I lay down but didn't sleep. And in the morning, when Rick showed up with groceries and mail, I forced myself to stay at the desk where we studied and do what I always do, which is glance up and then look away because he was hard to look at. If you looked at him too long, you could feel his anger like water in a kettle. I had never considered asking him for help or telling him anything, even before Lucy told me about his past and how they had saved him from drugs and his guilt.

"He came and left and everything seemed normal. I slept that night, relieved and grateful because I thought he hadn't told them and it would just be forgotten. Another day passed, and another night of sleep. I felt my nerves settle down and when they did, the disappointment poured in. I realized then that I was right back to where I had been, and that I had exhausted myself and worried Emma for nothing. Just to be back in the same place.

"It didn't help that Emma was mad at me, and not just pretend mad for our plan. She was mad because I had failed.

"On the third day, Emma and I came downstairs to breakfast

set at the table. Usually we just made some toast and took it to our desks. Lucy didn't like us being around the baby. 'Sit down,' Bill said. It was strange that they were both there in the kitchen like that. But we did what was asked of us and sat down. Lucy poured us some juice and then gave us plates with two toaster waffles and syrup. Then she sat down as well, with the baby in her arms and Bill standing behind her.

" 'We've been thinking,' Lucy said. 'Maybe you girls have been here long enough. Maybe it's time to go home.'

"I felt a rush of happiness! I thought Rick had told them about the boat and the rocks and the oars that wouldn't steer me out of the current and now they were just going to let us leave. We weren't prisoners. How stupid we had been! Why didn't we just ask to leave? All this time, they would have let us go! And then I felt guilty for thinking bad things about Bill and Lucy, for being so stupid and melodramatic.

"Emma looked at her baby and started to cry. 'Really?' she asked. 'We can go home now?' Lucy smiled. 'Of course! You always could.' They told us to finish eating and then go pack our things, which we did. But before that, when we were at the top of the stairs, Emma about to turn left and me right, she grabbed me and hugged me and told me I had saved us all. I packed so fast, you can't imagine! I put things into three plastic bags because that was all I had, and I left whatever didn't fit inside. Emma and I were on the dock within half an hour. It was February, and the cold is hard to describe. It cuts into you.

"Bill and Lucy were there, with the baby. Rick was in the boat waiting with the motor running. I hugged them both. I thanked them for everything they'd done for us. Emma did the same. Bill took our bags and put them on the boat. Then he helped us step over the railing and into the boat. Lucy was standing right next to us, holding the baby. Emma reached her arms out to take her, but the boat started to move, to pull away.

"'Wait! Stop!' Emma yelled at Rick. He shut the motor. We were ten feet from the dock, Emma's arms stretched out as far as they could go, reaching for her daughter. 'What's wrong, love?' Lucy asked her. She had the most evil look on her face. 'My baby!' Emma said. 'Oh, no,' Bill called out. 'Julia's not going with you. Why would you think that?' Emma started yelling at them, screaming all sorts of terrible words. It was as if the whole eleven months of being deprived of her flesh and blood had infected her with poison that was now gushing out like an exploding volcano.

"'Give me my baby, you stupid old bitch!' She was yelling things like that. Rick just stood there looking out at the ocean. The boat was drifting into the harbor, and I knew it would soon get pulled into that place on the west side of the island. It was quiet like the night I tried to leave, only the water lapping against the boat and the wood dock creaking as it rocked back and forth. I couldn't believe what was happening, even though I knew what was happening.

"Then Bill held up a piece of paper. 'She's not your baby, Emma. She's our baby. "Certificate of Live Birth. Baby girl, born to Lucille Pratt and Bill Pratt."' He was reading from the document, a birth certificate he said he had made and filed with the town hall in Portland. That's what he said. Rick started the boat. Emma screamed like I've never heard her scream before. I didn't know until that moment how much she loved her baby. How hard she must have been suffering. 'I'll come back with the police! I'll prove she's not yours! I'll prove it!' She waited for a reaction but there was none. The boat just kept moving. And then I realized what they were going to do.

"'Emma!' I screamed at her twice. The first time I screamed,

'They won't be here when we come back! They'll be gone. With your baby! And with that piece of paper, they could go anywhere!'

"Emma looked at me, horrified. Then she climbed onto the edge of the boat and jumped into that freezing-cold water. The thing about the cold water is that when you are in it, your heart starts to pound wildly, like out of control, and then you can't breathe well. It feels like you have an elephant on your chest, and I could see Emma already struggling as she tried to swim.

"I screamed the second time, this time just her name. 'Emma!' But she didn't look back. She just kept swimming and gasping for air through her heavy chest and pounding heart. Rick steered the boat around. We weren't more than twenty feet from the dock by then, but against the current, and Emma swam to it and climbed up the side of the dock. Bill and Lucy looked at her, at both of us, with this sort of smug expression. Like we were naughty children who deserved to be punished. Emma ran toward Lucy and her baby, soaking wet and shivering, but Bill grabbed her by both arms. She was like a wild animal, thrashing against him, her long wet hair sending pellets of icy water all over the dock. 'Give me my baby!' Lucy squeezed the baby tighter and tried to block the sight of Emma, of her own mother, from her eyes.

"Bill started screaming back at Emma. 'I'm so sick of you girls! You selfish girls who don't know what's right!' There were more things—horrible, crude things—about girls and sex and babies, and I realized that tolerating us to keep Lucy happy with the baby had worn out his patience. He was sick of this world where ungrateful girls have babies all the time and his precious wife could not. He started to push Emma back toward the edge of the dock. She looked at me, and then the ocean, and then he just gave her a shove and she was back in that water! She came up from beneath the surface and swam again to the edge of the dock and tried to climb out. But Bill wouldn't let her. He kicked at her fingers with the toe of his boot until she let go and went back in the water.

"She did it three times. I could see her lips turning blue, her fingers red with blood. She was hysterical, not thinking straight. She was screaming from the water. Bill was screaming from the dock. I was screaming from the boat. And then, Bill did the most horrible thing. I couldn't believe it when I saw it with my own eyes. He went to Lucy and took that little girl, that baby, from her arms. She said nothing at first. I think she thought he was going to take her up to the house. But he didn't! He walked to the other side of the dock and he held that baby over the side by one arm, dangling her in the air. And he said, 'I swear to God, I'll let her drown!' Emma couldn't say the words from her frozen mouth but she was shaking her head, thrashing it back and forth. She tried to swim toward them, but Bill then lowered the baby to the edge of the water. We all could see that she would sink beneath the black surface before Emma could get there.

"When the boat came close enough, I jumped onto the dock and reached in for Emma. I grabbed her arm and pulled her to the edge, and then back onto the platform. She was so heavy that she could barely help me. I pulled at her shirt, her pants, pulling her to the edge of the wood planks and then rolling her until she was out of the water. 'We'll stay,' I said. 'We'll stay and we won't cause any trouble. I promise! Please!' Bill cradled the baby, who was screaming so loud by then, and walked away from the edge where he was standing. He gave the baby to Lucy, who stood silently, watching. Looking back, I think she knew Bill would never have dropped that baby, her baby, into the water and let her drown, because she had been silent. But it didn't matter whether he would or he wouldn't. All that mattered was that we had no way out. If we left without that baby, we would never see any of them ever again.

"But it was more than that thought that made me say those things about staying. There were two thoughts. The second was this—when Bill was dangling that baby over the water, and when he was kicking Emma's hands off the dock, making them bleed, I looked at Rick, at the expression on his face. It was something I had not seen in the year and a half since we'd been there. His face sort of flinched, and I imagined him on the deck of that boat in Alaska, watching those men attack that woman. And I knew then that I would be able to make it out of there."

Cass stopped speaking. That was it—the whole story—and she had nothing more to say about it. Abby clutched a pen in one hand, the notebook in the other. She could not remove her eyes from her subject. Cass had told this story start to finish without looking up once. Was she concentrating? Was she afraid to see the look of disbelief on her mother's face?

The room felt as though it were being swallowed by the silence.

"Can I get something to drink?" Cass asked. She was eerily calm, given the story she had just told.

No one moved. They were waiting for Abby to agree or disagree. She was thinking now about the way Cass had told it—and the ones before it. The counting of things. The precision. And today, the lack of emotion.

"Abby?" Leo said, pulling her back into the silent room.

"I'm sorry. Yes, let's take a break."

Everyone started to rise from the sofas and chairs.

Abby smiled and did the same, her eyes fixed on Cass. She had been so consumed with Judy Martin, the narcissistic mother who'd driven her children to run away—only now that was not the story being told. So, the narcissistic mother who'd done . . . what, exactly?

She watched Cass stand and run her hand several times over the front of her shirt, smoothing the wrinkles. She noticed, too, how her eyes would look down and away like she wanted to hide. And the numbering of things, the affectation Abby had come across in her research years before, and had seen in her own sister.

But there were some things, some moments in her story that were not counted or numbered, like how long she hid and waited in Emma's car the night they disappeared. And how long Emma's labor was before the baby finally came.

And how could she be so unemotional telling this most horrific story about watching a baby nearly dropped in that cold, black water?

Abby tried to finish the sentence. *Judy Martin, the narcissistic mother who wreaked havoc on her children, leaving one a pregnant teen and the other introverted and insecure, with abnormal social instincts and obsessive-compulsive disorder.*

Or maybe, something else. There were times when Cass would look into Abby's eyes so intensely, it was like catching a glimpse of the sun. And each time it felt like she was sending Abby some kind of message in a secret code.

Was she playing her? Was she playing all of them? The question remained, and was even stronger today.

What if the sentence ended like this?

Judy Martin, the narcissistic mother who created a narcissist.

And not just Emma, but maybe Cass as well?

Abby followed them all out of the room, just behind Leo. She wanted to grab hold of him, shake him until he could help her sort out her own mind, which was spinning now, round and round like a dog chasing his tail. So many thoughts.

You know too much. Maybe Meg was right. She was so tired now, it was hard to think. She needed sleep.

You have to move forward. What did any of this matter? What Judy Martin's narcissism did to Emma? What it did to Cass? They would find the island and find Emma, and then they would know and this would all be over.

And then Witt's words, which kept finding their way off the page of Abby's notes, where she'd written them three years ago.

She is evil.

Abby knew what that meant. She knew this kind of evil inside and out. She knew what made it stronger and what made it weaker. And she knew how to get inside it, to become part of the splint that held it together.

As they walked from the house to their cars, wrapping up the day and saying their good-byes, Abby could see the plan taking shape to do just that.

ELEVEN

Cass—Day Three of My Return

On the third day of my return, I awoke to three surprises. The first was that I had actually slept for more than two hours in a row. After the visit with Hunter, I could feel the exhaustion in my stomach like a sickness. Like I wanted to vomit. It was in my head as well, throbbing like a headache, but also mixing up my thoughts so that the worst of them were able sneak past the better ones and start to seem real. I needed to reset my brain so that the bad thoughts could be contained. And I needed to remove the distractions of the headache and the vomit wanting to come. The only greater obstacle to thinking clearly than pain and vomit is fear.

I took two of Dr. Nichols's pills and had one glass of wine. I locked my door and slid the dresser in front of it. I should have done that first because I was nearly incapable of finishing the job after the pills and the wine. I lay down in the bed in the guest room and I slept for eight hours.

I did not take any medicine on the island. And I did not intend to keep taking the pills Dr. Nichols gave me after Emma was found. But until then, I would do what I had to do. As I was swallowing them down with the wine on that second night of my return, I thought that it was ironic that it was now—safe at home—that I needed the pills just to sleep, and to reset my brain so I could think.

Lucy used to say that, when she took her pills at night. *I need a good night's sleep so I can reset my brain. Sometimes your own thoughts can do you in if you don't get rid of them.*

I could see her thoughts, the ones that might do her in. The way she would stare out at the ocean gave her away. The Universe had been so unfair to her and it made her angry. It made her want justice. It made her believe she was entitled to justice. And that justice came in the form of a child. She would smile and nod to herself. *Yes.* I could see her thought. *I deserve a child.* But then her face would grow conflicted until the sadness beat down the self-righteousness. Until she began to wonder if what she was doing was divine justice, or if it was just plain crazy. And she could not afford to have that thought and still hold another woman's child in her arms.

I knew about crazy thoughts from the island. You have no idea what it's like to see land not that far away, to see lobster boats and yachts and motorboats just far enough that they can't hear you or see you well enough to know what you're doing if you were to jump up and down and make signals or fall to your knees in total despair. It makes you think that anything is better than this, even drowning in the current or freezing to death in the cold water. I had two parts inside me, like Lucy and Bill, with the one crazy part wanting something so bad, I was willing to do crazy things to try to get it, and the other part knowing it would kill me, actually physically kill me. That part of me was stronger than the crazy part. Otherwise, I think I might have died trying to leave that place.

I had other crazy thoughts on the island. Thoughts about deserving what I'd gotten. Thoughts about being an ungrateful teenager who was worthy of the disgust I had seen on Bill's face that day on the dock. They crept in when I wasn't looking, alongside the image of Rick's face and the plotting of how to use this to escape. And just like the fight between the crazy part that wanted to brave the frigid water and the sane part that stayed on the land, this part of me that felt I was so wretched, I deserved what I'd gotten waged war with the part that felt worthy of seeking revenge.

When I returned home, those thoughts found their way back into my consciousness, mixing with thoughts from my childhood about my profound unworthiness. I don't know how, but they are related, these thoughts. They must be because they felt familiar, like old friends I hadn't seen for a while but when I saw them I remembered them well and even welcomed them in no matter how terrible they were and always had been.

And they were terrible. They made me miss Emma so much. I don't know why. Sometimes when I hear the stories leaving my own mouth, I realize that Emma was not always nice to me. But something happens when you hold someone or when they hold you. It makes you feel better. It takes away the bad feelings of being worthless.

Those days when I was home, I could close my eyes and feel Emma holding me in the middle of the night. I could also feel that sweet little baby wrapped around in my arms, so tight. I would stroke her hair, which was so soft, just like Emma would stroke mine when our mother was asleep. I longed for those things. I felt as though I would die without them, like not having food or water. Without those things, I was lost in the bad feelings and I began to worry that I would never find my way out.

The second surprise that morning was a pile of new clothing outside my door when I finally woke up. They were my size and they were very nice. A pair of lightweight khaki pants, cropped at the ankle, and a button-down shirt that I could either wear long-sleeved or short-sleeved. The sleeves had a button and little tab thing that held them rolled up. There was some nice underwear from Victoria's Secret and a pair of flip-flops.

I brought them into the guest room and lay them on the bed. A question rushed into my brain and I knew then at that moment that the sleep had done its job and I was again thinking clearly. Very clearly.

When, exactly, had my mother purchased the clothes? They were outside my door at eight o'clock. I had gone to bed at midnight. No stores are open then. No mail is delivered then. We had not had any visitors. All of which meant that my mother had purchased or somehow obtained the clothes the day before but had chosen not to give them to me. Instead, she left me to wear her fat clothes and Hunter's old sneakers. Since the only thing that happened the afternoon before was the visit with Hunter and his girlfriend I arrived at the conclusion that my mother had not wanted me to look nice for Hunter. And this made me smile like before. I smiled the whole time I was putting on those clothes because I understood. Just like with Hunter's long hug, there is something about understanding that comforts me, even if I don't like what I understand.

I found out about the third surprise when I got downstairs. Dr. Winter was waiting for me. So was Agent Strauss. They were waiting for the sketch artist to come again. My father and Mrs. Martin had been asked to gather as many pictures of Emma as they could find from the time she was born. The sketch artist was going to do some kind of time lapse image of her in case the

Pratts had started to run and Emma had gone with them. I didn't like the sound of that because it meant they were still wondering why Emma hadn't left with me—if she was staying voluntarily and if, by inference, I had not been held captive either.

They were in the kitchen with the officer who watched the house from the street and kept the media trucks from coming down the driveway. They were having coffee. Mrs. Martin was there as well, taking something out of the oven. It smelled like bananas and cinnamon. I won't lie. That sight, and the smell of Mrs. Martin's banana bread—which she used to make on Sunday mornings with Emma—reached inside me and grabbed my heart. I almost looked around for Emma but I stopped myself. I was so grateful then for the sleep, for the pills and wine, for Dr. Nichols.

"Good morning, sweetheart," Mrs. Martin said. "How did you sleep?"

I told her I slept well. I thanked her for the clothes. She said we would go shopping later if I wanted, or maybe on the computer so I wouldn't have to face the reporters. She said she didn't get more than one outfit, because I might want to pick things out myself, from any place I wanted. She said it with a tilted head and a sweet, closed-mouth smile.

I had told people many things in the two days I had been home. In between the formal interviews with Dr. Winter and Agent Strauss were dozens of questions about my life on the island. What did I do all day? What did I eat? Who cut my hair? How did we get clothing? Did we play games or listen to music? And how did we not go crazy without the Internet or any way to reach the outside world?

It is probably hard to imagine that my life on the island after that day on the dock was anything but a constant state of urgency to escape. That every minute of every day was not spent plotting and worrying and mourning the loss of my freedom. The loss of my life. Or that the rest of it wasn't filled with those thoughts of deserving what I'd gotten because I was so unworthy, and that I should feel grateful for the home I had been given. But human nature does not allow for that. No matter where we are and what we are subjected to, we will eventually settle into the new reality and try to find pleasure, even if it is nothing more than a warm shower or food or even a glass of water. I think if I had been kept in a cage in the darkness with nothing but one piece of bread and one glass of water a day, I would eventually have come to find happiness in that bread and that water. And so on the island, there was laughter and there was friendship and there were moments of pleasure in between the sorrow and the urgency and the self-loathing.

Mr. Martin, who has been very successful in business and supposedly very smart, asked me even more questions every time I gave an answer, especially about how Bill paid for things. Mr. Martin was very skeptical. How did they buy the island or pay rent? How did they pay the boatman? How did they pay for the gas that went into the generator and the food and the books for us to study? That required money. Money required a job. A job put you in "the system" he kept saying.

My mother had asked me about my clothes. I had shown up wearing jeans and a T-shirt from Gap. My shoes were hiking boots. I picked things out of catalogs, and the boatman would buy the clothes and bring them to the island. Or maybe they ordered them through the mail. He did not bring packages to the island. Everything was opened, envelopes gone. The address labels were always torn off the catalogs. Nothing came onto the island that had a name or an address. I knew the Pratts were called that name only because that's what Rick called them. *Mr. Pratt* and *Mrs. Pratt.*

Mrs. Martin was obsessed with the fact that I had not been to a store myself since the night I disappeared. She had mentioned this to Dr. Winter the morning of my second day.

Dr. Winter, can you even imagine what it would do to someone to never leave a place? For three years . . . not being out in the world. Not shopping for your own food and shampoo, not going for coffee or lunch, not seeing movies? Not even shopping for your own clothes!

She said it like she felt sorry for me. But I knew what she was doing. She was trying to plant the seed that I had gone crazy because of what I went through. *Can you imagine what it would do to someone? . . .*

In the kitchen that third morning, after Mrs. Martin offered to buy me clothes and placed the banana bread on the counter, she walked to me and stroked my cheek. It made the others melt. I could see it on their faces. How nice this was, mother and daughter reunited. Mother caring for daughter. I looked at Dr. Winter. I searched her face for something, some sign of recognition. But I found nothing to comfort me that day. Mrs. Martin was very powerful and I could not forget that.

Dr. Winter was suddenly being very nice to her—and this was the third surprise. It was not a good one.

She told her it must have been very hard for me and Emma, and then she said something about how she liked to shop and would miss it very much, but anyone looking at Dr. Winter would see that she was not the sort of person who liked to shop for anything. She had worn the same jeans and the same boots and the same belt for three straight days. And her T-shirts were all the same type, as if she had found the kind she liked and then just bought a lot of them in different colors.

I didn't like that she was being so nice to Mrs. Martin. It was making her calm, giving credence to her theory that I was crazy.

I did not come back to make my mother calm. I came back to make her see what she had done to us, to make everyone see! I came back to find my sister, and time was not on my side.

There was some comfort for me that the forensic agents were all very skilled. Even on the first day, I could feel the importance of every word I said, every answer I provided. Imagine if the things you said resulted in federal agents taking to the streets and analysts scouring their databases—everyone in a large team of highly trained professionals jumping to a new task simply because you said the leaves turned orange in the fall or the air smelled of pine trees. After so many years of being powerless, of having no voice, of having no one hear me, I was overwhelmed.

Agent Strauss said he had been looking into agencies and crisis lines that claimed to help pregnant teenagers or had been investigated for illegal adoptions. And Dr. Winter told us that she had been working around the clock, tracking down her list of people from the past, people who might know something about the Pratts or Emma's pregnancy. She had already spoken with some teachers and friends of both girls. They had all heard about Cass's return and the desperate search for Emma, though so far none of them had anything to add that was helpful. They had been shocked to hear the truth about why we left home.

But despite all their skills, the FBI had no promising leads, even after searching up and down the Maine coastal region. There was no record of Bill or Lucy Pratt—not in the Social Security database or in any public documents they could find. They said most towns put things online now, but they were also looking at paper land records for islands, tracing ownership. They had even searched the public health records in Maine for birth certificates with the name Julia, or Pratt—girls born around the date I had given them. All of this was very time consuming and every day mattered. No one seemed to doubt that the Pratts would try to leave, and the worry this made me feel erased the relief from having all these agents working to find them. Worry, but also despair. Imagining this outcome, never finding the Pratts, never finding the baby, never finding Emma—I understood what my father had been through.

I told myself I would not be weak like my father. I would stay focused and help them in any way I could.

They had enlisted many local police to knock on doors in the villages. No one recognized the drawings that I had helped make with the sketch artist. No one could recall anyone fitting the descriptions of the Pratts or the boatman. And they had begun an investigation into the incident in Alaska, hoping to identify the boatman from his time on that fishing boat where the woman was raped.

"Having an age-progressed drawing of Emma could really help," Agent Strauss said. People would notice an older couple with a young woman and child. More than just an older couple alone. And with my help, they could get close to a real photograph of Emma the way she looked now.

I agreed to help, of course, and went into the living room, where my mother had set out all her fancy photo albums, the ones with the brown leather bindings with the years engraved in gold. Dr. Winter and Agent Strauss followed. Agent Strauss had yellow Post-its and he said we should tell him when we saw a photo of Emma from each year since her birth—pick the best one, he said, or maybe two with one having her profile. Dr. Winter said she would do this with me while Agent Strauss and my mother went through her computer in her study for photos that were stored there. But that was just an excuse for Dr. Winter to be alone with me.

In fact, this entire project felt like an excuse. Three years was not that long. We had been almost grown when we left. How different did they think she could look? But I went along with it.

We looked at photos. We picked the best ones from each year. Dr. Winter asked a lot of questions as she saw changes in my sister. One of them caught her attention—it was the year Emma turned fifteen.

"Why did she cut her hair?" Dr. Winter asked me.

It caught me off guard and I sort of gasped and put my hand over my mouth. I had not expected her to ask me about Emma's hair.

"Did she tell you anything, Cass? About why she cut her hair?"

Dr. Winter started turning the pages. She saw Emma with long, dark hair in the summer and early fall, and then the short cut just before the leaves were turning. It was above the ear, with severe angles and jagged corners.

"How did we not see these before?" she asked.

I shrugged. "I don't know," I said. "It wasn't a secret."

Dr. Winter's face became curious. "This was the year those nude photos were taken, wasn't it? Emma topless? Posted on the Internet?"

I was still silent, but I had forced my hand to drop back into my lap.

"Your brother told me about the photos. So did your father. Three years ago, during the investigation. How everyone thought it was Hunter. How Emma lied and said it was a friend goofing around, but then she couldn't explain how Hunter got access to them."

"Yes." That was all I said.

"Did Emma feel so humiliated by the pictures that she cut her hair to feel better? Sometimes people do that, you know?"

I shook my head.

"Then why? Why did Emma cut her hair?"

"She didn't," I said finally.

Dr. Winter looked confused. "What do you mean?"

"Emma did not cut her hair," I said more clearly.

"I don't understand," Dr. Winter said. She got up and moved closer to me. She placed a hand over my hand and squeezed it tight.

"No one told you about this? Before?" I asked. I never imagined this secret could be kept. Not with all the FBI agents and their skills and cunning. Somehow, Mrs. Martin had managed to do just that.

"No, they didn't. Should someone have told us?"

I nodded.

"Can you tell me now?"

"That was the year of the photos. At the end of the summer. They got posted and my parents freaked out. They traced it back to our home computer, so everyone blamed Hunter."

"Do you remember why they blamed him?"

"I don't know," I lied. "I don't know that much about it."

I did not want them getting distracted by talking to Hunter. I didn't want them to get distracted by anything. And I did not want them digging into the things that happened in this house.

Another curious look came across her face. "So, Witt punched Hunter and Hunter slashed his tires, right?"

"Yes. And after all that, I asked to live with our father. I thought that maybe that would finally be enough."

"No one said anything about that—and I didn't see any court filings. I went through the entire case history. Did your father ever file a motion for custody?"

I couldn't believe it. I couldn't believe they didn't know. And now I would have to tell them and they would have to believe me.

"My father called the lawyer he had used in the divorce and she sent a letter to my mother's lawyer threatening to file a motion to change the custody arrangements if she didn't agree to it. My mother went crazy. I guess she started calling my father and making all kinds of threats, things she would tell the court about him that weren't true. But he said he didn't care. At least, that's what he told me he said.

"We had been at his house for the weekend, me and Emma and Witt. We were all talking about it. I was relieved. Witt was sort of calm about it, like of course this was what had to be done. Emma seemed excited but in a nervous way. Like she knew it was going to incite our mother and she wanted it to but was also a little scared."

"You weren't nervous?" Dr. Winter asked. Her mind seemed busy. Thinking.

"Of course. But I thought that I had our father behind us that time."

"So what happened?"

"We got back to our mother's house. She was pleasant but also cold as ice. She made us a nice dinner and we all sat in silence. Hunter was gone, back to school, and Mr. Martin was in the city for some event. So the three of us just sat there, staring at our food, eating and not talking.

"I went to bed around eleven. I woke up at two thirty to the sound of Emma screaming. I ran into her room." I stopped there. It was hard to tell this part. To remember it.

"What happened, Cass? What happened to Emma that night?"

"She was there. Mrs. Martin. She was in Emma's bed, straddling her. She had a pair of scissors in her hand . . . she had cut off her hair . . . her beautiful dark hair that fell almost to her waist. Oh God. . . ."

I was shaking my head and staring at my folded hands, which were squeezed together so hard, my knuckles were turning white.

"Emma woke up after the first cut, but it didn't matter. Mrs. Martin had managed to take off almost an entire side, right above Emma's ear.

"I screamed, 'Stop! It wasn't her, it was me! I asked to leave, not Emma!' But she didn't stop. Emma was trapped under the blankets and Mrs. Martin's legs, so she punched at her. She gave her a black eye. Mrs. Martin threw the scissors on the floor and got off the bed. When she was leaving, she looked at me and said, 'That's what you get for betraying me again!'

"Emma cried all night, cutting off the rest of her hair herself to make it even. I stayed with her but she wouldn't even look at me. 'This is all your fault!' she kept saying. The next day, she pretended to go to school but walked into town and sat outside a hair salon until they opened. They tried to fix her hair the best they could. I didn't go to school either. I went to see my father and I told him not to file the papers. I told him I'd made a big mistake and begged him to stop."

Dr. Winter did not know what to say. If they had known this story, if anyone had known, maybe they would have looked harder for us, and in the right places. They had never seen or heard about Emma's short hair. I knew then that this album had not been among the stack three years ago when they came to this house to look for us. It had already been buried in the trunk upstairs where I had found it the first night I returned, under piles of neatly folded blankets. I thought it should be here, with the other nice photos from our childhood, so I brought it down.

"Did you tell anyone? How did your father not figure this out?"

"Our father sees what he wants to see. We gave him an out and he took it. He's not a fighter. He loves us, and he tries. But he's not a fighter."

Dr. Winter looked at me closely. "So who knew? Did you or Emma tell anyone, try to get help?"

I shook my head. "My mother told Mr. Martin because he heard the screaming and came out of their room. I don't think any of us told anyone else."

"Cass," Dr. Winter said. She took my hand again. "I'm very sorry this happened."

I wanted to squeeze it. I wanted to fall right into her and let go of everything I had been holding. But I would not be weak.

"That was the last time I asked to leave."

"And how were things the next day? When Emma came home with her new haircut and the custody challenge had stopped?"

"We came home at the time school got out. Our mother was in the kitchen. She'd made us brownies. We all sat down together, ate the brownies, and she said something like, 'Nothing will ever tear us apart. Do you understand?' Emma and I nodded. And that was that."

I must have been very bad at hiding my feelings because she asked me then, "Why did you come here, Cass?"

"This is my home," I answered. But that was a lie. I came here because it was my only hope of finding Emma.

"You could have gone to your father. You could have gone to Witt. Don't you see that I can help you, we can all help you if you let us? Don't you want to find Emma?"

That was the moment I felt strong again. I looked at her calmly. "I am," I said. "I am finding Emma."

And then I said what I had been waiting to say with my mother gone from the room.

"Has anyone spoken to Lisa Jennings?"

"The school counselor? Yes. We interviewed her extensively three years ago. She didn't have much to say that was helpful, though she felt she knew you girls somewhat. Why?"

"She talked to Emma a lot that fall. I had a class across the hall from her office, and three times I saw Emma come out of there. I bet there were a lot more times. Maybe she was helping Emma. Maybe she's the one who found the Pratts."

Dr. Winter was very surprised. "Why wouldn't she tell us if she knew something that important?"

I thought it was obvious, but I spelled it out anyway. "Well, if she put Emma in touch with the Pratts, she could get in trouble, couldn't she?"

It was then that Mrs. Martin came back in the room. She was suspicious because her back was very straight and her eyes very narrow.

"Did you find anything useful?" she asked.

Dr. Winter closed the photo album with the pictures of Emma's short hair.

I looked at my mother and smiled, because she was about to find out that she was not the smartest woman in the world. And I had just raised the stakes in a game she didn't even know she was playing.

TWELVE

Dr. Winter

Lisa Jennings. Abby heard the name inside her head. She could picture her notes from the original investigation. Lisa Jennings had not mentioned any meetings with Emma Tanner.

"We'll need to track her down," Abby said to Leo when they were finally alone in the Martins' living room. The photos had been chosen and given to the sketch artist, and now everyone was taking a break. "She's not at the school anymore."

"Okay. And what about this incident with the hair? How did we not know about this?" he asked.

Abby shrugged and told him what Cass had just told her before her mother insisted she have a rest. "She doesn't know. She assumed we'd seen the pictures and asked about it."

The truth was, this was textbook behavior for a narcissist mother—finding a way to divide the alliance that was rising up against her, using violence and terror to bring her subjects back in line.

"All right," Leo said. "I don't like it, but let's move on to the boatman, right?"

"Sure." They had so many questions, so much ground to cover

now. They were on the third day of the investigation. Abby was getting worried.

"I'll go round up Cass. Maybe we can keep Mom away a little longer."

Abby smiled. "Good luck with that. Cass doesn't want to be more than a yard away from her."

Leo left to find Cass. And Abby was left with the harrowing image of Judy Martin attacking her daughter while she slept, cutting off her hair with a pair of scissors.

Vivid images from her own childhood had already begun flashing before her, like they'd been stored in a secret box that Cass had just opened. Little Meg, hiding under a table as their mother searched for her with a belt in one hand and a bottle of vodka in the other. Their mother wearing a see-through top to their school to watch them in a play. Their mother flirting with a young landscaper out on the lawn. There were so many. Too many. But they were nothing close to the image of Judy Martin with those scissors.

Abby's father had left when she was five. It's not easy to live with a narcissist. The constant pushing and pulling to reconfirm your love and commitment grows very tiresome very quickly. For all her manipulative skills, Abby's mother had misread their father. He had been drawn to her beauty, her charm, which was undeniable, but he wanted a normal life and he found a new woman who could give that to him.

The divorce came as a shock to her mother. Losing her husband dismantled the fragile alter ego that had been protecting her, the delusions of her elevated place in the world. The delusions of her power and control over people. She reacted violently, first by contesting every step of the divorce—not showing up for court, refusing to follow orders that the judge issued—anything to prevent it from ending. But it did end eventually, and when it did, she drowned herself in alcohol. She died one rainy night driving back from a bar, high on cocaine and a blood alcohol level of .22. Abby and Meg had gone to live with their father and his new wife. Both had passed in recent years.

Something had shifted today. Abby could feel it. She was beginning to see the forces at play, to see the patterns in Cass's behavior and demeanor. Cass had resisted their ongoing efforts to speak with her alone. She wanted her mother there, but it was not for comfort. She wanted her mother to hear the stories about the island and the horrible things that were done to her daughters and her granddaughter. She became desperate and tearful when her mother reacted with surprise or outrage or disbelief. *Yes*, Abby had concluded. It was the disbelief that caused the greatest shift in Cass's demeanor, like she was panicked.

And then there were moments when she tensed up and grew quiet. When her eyes searched furiously among the audience, gauging their reactions, their emotions, to what was being said by Judy Martin. She did not like that Abby was being kind to Judy. She was starting to see Abby as an ally—but in what war? Finding the Pratts? Finding Emma? Or something else? There was no doubt Cass Tanner had a plan that she was not revealing.

But Abby had her own plan for Judy Martin. She had studied these people. She knew them inside and out. Judy Martin had to trust her; she had to believe that Abby was under her spell. And then it might come—in the things she didn't say and the ways she didn't react. Judy had to trust. And Abby had to be patient.

She'd gone home last night, after the second day, after hearing the horrible story about the dock and the retaliation for Cass's first attempt to escape. She'd stared at the sketches of Bill and Lucy Pratt, of the boatman Rick, and the truck driver. She had written a preliminary analysis of their psychology, the possible traumas that were at play, and she had spoken to the field teams about her theories. The boatman was easy. Childhood dysfunction had led him to the brutal life on that fishing boat at such a young age. And the rape of that woman on the boat had debilitated him with self-hatred.

As for the Pratts, they had also suffered some kind of trauma. And it had to do with a child. Their desperation to have a baby, but also the lack of compassion for Emma's daughter as she screamed in terror over the cold, black water—they had grown immune to that kind of attachment. Now the baby was no more than a psychological object. It was not real. Something had numbed them to genuine love.

It was just a working theory, but they had to start somewhere.

When Leo returned with Cass, Judy was right beside her. He gave Abby a look that said he had tried but failed to get Cass alone.

"If you're ready to start again, we want to hear more about the boatman, Rick. Everything you can tell us about him will be helpful," Abby said. "You told us he helped you escape. And that the first time you tried, he turned you away."

"Yes," Cass said.

"And you said that something changed after that incident on the dock, when they tried to make you leave without the baby."

"Yes."

"He had a look on his face, like the Pratts may have crossed the line," Abby said. "We want you to finish the story, fill in the gap between your first escape attempt and your final escape that brought you home."

Cass looked at her hands again, concentration pulling across her face. "Do you think you'll find him soon? Now that you have the sketch?"

Leo answered her. "The problem is that he has no incentive to come forward. He participated in kidnapping. And he already has a guilty conscience from the incident with that woman on the fishing boat in Alaska. Then there's the loyalty to the Pratts, whatever might be left of it. It may come down to finding his family. Seeing if they know anything. Did he ever mention that? His own family?"

Cass shook her head. "No. He never did."

"Okay. That's fine," Leo said. "Why don't you tell us what you can about him."

Cass nodded slowly, then began to speak about the boatman. "I thought a lot about loyalty." Her voice was steady, as if she were explaining a term paper she'd written in school. ". . . I think it's founded on one of three things. The first is debt. For example, if you saved my life, I may be loyal to you forever. The amount of loyalty and the time it lasts will depend on the debt that is owed."

Leo leaned forward, confused and about to interrupt her. It was a strange way to begin her story about Rick, and how he went from turning her in to helping her leave. But Abby reached out and touched his hand, shaking her head. Stopping him. This was exactly what she wanted from Cass. The truth would come as much from the digressions as from the story itself.

"What's the second one, Cass?" Abby asked her.

"The second is money. If you pay me to be loyal, then I will be loyal as long as I need the money."

Leo nodded. "I can see that. Do you think it was money that made Rick so loyal?"

"Well, the third thing is about keeping secrets. If I know you will keep my secrets, then I will keep yours in return. This is the most pure form of loyalty, I think. But like most pure things, it is also the most vulnerable."

"Because secrets can hurt you?" Abby offered.

Cass nodded, her gaze somewhere on the table in front of her clasped hands. "I did a lot of thinking about Rick after that first time I tried to leave. I thought about how he didn't seem to care about anything. The fishing boat may have done bad things to his mind like the Pratts told me, but there was a reason he was on that boat to begin with. Why would someone choose to do that at eighteen?"

Abby drew a long breath and leaned back in her chair. She was buying time before answering the question.

"Sometimes people do things like that to escape emotional pain. Extreme things that cause them to focus their attention away from the cause of the pain."

Cass glanced up then, an excited look on her face. "Yes! I think that's it. I think he was already in pain. The thing is, the Pratts did pay him, but he could get work as a boatman any-where. And from the way he dressed, I didn't believe they were paying him more than other people might. So that left two things—debt and secrets. The Pratts helped him get off drugs. They paid for some rehab program and let him go to meetings every Wednesday night. If we ever needed something on a Wednesday afternoon or evening, we were out of luck. Lucy told us that every Tuesday because, as she said, 'I don't want to hear any complaining tomorrow if you don't have ice cream or a new DVD.'

"In my mind, he had paid off this debt. The Pratts had gotten him off drugs, and they'd helped him with his conscience, but he had helped them with our kidnapping. He had taken my rowboat and put it back on the dock. And then he'd told them about my failed escape, and because of him, Emma and her baby were nearly drowned, and we were forced to stay—"

Cass stopped herself. Her face had turned red like she was about to scream or cry or pound the table with her fists. She was so different from other times when she'd told stories that should have been hard to tell. Even harder than this one. But she had been remarkably calm.

Abby touched her hand. "I understand what you're saying. He repaid that debt."

"So you think it was about secrets?" Leo asked.

Cass nodded.

"The secret he had about Alaska and how he didn't help that woman?"

She nodded again. "As far as he knew, the Pratts never told a soul about what he had witnessed in Alaska, what he had let happen in front of his own eyes. But I knew, didn't I? I know I'm still young. But it shocks me some of the things I know that other people don't."

She turned her eyes back to the spot on the table.

"Your secrets are never safe. Not ever. Unless you never tell them to another person. It was so obvious. Lucy felt worthless for not having a baby. Helping Rick was one of her shining moments and it made her feel like she was a good person even though she couldn't have a child and had to steal Emma's. But she hated herself so much that it wasn't enough just to have it inside her, to know it herself. She needed us to know about this wonderful thing she'd done for Rick, and that need trumped any trust that Rick had placed in her.

"Do you ever feel conflicted by this?" she asked, her eyes now on Abby.

"I'm not sure I understand."

"I know that we all need people. I mean, we need to trust people and we're always seeking out love, aren't we? But I can't ignore what's in my head. Everyone I could ever trust, everyone you could ever trust, could betray you. It doesn't matter who they are or whether they mean to do it. Your friends. Your husband. Your wife. Your siblings. Your child. Even your parents. Some people just do it and they don't care. They don't think twice about it. But others do it and they justify it in their heads so you can't even blame them. They have their reasons. Do you know what I'm talking about?"

Abby nodded cautiously.

"That's what I meant when I said this kind of loyalty is vulnerable. Because your secrets are never safe and that person who has your loyalty will betray you one day. That's what Lucy did to Rick. Do you see?"

Leo answered her question. "Yes, Cass. I see."

But Judy Martin did not see, and she could not stay silent for one more second. Something about this had gotten under her skin. "This is very silly talk, sweetheart. If this was true, we would all be killing each other, wouldn't we? Some people can be trusted. If you choose the right ones. And if you are the type of person who's worthy of their loyalty. That's what I believe," she said, finishing with a determined nod.

Cass ignored her and continued.

"When I was on the island and I came to these terrible conclusions, I was not sad. I added these conclusions to the expression I had seen on Rick's face that day on the dock. Suddenly my plan to escape felt real, so real that it filled me with excitement.

"One day I was sitting on the dock waiting for the boat. Rick tied up the boat and tucked the keys into a small pouch he carried around his waist so we couldn't steal it. He looked surprised but didn't ask me why I was there. I watched him do his work and then grab some bags of groceries. 'Can I help you?' I asked. He said no. He started to walk and I followed him. And then I just blurted it out. 'I'm sorry about what happened to you in Alaska.' He missed a step, stopped, but did not look back at me. He started up again and I let him go. That was enough then. I had planted the seed."

Abby knew exactly what she had done. "You were letting him know that they had betrayed his trust. They had gossiped about a horrible thing he had done, that he was deeply ashamed of."

Leo spoke then. "So you could sever the loyalty?"

Cass nodded. "It was the beginning, yes. It took a long time for that to eat away inside him, but it did. And when it did, it left a void."

"A void which you filled?" Abby asked. She already knew the answer. It was the next logical step in this plan of manipulation.

"Yes."

"Were you intimate with him, Cass? Do you know what I mean by that?"

Cass nodded and looked up abruptly, her eyes sharp and focused, and directed at Abby. "Yes," she answered.

Judy gasped and covered her mouth with her hand like she was horrified. "Cass!" she said. "How could you not tell us this right away?"

Abby ignored her. "How did this happen? And when? Can you tell us that?"

"It took me a long time, but I used that power, you know? With sex. Sex power. It's how women get power over men, right?" She was looking at her mother then. The room grew quiet for a moment.

Abby wanted desperately to go down this road, but not now. Not with Judy here. So she moved on. "You created the void and then filled it with something new."

"Yes. I filled it with something new. I filled it with pieces of me. And every time I gave him a piece, it would take me days to remember why I was doing it," she said.

Abby nodded. "It must have been very hard to be with someone like that. For reasons that are not known to him, only to you."

The room grew silent for a long moment before Leo pushed forward. "So when you were able to sneak out one night, he was there waiting. With the boat and the friend with the truck on the mainland?"

"Yes," she answered again. "Like I said. It was not easy. And it took a long time. It took months."

"And in all that time, there must have been conversations. Does anything stand out? Anything at all about where you were, where Rick was from, how he knew the Pratts, how they paid him—?"

Cass started shaking her head wildly. "No! Don't you think I would have told you? He barely spoke to me. And if I had pushed him on anything like that, he would have stopped believing that he could trust me!"

"Okay, Cass. It's okay. What about the truck driver? Did Rick say how he knew this man?" Leo was not giving up.

Cass shook her head.

Abby jumped in then. "Cass, we need you to see another doctor. An adult doctor."

But Cass refused. "I want you to do that examination, the one my mother keeps asking for. The one that will prove I'm not crazy."

"No one thinks you're crazy, Cass," Leo said.

"We'll do it tomorrow," Abby agreed.

"Okay." Cass seemed relieved. "Are you still going to find them? Find the island? Find those horrible people, even though I did what I did with the boatman?"

Leo looked at Abby. She could see the father in him screaming to come out. This was one of those moments when Cass seemed like a child, and it stood in glaring contrast with the other moments when she was wise beyond her years.

All of this was alarming to Abby.

"We will find them," Leo said with conviction. "And we will find your sister."

Cass appeared neither surprised nor comforted by the reaction she had provoked. It was something else, something akin to satisfaction, which meant it was calculated.

Cass Tanner was taking them all on a journey, and the only way they would find Emma was to go along for the ride.

THIRTEEN

Cass

Our mother had taught us about "sex power" around the time when Emma was thirteen. It was just after Mrs. Martin had started having sex with Mr. Martin behind our father's back, and so I think she was very pleased with herself because she had discovered that this power had not left her. Mr. Martin was very powerful, and my mother was getting older.

It's not just about age and beauty, girls, she used to say with that smile I hated. *It's how you make them feel—like they're the ones who are powerful! Like they make you melt like no other man. It's a trick women play. Think of it like a game.*

She gave us lessons like this whenever something came up that seemed relevant to her. A woman with big breasts and a low-cut shirt at the club—*See how all the men are trying to talk to her?* Things like that. Emma always listened but pretended not to. I always pretended to listen when I was actually blocking out the sound of her silly voice and her even sillier words.

When I first met Dr. Winter, I knew she had never used Mrs. Martin's sex power on a man. I don't know how I knew this. Maybe because she was still single. Maybe because she did not react to Mrs. Martin the way most women do, which is with a mix of envy and contempt because they wish they had her sex power but hate that they need it to get things in life. I think that when you see a woman who has sex power but chooses not to use it, she is someone you can trust.

I considered then the possibility of trusting Dr. Winter. I considered falling apart in her arms the way I did with my brother when I saw him the next day, and telling her about my mother and the things she had done. But I had learned my lesson years before with that woman from the court, and with my father. It's like I keep saying—people believe what they want to believe, and I had no idea what Dr. Winter wanted to believe. I feared I had already told her too much with the story about Emma's hair.

Sex power has its limits. I knew this because of the things that had happened at home before I left. I knew this again when I saw Hunter and his girlfriend. And I knew this from Mr. Martin and how he looked at Emma when Mrs. Martin was right there for the taking, every second of every day.

I knew this before the naked photos of Emma were posted on the Internet. So when I saw them, I knew who had taken them.

The IP address was traced to our Internet at our home, which meant they had to have been sent from the desktop computer we all shared, or Hunter's laptop. Neither of them had any stored photos of Emma without her top, so it was also assumed that they had been deleted. We could have had the computers sent away to see if they could find traces of them in the deleted files, but Mr. Martin refused. He told my mother that because Emma was a minor, if a technician found traces of naked photos, they could all be accused of child pornography because the computer technician would have to turn the information over to the FBI. The technician confirmed this. He told Mr. Martin that this very thing had happened in divorce cases—a suspicious wife let him poke around the deleted files of her husband's computer, and he found images of underage girls from sites that pop up when you're surfing porn. The husband probably wasn't looking for underage girls when he was doing his porn surfing, but that's what he got, and once it's on your computer, it never really leaves.

Mrs. Martin could not argue with that. I think she was relieved because she didn't want to know anything about the photos.

So everyone assumed Hunter had taken them and posted them to the Internet. Witt punched him in the face. I asked to live with my father. And my mother cut off Emma's hair.

But it was not the events after the photos were posted that gave Mr. Martin away. It was everything that happened before.

It started the previous spring, with that evil boy from Hunter's school that Emma had sex with. Emma did not speak to Hunter for weeks after that incident, because Hunter called her a whore and laughed at her. But this didn't last long.

Hunter missed Emma. He missed snuggling with her on the couch watching scary movies and he missed getting high with her and he missed sneaking out with her to go to parties at the beach. He missed her smiling at him and flipping her hair and telling him things about her life. So when she came back from her summer program, Hunter made nice with her and they went back to their usual fighting but then getting high and laughing and snuggling on the couch. That didn't last long either.

In early August, Emma started dating a new boy from our club. Hunter became insane with jealousy again. He was as cruel as he had ever been. He did lots of small, petty things like stealing all her underwear and hiding her phone so she couldn't find it. But the worst part was how he just kept calling her a whore.

Good morning, whore. How was the movie, whore? Lose your phone again, whore?

My mother did little to help. Every time she spoke to Mr. Martin about it, he got angry with her because he felt like she was criticizing his son. That's what he said. But he was also angry with Emma for hurting his son, and for the way she made them both feel, which was wrong for both of them but especially for Mr. Martin.

One night late that summer, Emma came home from a party she'd gone to with that new boyfriend. Hunter was waiting for her. *You're such a little whore!* he said. She ignored him and started to walk upstairs. Hunter followed her. *Get away from me, loser!* she said. But he didn't. He followed her to the upstairs hallway and pushed her against the wall so hard that one of Mrs. Martin's framed pictures crashed to the ground. He used his forearm to press into her chest and then stuck his hand down her pants. *Is that what you let him do to you? Huh? Like this?*

Emma just stared at him. I was standing in my doorway, frozen. It was such a strange and scary thing to see, but somehow Emma was not afraid. I could tell by her expression. She was defiant. He could put his hand in her pants. He could even kiss her and stick his tongue in her mouth. It wouldn't matter. Emma had power over Hunter and she was never going to give it up by letting him have her. She was going to use it to torture him.

The next day, Emma was in her bedroom. She was getting dressed for another party and wouldn't let me in to watch her. She said she wanted her privacy and that I was being a pest. Mr. Martin was driving her because our mother was at a charity function.

I heard Mr. Martin call her name from the bottom of the stairs. Emma did not respond. This made me curious, so I turned off my music and listened. Footsteps bounding up the stairs. Another shout for Emma from down the hall. A knock on her door. The door opening. Then silence.

Very softly, I opened my door. Mr. Martin had disappeared inside Emma's room. It was silent in that room for a moment, and then Mr. Martin walked out, a little dazed. He looked at me standing in the hall. He looked the other way, then back at me. His phone was in his hand. Shame was on his face.

Tell your sister to hurry up.

I walked to Emma's room and found her smiling in front of her mirror. She was wearing a sundress with spaghetti straps and Dr. Scholl's on her feet. Her long hair was straight from her iron, and her lips were bright, bright red and shiny with gloss. Her face was flushed.

This is exactly how she looked in the pictures that got posted on the Internet—the dress, the hair, the makeup and the room. In one of the pictures, she had dropped the top part of the dress to expose her breasts. Of course, when I saw the pictures, unlike everyone else, I knew the moment they had been taken. And I knew who had taken them.

Emma never told me what happened, but I imagine it was something like this: She was mad at Hunter for putting his hand down her pants and calling her a whore all summer. She lured Mr. Martin to her room and probably asked him to take a picture of her to post on Instagram or something equally innocent. Then she dropped the dress. And Mr. Martin was tested. Finally, after all these years of watching her and envying his son for being so close to her, she was his. Just for a moment. And rather than walk away, he snapped one last picture that he would save to his phone so he could remember the moment and satisfy his urges. It's a slippery slope, giving in to a wanting as strong as his. Even if you just give in a little.

I concluded as well that Mr. Martin would never have posted those pictures online. It served no purpose for him, and the site they went to was nothing any grown-ups had heard of.

So, I don't know when she did it, but Emma must have told Hunter about the pictures and Mr. Martin. And Hunter retaliated by finding them and posting them online. It was all-out war, and that war would rage in our house for two more years. Until the night we disappeared.

It was on the third night of my return that Witt came to visit. I decided to stay with my father that night. I thought it would be a relief, but he was not doing very well and I felt myself being pulled into his emotional storm.

I know Dr. Winter spoke to him about how to speak to me. She told him not to be overly emotional when he asked me questions about my time on the island, not to sound judgmental. My father had a lot of trouble with this. I know he tried. I could see the strain in his entire body as he held back his questions, held in his agony for his daughters. The veins that ran down the sides of his forehead, and his neck, and up his forearms were popping out from beneath his skin as we sat at the dining room table eating takeout.

"You must have missed Chinese food. It was always your favorite."

I told him that I had missed it very much.

"What about television? Did you get to watch any of your favorite shows? Did you see any movies?"

I told him some of the movies and things we watched. We had a satellite dish, and it seemed like it was not legal, because it didn't work all the time. I asked him if he had seen the same shows or movies.

Something about this made my father cry and leave the room. Actually, he asked me if I minded if he left the room because he had to cry. He said he would go and get us some ice cream. I thought that was considerate. But at the same time, I was mad at him. I wanted him to be stronger.

I could see Witt was barely tolerating him, the way he always did. His lack of respect for him would never go away, and I thought it was odd that this bothered my father less than Mrs. Martin choosing Mr. Martin and leaving him. But I suppose it all goes back to one of Mrs. Martin's lessons about how everyone wants what they can't have. I never want to want anything after seeing the damage wanting brings.

Well, maybe that's not true. I would never stop wanting to find my sister.

Our father had always been this way. We had to see his feelings and, to a large extent, feel them as well, because that's what normal people do, especially when they are very young and are learning how to be empathetic. He was always sorry for being weak. From crying in front of us to settling the custody case to sleeping with our mother and breaking up his family with his first wife and Witt. But I was tired of sorry. From him. From the millions of people who were watching my story and making their dumb comments on TV. From everyone who said, "I'm so sorry." Sorry happens after something bad has happened, after people have let it happen. It had become contemptuous to me, all these I'm-so-sorries.

Being alone with Witt nearly destroyed me, pieces of me crumbling, falling to the floor, and I had no idea how to piece me back together. That sounds bad, but it was the opposite of bad. When my father left, when I heard the door close, I fell into Witt's arms all at once and sobbed. He had heard my stories from the island and he didn't ask me any questions at all. Not one. He told me everything was all right and that he would make sure it stayed that way. Witt said I could come and live with him and his wife. We talked of logistics and strategies to get through this time of finding Emma—and we would find her!—and then of the future, when the media trucks were gone and my fifteen minutes of fame were over. He was going to get me tutoring so I could take the GED and get my high school diploma. And then I would go to college if it was the last thing he did. He said these things very fast into my ears as he held me while I cried. I nodded and said okay over and over so he knew that I heard him and that I believed him. But I did not believe him. Not completely, the way I pretended to.

"What's happened, Cass? Are you worried we'll never find her?" Witt pulled away and looked me in the eye.

"Yes," I said.

"Why? Has something gone wrong with the Bureau or that doctor? . . ."

That's when I told him about the conversation I had overheard between my mother and Mr. Martin when they were behind the closed door of their bedroom:

Jonathan, she's out of her mind. Did you hear what she's saying? Talking about these people and Emma's baby . . . it's crazy talk!

So what? Don't you see? They have to realize it on their own. You can't be the one to tell them she's crazy. Let them find out through their investigation. They'll find the island, and that boatman.

What if she's not?

Not what?

Not crazy. What if I'm the one who's crazy?

I am not having this fucking conversation one more time! I swear to Christ, Judy . . . sometimes you can be so fucking stupid—

Don't be angry with me. I'm scared. The things she's saying—

Cass is not right in her head. End of story.

They went on to discuss all the ways I seemed "off." I sounded paranoid. If they told Dr. Winter or Agent Strauss that I did not seem myself, the search for Emma could be diverted to a search for my sanity. This was another reason I asked to sleep at my father's house. I needed to see myself through Witt's eyes so I would know for sure that the Martins were wrong about me. And that even if they were right, if I had lost my mind, that no one would believe them and they would keep looking for my sister.

Witt laughed a little bit. It was not because he was happy or found any of this funny. It was the laugh people have when they are thinking about vengeance.

"Good. Let them think you're crazy! Let them fight about it and worry about it. My God, you and Emma did plenty of that when you were kids. Look—this is easy. You'll pass the psychological examination tomorrow, and that will be the end of it."

"And they can keep searching for Emma at all cost."

"Yes. They will keep searching for Emma. And they will talk to the counselor at the school. And one way or another, Emma will be found."

I asked him then what he thought when he heard my story and when he looked at me. Did he think I was crazy? Mrs. Martin had a way of making people forget what's real. Maybe she had done that to me.

"No!" He said it emphatically.

Too emphatically. But I did not ask again.

He put his arms around me. "No, Cass, no! I promise you."

I kept crying, right into his chest, my tears soaking into his shirt. I wanted to go back in time, even to the bad times, when Witt and Emma and I were together in this house. Maybe my father was right. Maybe it was dangerous to have things like that because when they're gone, it breaks you into pieces.

Witt didn't know what to make of me then. But I could see everything wash away except his love for me.

"Come home with me now. Right now! You've done everything you can do to find Emma. You've been through too much, Cass."

Our father returned with ice cream then. I stopped crying and Witt stopped telling me to go home with him. We ate the ice cream with our father at the kitchen table.

I thought about what Witt said as I calmed myself down. I thought about getting in his car and never coming back. Relief washed over me and it felt like nothing I have ever felt before, like someone had just injected me with a powerful drug that takes away all your pain. I needed the pain to stop.

But I could not get in my brother's car and drive away to a new life. Not now. Not yet.

I was not finished with Mrs. Martin.

FOURTEEN

Dr. Winter—Day Four of Cass Tanner's Return

On day four of Cass Tanner's return, they sat in the parking lot of Danbury High School talking about the boatman, who had just been identified as Richard Foley. The ID had come in that morning, and everything else was now on hold. It was their best lead. If they found the boatman, they would find the island, and—they all hoped—Emma and her baby.

"Are they sure?" Abby asked.

"How many gang rapes of government officials from the Department of Fish and Game do you think there are in Alaska?"

Field agents in Alaska had found an article in the *Ketchikan Daily News* from seven years back about a fisherman's account of the rape.

"They talked to the reporter. Foley refused to disclose the name of the woman, and without corroboration, the paper couldn't print the names of the men involved."

Abby considered this. Seven years was a long time. But small towns had long memories.

"So, listen to this. The reporter said Foley lived in Ketchikan for about three years. Cycled on and off the boats. He left after the incident, according to his own account, and returned seven years later to make amends for his silence."

"Too late to prosecute?"

"The DA said they couldn't do a damned thing without the woman's cooperation. Everyone knew who she was. It's a small town. But she wanted no part of the story after all that time. Said she'd moved on. The article was tucked away in the back pages, and nothing ever came of it."

"And Foley?" Abby asked.

"Came and went in a day. Guess he wasn't in the mood to catch up with his old fishing buddies."

"Whereabouts?"

"They're looking. Asking around town if anyone remembered him, remembered him talking about where he was from or where he was going. They got his social from the employer up there. Got his old local address, too. They'll canvass the landlord if they can find her. She sold the building not long after he left."

"But nothing from the social?"

"No. He was only eighteen. This was his first W-2 job. And apparently his last."

Abby could feel Leo's eyes on her. He had been doing a lot of that—studying her when she was looking away, when he thought she wouldn't notice.

"You sleep?" he asked.

She nodded yes. And then shook her head. "A little," she answered finally.

"This is a tough one," Leo said, looking at the picture of Foley.

"Why do you say that? We have the boatman." Abby looked at him, puzzled. He had been the one telling her that they would find the island, that they would find Emma. They had Cass, they had an actual person who knew what had happened. And now they had Richard Foley. Abby had finally started to believe him.

"We have the boatman's *name*. Not his location. Big difference, kiddo," Leo answered.

Richard Foley's family had not seen or heard from their son since he left for Alaska after turning eighteen. He had been a difficult teenager, and they were relieved to see him go out into the world. They had envisioned him working hard, finding purpose, and perhaps gaining an appreciation for what it was like to be a responsible adult. They always thought he would come home to Portland, where the family had lived for three generations.

Abby was not there when the family was interviewed. His mother, father and two older sisters had been shocked to learn that Rick was involved in the case of the Tanner sisters, the story that had been all over the news for days. They had provided names of friends, other relatives, dental and medical records—anything and everything that was asked of them. To their thinking, he had helped the younger sister escape and could now be on the run or in grave danger from the kidnappers who lived on that island.

Danbury High School was an hour north of the Soundview Academy, where the Tanner sisters had attended school. Abby had been through her notes from the interview with the school counselor, Lisa Jennings. The woman claimed she didn't know Emma well and had never met with her alone. Agents in New Haven had run her name and found nothing of concern. But Cass insisted that the woman had counseled Emma, that they had grown close. She seemed preoccupied with this lead. There had to be a reason.

"Catch me up," Leo said.

Abby pulled some notes from a bag. She didn't need them to recite the brief history, but she read from them anyway. "Worked as a counselor at Soundview for six years. Left at the end of the school year following the girls' disappearance. Thirty-four years old. Unmarried. Has a degree in social work from University of Phoenix."

"And the original interview?"

Abby shrugged. "She had a lot of opinions about the girls, but she also said she only knew them peripherally, seeing them in the halls, faculty room gossip. It was helpful three years ago to get a picture of who they were, but nothing there helps us even guess who the father might be, or who might have helped Emma run away."

"All right. Let's go solve this little mystery so we can get back to Richard Foley."

Abby followed him up the steps of the school, to the receptionist and then down a narrow, gray hallway to the office of the school counselor, Lisa Jennings.

This was a far cry from the white marble floors of the Soundview Academy.

They sat in metal chairs around a small coffee table adorned with a neat stack of teen magazines. Lisa Jennings was every bit as beautiful as she had been three years before, though her face had begun to hollow beneath her cheekbones, small crow's-feet now visible at the corners of her eyes as she marched into her midthirties. On her finger was a diamond engagement ring.

"It's so nice to see you again, Dr. Winter, under happier circumstances," she said, smiling broadly.

Abby returned the gesture. "Yes, it is. And congratulations. That's a beautiful ring."

Lisa fanned her fingers and admired the diamond. "Thanks. Only a few months to go until the big day!"

"That's very exciting," Abby replied.

Leo was not in the mood for small talk. He sat on the edge of the chair, legs straddling the corner of the table, elbows on knees. "How much have you read about Cass Tanner's return?"

The woman was startled by the abruptness of the question. She settled back into her chair, hand to face as though thinking about her answer carefully. "I've read everything I could find, of course."

She recited the facts that were public—how they left because Emma was pregnant, how they lived on an island off the coast of Maine with people named Bill and Lucy Pratt. How there was a boatman named Richard Foley who helped Cass escape, and how they believed Emma was still on the island with her daughter, now two years old.

"Is there more?" she asked.

Abby jumped in. "We're trying to find out who might have put Emma in touch with the Pratts. That's probably not their real name, so we're having to work backwards, looking for any connection from before the disappearance."

"Well, I wish I could help you, but I had no idea Emma was even pregnant, let alone trying to find someone to help her run away."

Leo looked at her curiously. "That's strange. Cass told us you and Emma had grown close. That Emma had started coming to your office more and more that early fall. She was certain you might have something that would be helpful, even the name of a boy she might have been dating."

Lisa Jennings shook her head. "That's not true at all, actually. I tried to speak with Emma on several occasions over the years, given the turmoil in their home with the divorce. She had no interest. I think I told you before that Emma had a very strong external wall, and she seemed very sure of herself. Confident. Some might say arrogant."

Abby finished the thought. "But behind that wall, you said she was insecure. Why did you think that?"

"Well, if I recall, it was really based on comments made by some of her teachers. And also the way she used her appearance to attract friends. Boys, in particular."

"Huh," Abby said, fanning through her notes. "What was it about her appearance? I'm sure I have it in my notes, but I'm working on very little sleep—"

"Sure—you know, she wore heavy makeup sometimes. Eye liner and lipstick. She always wore her hair down, and it was meticulously straightened. She liked to show off her legs, so short skirts and tight pants. We had a dress code, but the girls always found the loopholes."

When she stopped speaking, Abby and Leo let silence fill the room to see if she would fill it. She did.

"Then there was the time she had that very short hair, and all the girls thought she was being very courageous. The boys were curious as well. It was as if she had decided to make a statement about the pressure on girls to please boys. And of course, it only made the boys want her more. She let everyone believe she was bold like that. She liked that people believed that about her."

Leo slipped his phone back in his pocket like he was getting ready to leave. "So Emma did not come to see you?"

"No. Never."

"And you did not know of any boyfriends at the time of her disappearance?"

"No."

"And you had no idea she was pregnant?"

"No, none at all."

"Is there anyone you can think of who might have helped her with her plan to run away? Any teachers or friends or parents of friends who may have had views on abortion or adoption or who were involved with troubled teenagers?"

She shook her head. "No. I would have told you back then. We all racked our brains trying to understand what might have happened to those girls. I remember answering all of these same questions—about men and friends and teachers and parents. I'm sorry. I left at the end of that school year."

Abby was not ready to pack up quite yet. "Can I ask why?"

"I just needed a change. Public schools have different demographics. I can do more good here."

"And public schools pay more, don't they?"

Lisa smiled. "Yes. That, too."

"I thought it might have been because of your fiancé," Abby said.

"We met after I started work here. He teaches history."

"Well," Leo said, standing now. "Thank you for your time."

Abby followed, reluctantly. She needed an answer to the one question Lisa Jennings could not answer. *Why did Cass lead us back to you?*

"I'm sorry I couldn't be of more help. I will keep thinking about it and let you know if I remember something."

"Thank you." Abby gave her a card. Leo did the same. They turned for the door.

"Her family must be elated. Please send them my regards," Lisa said as a parting gesture.

Abby turned to face the woman, suddenly curious but not sure why. "Her family is complicated, as you know."

"Yes, sadly. I was aware of the situation with the parents. I'll never forget the real reason Emma cut her hair so short. We all thought that might be the end of the turmoil, however terrible that was."

Leo stopped now as well. They both looked at her, then back at each other.

"I don't know if things are ever really over in a situation like that," Abby said cautiously. A new door had just been opened and she had no idea where it would lead.

"Or with a person like that. I thought it was child abuse. When I heard how Mrs. Martin cut her daughter's hair in the middle of the night, well, I tried again to speak with the girls. Maybe that's what Cass was remembering. I tried to help. But they would not talk about it—or anything, for that matter. You know, sometimes I wonder if I should have reported that to social services. I wonder if I could have stopped that runaway train. But you have to understand, I was following protocol. It was not a reportable event according to the school, and I worked for them."

Abby flipped through her notes again, stopping on a random page. "Right, I remember that. Judy Martin cut her hair to punish the girls for wanting to live with their father. That must have been very difficult. It's a shame they didn't confide in you."

Lisa Jennings held her palms to the sky. "Teenagers . . ."

"I remember being one," Abby said. She smiled and touched the woman's arm warmly. "Do you remember who told you about that—I mean, if the girls didn't say anything?"

"Oh," Lisa said. She was taken aback, then struggled to regroup. "You know, I think it was their father, Owen. Strange I can't remember. It was a long time ago."

Abby smiled. "Yes, it was."

"And I'm sure you did everything you could," Leo said. "You know what they say about hindsight."

They said their good-byes. Abby rushed down the hall and out the door. Leo was right behind her. Neither of them spoke until they were outside, barreling down the stone steps to the parking lot.

"Holy shit," Leo said.

"I know." Abby was out of breath. Her heart was pounding. They stopped on either side of the car, looking at each other over the roof.

"What did Cass tell you about that story?"

"That only four people knew that it was Judy who cut off Emma's hair."

"Cass, Emma, Judy—"

"And Jonathan. Jonathan Martin."

"Which means Owen Tanner could not have told her. No way Judy told her. And she would have remembered if one of the girls had told her."

"She said she never met with the girls," Abby continued.

"Which means Jonathan Martin told her. But why?"

Abby could see her thoughts playing out across Leo's face. "The same reason she just lied about it."

FIFTEEN

Cass

After my visit with Witt, I returned to Mrs. Martin's house and began my mission to prove myself sane. It was day four of my return.

Mrs. Martin was beside herself with happiness. I had finally submitted to that psychological examination she wanted Dr. Winter to give me. It didn't matter that it came back "normal." What mattered was that my emotional state, my sanity, was now being discussed and examined along with the search for Emma.

When I first heard the words "psychological examination," I imagined having to lie on a table with electrodes connected to my brain. I imagined it would be physically painful somehow, like shock therapy. But it had nothing to do with my brain. It was just a lot of paperwork, 567 questions on a form called the MMPI 2, whose answers were meant to indicate one thing or another. I could see the conclusions they would draw from the different answers. "I have bad thoughts more than once a week," for example. Why would anyone answer yes to that? "Evil spirits possess me"? "I have acid in my stomach most of the time"? "If someone does something bad to me, I should pay him back"?

The questions jump around because they are trying to catch people who think they can trick the test. There were a few questions about sleep and other physical symptoms of stress or anxiety but then a question about self-esteem, for example. Some of them were very tricky, asking about authority figures and whether you sometimes feel alone in the world. No one understands you. I could see that if I answered them in a way to appear perfect, the test would flag me as being a liar. No one is perfect. And we all feel alone sometimes.

It was not hard to answer the questions and be found sane. It was not hard to also alert Dr. Winter to the extreme emotional stress I was under, both from my experience on the island and my obsession with finding my sister. "I have trouble sleeping." "I can't stop thinking the same thought over and over." "I have trouble concentrating." These were all answered with a yes.

Mrs. Martin was not only happy because the professionals were looking into my sanity; she was also happy because she was able to trust me again. I could see it on her face and from the amount of time and attention she gave me that afternoon. We went shopping for clothes. We got manicures. We went out to lunch. She talked more about town gossip and I pretended to care about all of it. She talked to me about being a woman, about my future and the things we needed to do for me, like getting a tutor and taking a vacation together, maybe to a spa in Florida. And at random moments, she would stop what she was doing and stare at my face. Her hand would cup my cheeks and she would shake her head and say how gorgeous I had become and how lucky she was to have me back.

And in everything she did and said to me, there ran an undercurrent of sympathy. I was crazy. Poor, crazy Cassandra.

Mrs. Martin has a switch. It goes on and off depending on

how she feels about you. If you adore her and are on her side, and if you make her feel good or look good to others, she trusts you and so she loves you. If you are a threat to her in any way, or competing with her for anything she wants or needs, she despises you and will dedicate herself to destroying you. In between, there is a neutral position in which she is indifferent. You have been fully neutralized, meaning you can never harm her. And you have nothing to offer her that she wants or needs. You cannot make her appear good or bad. You cannot make her feel good or bad.

It was easy to see the position of her switch with my father. After the custody fight, after she'd won, it was in neutral. My father would always love and desire her. He could not take anything from her. And she had beaten him publicly and won her daughters. She did not think at all about my father, except for that brief incident when I tried to leave her house and live with him. She took care of that with a pair of scissors—cutting off Emma's hair to punish me, and I was punished because when Emma had to go to school like that, I felt her humiliation way down in my stomach, worse than if my own hair had been cut off. I always wanted my father to find a beautiful woman and marry her just to see my mother flip her switch to loving him again. She would have loved him to death, or at least until she won back his desire and could trust him again. But he was too close to see any of this.

It was very different with Mr. Martin. My mother never rested in her efforts to keep his desire, because it was always in jeopardy. Emma was a constant reminder of this, and as she got older, it got worse and worse. Mrs. Martin didn't really love anyone, not the way I think of love. So I use that word more to describe how she acted toward people. Her switch for Mr. Martin was always on love.

With Emma, she could go back and forth in a matter of minutes. Emma made her feel proud because she was so desirable. The love switch was on. But then she would catch her husband looking just a little too long at Emma, and especially Hunter and Emma when they were together, and the switch flipped to hate. Emma was a proficient operator of Mrs. Martin's switch. She had studied the circuit board for years and it came to her like her first language. It was effortless. Maybe even subconscious.

Before I disappeared, I spent most of the time in Mrs. Martin's neutral position. I had no power to help her or hurt her and she was too busy dealing with the threat of Emma, the lightning rod, to even notice me. When I returned, things were all mixed up. First, when she thought I was crazy but no one else could see it and they were all believing me and feeling sorry for me, she hated me. I could feel it, even through her plastic smiles and bony hugs. But now—now that she was the dutiful mother whose long-lost daughter was mentally disturbed and in need of help, now that the things I said were not a threat to her, she could love me again, and this was a great relief to her.

"I know you were in your room that night," she kept saying that day. "You weren't hiding in Emma's car. You didn't go with her to the beach, did you? You'll remember when you get well." She said this with a smile while our nails were drying.

I knew when this was over, the switch would move again. And that it would move for the last time.

Later that day, Richard Foley's boat was identified. The owner of the boat ran a commercial dock in New Harbor, leasing slips and watercraft—long-term rentals for local residents and lobstermen, and seasonal rentals for the tourists and vacationers. The boat had been found six days before that off the coast near Rockland over thirty nautical miles north of the dock where it was from. But it was not until day four of my return that the dock owner put the pieces together and contacted the FBI. He said his wife saw the story and the picture of Richard Foley on a news show that morning. They had been renting a boat to Foley for five years, but under a different name. He paid cash, even for the six-thousand-dollar security deposit.

I could barely contain my excitement, and my fear. I knew they would find the island now and I could taste the vengeance that was growing closer. But this news had done nothing to upset my mother, and I was beginning to think that nothing would. She had grown stronger without us here, without Emma constantly chipping away at her façade of perfection. And even though I had been proved sane, she had convinced herself that people doubted me because I had taken the test in the first place. And so there was just as much fear as excitement.

There was also something else when I heard the news about Richard Foley being identified and his boat being found. It was so easy to answer that one question. *Were you and the boatman intimate?* But there had been nothing easy about it, and I could not chase the memories from my brain when I heard the news, and when I heard his full name.

I was Richard Foley's lover for 286 days. I will say very little about this because it is still mixed up in my head. When I think about it, I feel sick in my stomach with shame and disgust and also from the knowledge that there is evil in the world and that evil can dress up as love so convincingly that it blinds you to the truth. Those are all very sickening things and I don't like to feel them.

I knew three things about Richard Foley. First, he was not easily conquered by that kind of power Mrs. Martin had taught me about. However strong his desire was, his will not to give in to it was even stronger. The second thing had to do with his experience in Alaska witnessing the assault of that woman. He had a conscience, and he had morality. He had been so disturbed by what he saw that he became a drug addict just to shut it out of his brain. And he had then cleaned up and made amends by returning to Alaska and telling the story to the newspaper with the names of the men who had done it. The third thing I knew about Richard Foley was that the first two things fit together like a hand and glove.

It was not complicated. I started taking long walks at the times I knew the boat was coming with supplies or to take Bill to the mainland. I waited until Rick was alone on the trail, and I would be there as well, not every day, but many days. Our paths crossing had to appear coincidental. And on those days, I walked slowly, with my arms folded around my body, and my face swollen with despair. Sometimes I would be sitting on the dock, staring out at the ocean that held me prisoner, silent pleas flowing down my cheeks. I would not look at him or even acknowledge him for several weeks. I did not speak until he did.

It began in March one and a half years after we'd first arrived there in his boat. I was on the path to the dock, the ground packed with snow. The trees bare. I had stopped walking and crouched against a tree, knees to chest, rocking back and forth with violent shivers. Rick saw me and stopped for a second, like I had startled him and then shocked him. He got a hold of himself and walked past me, but then he stopped, turned and, for the first time in all that time, spoke to me.

You should get back to the house. The rain's coming. And it's too cold out here.

I looked up at him, met his eyes, and then reached out my hand. He hesitated, but took it and helped me to my feet. I had been crying, so it was not hard to start again, to make the tears fall and the breath heave in and out. He started to let go, but I reached out and grabbed both his forearms. I grabbed them tight like they were ropes from a lifeboat trying to drift away and leave me to drown. I pulled on those arms and pulled myself closer to him and then I rested just the very top of my forehead on his chest. I did not move any closer than that. I did not try to hold him or make him hold me. I waited for him to push me away, but he didn't. He just let me hold his arms, the top of my head on his chest, until I had finished crying.

When I was done, I looked up at him again for a second only, wiped my face and then marched back to the house.

I had learned a lot from Mrs. Martin, and from Emma. I had gotten smarter from them. Everybody needs something. And what Rick needed was to do what he had failed to do years before on that fishing boat. He needed to save the woman. So I became a woman he could save. I let him save me with small moments like the one on that trail. And then he saved me some more by listening to me talk and keeping me company on my walks. And then he saved me the most by loving me and letting me love him.

Now, at the same time I had planted the seeds to undermine his loyalty to the Pratts. That is the part I told to Dr. Winter and Agent Strauss. Nothing I had to offer would have been enough to overcome that loyalty, so I had to break its back first. I did not take any chances. And I was patient. So incredibly patient.

There were many days when I thought I didn't have one more drop of patience. My desire to leave, to be free and seek revenge, was growing too big. Every day, seeing Lucy with the baby, pretending it didn't make me want to kill her, stealing moments with the baby because I loved her as much as I loved Emma. Maybe even more. I loved her smell. I loved her laugh. I loved her pudgy arms and bright blue eyes. It was the first love that I knew was pure because she was too little to do anything to force me to love her, or trick me into loving her. I loved her so much that it was torture to see her so close and not be able to hold her. From that wretched day on the dock, it took 247 days to break Richard Foley. And then it took those 286 days more to conquer that loyalty so he would help me leave. I held this painful desire all that time.

I don't know exactly when it happened, but my wanting Richard Foley to manipulate and control him so I could escape the island blurred into just wanting Richard Foley. I had to truly want him to make him believe me. And so with every interaction, every look, every moment getting ready to see him—brushing my hair, choosing my clothes, pinching my cheeks so they would be flushed with pink—I thought of nothing else but his hands on my body, his mouth on my mouth, his skin touching my skin. I thought about him at night. I thought about him when the air turned warm or the sunlight reached my face. The desire to leave became all mixed up with the desire to have this man.

I can see him now, his tortured face as he held my cheeks in his strong hands. He did not want to do it, but he was too beaten down to fight me anymore. I had done that; I had beaten him down with my words and my power. I looked at him with desire, and it was pure and true, even though I made myself pretend to pull away. He held my face even stronger and drew it to his. It was a kiss I will never forget, and not only because it was my first kiss, but also because we were both starving, drowning, dying, and this kiss was all that could save us.

We lay down in the tall grass just before the rocks on the west side of the island. He stopped looking at me and I felt as though the connection that had been in that place, in our eyes and our thoughts and our words, shifted to our bodies and that was where it would stay for all those days we were lovers. I would be waiting for him somewhere—the grass, the dock, the shed that held the generator. And he would kiss me and remove my clothes and place me where he wanted me. Sometimes face-to-face. Sometimes he was behind me. But I was always beneath him, feeling his power over me the way I had used my power over him. It's hard to describe. It's hard to think about now. But he was gentle with his power, no matter how much rage he wanted to unleash in those moments. And he could have. He could have raged on my body—with the rage that had driven him from his home when he was young and the rage of hatred for himself for not helping that woman on that fishing boat. Holding back the rage somehow healed him, bit by bit like little drops of water seeping from a large pool.

On day four of my return, my thoughts turned to being with Richard Foley. My body missed his body. And my mind was twisted in knots. That is where desire begins, and it does not just vanish the minute we command it to. I felt things I didn't want to feel. Longing. Hunger. Disgust. I thought I had left those feelings on the island, and so I wondered that morning if these feelings had been with me here as well, in this house, waiting here for my return.

I took a shower, a long shower, to wash them all away.

The war in our house after the incident with the photographs had hot periods and cold periods. The cold periods were not moments of peace, but rather moments of regrouping, rearming and strategizing. Cold war. I don't know exactly when Hunter found out that his father had taken the pictures of Emma with her dress pulled down, but it was during the three weeks after they were taken and the time Hunter posted them on that Web site. I think it all happened quickly, and was driven by his fury at Emma and his father. As much as Mr. Martin worshipped and adored his son, Hunter idolized and admired his father. He loved to tell embellished stories about Mr. Martin's business conquests and wealth, and even insinuated that his father had side dealings with organized crime. His father had wounded him deeply by coveting Emma and giving in to his desires. And Emma had been vicious by using his father as a weapon against him.

Posting those pictures was done without much thought or planning. Hunter paid the price by having his face punched by Witt and being blamed for everything by Mrs. Martin. I think if he had not been driven by his emotions, his own fierce rage, he would have come up with a better plan.

He learned from this mistake.

The cold war in our house went on for months, with Mr. Martin avoiding Emma so he didn't have to think about her breasts, Hunter staying at school as much as he could to punish his father, and Emma gloating at her victory in the last battle, even though it had cost her the boy she'd met over the summer. *There are always more boys*, she said. The cold war ended with a devastating attack over spring break when we all went as a family to St. Barts. It was a quick and decisive strike. Yet it was so subtle that I nearly missed it myself—and I had devoted myself to observing the war as a matter of survival.

I can see that now, being older and having been through everything that happened on the island.

The teachers at the Soundview Academy told us that human beings have a natural desire to learn. What I think is more accurate is that human beings have a natural desire to learn the things they have to learn to survive. On the island, that meant learning about people—what motivates them, what their expressions mean, what causes them to act and react. And what they desire in their darkest, most secret places. These were things that could not be found in the textbooks Lucy bought, but I still managed to learn them. And I did it without even knowing I was doing it.

When I finally came home, it felt as though someone had injected my brain with this knowledge. I don't know how to describe it, exactly. It felt like I had put on ice skates for the first time and somehow just knew how to land a triple jump. I used this knowledge to help them find the island, and to find my sister. But I also used it on every memory that rushed into my brain. Things that had not made sense to me were now clear. Things that were done, by my mother, Mr. Martin, Hunter, Emma and even myself were now understood for what they were.

Not forgiven. But understood.

That spring break when the cold war turned hot, we rented a house up in the hills. It overlooked the ocean and I think it was the best house we'd had there in the three years we'd been going. St. Barts is a very fancy place. And very expensive. It is a French territory, so there is a lot of gourmet food and dance clubs that are open all night long. Models and movie stars go there, which was why Mrs. Martin had insisted on making it our spring break tradition after she married Mr. Martin. My father had refused to take her. He said it was too showy, and anyway, he loved to ski and made her go to Utah, where she would sulk and stay inside rather than make a fool of herself trying to learn. My father was an expert skier and he offered to get her private lessons. But she preferred to protest the trip.

Hunter always had a few friends from school who were in St. Barts during spring break, and he would meet them in town or at the beach. Emma had always gone with him. But this year she was not invited. I could tell this made her sad because she was stuck at the pool with me and our mother and then just me when the adults went out at night. She was so sad that she tried to make peace with Hunter by asking him to put suntan lotion on her back. I know this sounds like nothing. But she was doing more than asking for help with her sunscreen. She was asking for things to go back to the way they were. She was saying she was sorry about letting Mr. Martin take the pictures and that she forgave him for calling her a whore and not telling her about Joe's girlfriend before she had sex with him. And she was even willing to forgive him for posting those pictures on the Internet. These were very large concessions.

But as I have said, Hunter had learned his lesson about making his war plans without proper planning, and he had been plotting his next move for months. So he told her no. He could not help her with her suntan lotion.

I'm in a rush, Em. Cass can help you.

Emma stormed to her room and didn't come out all day.

The next afternoon Hunter did not meet his friends. He stayed home and sat by the pool with me and Emma and Mrs. Martin. Mr. Martin did not like the sun, so he would go to town every day, as he did on this day, to drink wine and walk around. This also served the purpose of not seeing Emma in her tiny bikinis. He avoided us the whole trip, which Mrs. Martin was happy about because it meant she could sit and read the kind of magazines that made Mr. Martin think less of her. I think if she had not been so happy, she would have seen what was happening and then she would not have been happy at all.

Hunter sat facing the ocean. His sunglasses were on, so we

could not tell if he was watching us or the ocean or nothing. A long time went by. Emma listened to music and texted her friends, laughing here and there, running her hands through her short hair. I was reading a book for school—*The Giver,* which is about a made-up place where people don't have feelings anymore. It was very awkward, being there with two enemies, pretending to be a family on vacation when really they were thinking of ways to destroy each other.

It was right before lunch when Hunter made his one deadly move, a move that would escalate the war and lead to everything bad that happened to Emma. And to me.

It's so hot today! Mrs. Martin said. She put down her magazine, took a sip of her rum drink, and reached for her suntan lotion.

Hunter, who had not moved since breakfast except to jump in the pool one time, got up from his chair and sat down on the edge of Mrs. Martin's chair. *I can do your back.*

Mrs. Martin smiled curiously. Maybe even cautiously. I could see her calculating how to answer, and because of my knowledge, I now understand why. If she said no, then she was admitting there was something wrong with her stepson touching her bare skin, rubbing it with lotion. But if she said yes, then her stepson would touch her bare skin, and rub it with lotion. She was undecided in that split second before she answered, until she noticed the hurt look on Emma's face.

That's so nice of you, sweetheart.

Hunter smiled. He took the lotion, squeezed some onto his hand, rubbed it with the other hand and then put both hands on our mother.

That was all that happened on that trip. But it was more than enough. Hunter went back to school and we would not see him again until the summer, when the next battle would be waged, this time by Emma.

There was a knock at the door on day four of my return. I heard it from my bedroom. Then I heard Mr. Martin get up to answer it.

Dr. Winter and Agent Strauss were at the door, but they did not ask to come in. Instead, they offered to speak with Mr. Martin outside on the porch and alone. I could see them through the arched doorway between the living room and foyer, the gestures, the surprised shoulder shrug, the exit and the door closing. I did not know for sure that they had found out what I needed them to find out, but I became instantly hopeful. Mrs. Martin had been increasingly unnerved with every day the island was not found and every day that I was telling my stories and being believed. The hushed conversations with Mr. Martin were more frequent; the worry lines were starting to march across her face.

But it was not enough. None of this had been enough.

Until the fourth day.

The very next day, they would find where Richard Foley lived, and that would lead them to the island. But on day four, they had found the other thing that I had needed them to find. It had been worth the torturous waiting, the whole day with Mrs. Martin's switch on love and treating me like a mental patient. It was worth her gloating and her arrogance. It was worth everything, even what it did to Dr. Winter.

SIXTEEN

Dr. Winter

On the evening of day four of Cass Tanner's return, Abby and Leo were back at the Martin house.

They sat on the porch in wrought iron chairs. Jonathan Martin crossed his legs, leaned back and smiled like he was at a cocktail party with friends from the club.

"How can I help you?" he asked.

Leo smiled back. This was his show and he was an exceptional performer. But he was working with very few props. "Lisa Jennings," he said.

Jonathan looked confused. "I'm sorry? Who?"

"The school counselor. From the Soundview Academy."

"Oh, right. I remember now."

Leo smiled wider. "She remembers you. Quite well, in fact."

Jonathan dug in deeper. "Why don't you just say what you want to say?"

"You had an affair with her. It was still going on when the girls disappeared," Leo said calmly. "You met at an open house for the school. She's quite attractive."

"That's absurd," Jonathan insisted.

Abby studied his face as Leo laid out the evidence. After their meeting with Jennings, they had gone back to the file and the two years of records that had been collected from Jonathan Martin's cell phone during the original investigation. The analyst who had gone over the records when the girls first disappeared had written a report, listing the phone numbers called and texted and the names of their owners. Dozens of calls and texts had been made to Lisa Jennings. Too much time had passed to obtain the content of the text messages between the two of them. There were no hotels or meals or travel. No doorman at her small walk-up who would have seen them coming and going. Essentially, they had nothing. Except her confession.

"I told you I was trying to help. That I was trying to get information from her," Jonathan explained.

Leo had accepted his explanation back then—that he was calling with concerns for the girls. Lisa Jennings had also been extensively interviewed, with no red flags appearing. The focus at the time had been on strangers, outsiders—people who could have kidnapped or harmed the girls, not the relationships between the people who had been trying to help them.

Looking back at it now, through the lens of suspicion, it was strange that Jonathan had contacted anyone at the girls' school. And now they knew why.

"We went back to see Lisa Jennings after we pulled the phone records, and that's not the explanation she gave us. She told us all about the flirtation at that school function, the slow seduction over text messages, and then the afternoons in her apartment. It had gone on for several months before the girls disappeared. Your stepdaughters."

Lisa Jennings had not held out for long. They explained to her about the lie she had told—hearing the story about Emma's hair from Owen Tanner. Owen had not known. From there, they had the phone calls and text messages. She was a millennial, accustomed to the indelible footprints of social media, so it was not difficult to convince her that the text messages had been stored by her carrier.

She'd had tears in her eyes when she told them about her realization that he never loved her, about how easy it was for Jonathan to cut it off with a phone call. It wasn't that she didn't understand. Of course it had to end, at least for while, during the search for the girls. The family, the school—they were under a spotlight. It was the fact that he felt nothing at all. No sadness, no longing, no empty spaces left behind. She had felt all those things. He had made her feel them—"I can see now that it was all a lie. All the tenderness in his eyes and the words on his breath—they were all lies. And he was very, very good at lying."

"Well," Jonathan said now on the porch. "She's obviously very disturbed."

Abby studied him while he and Leo did their dance. He was smug. He knew they could never prove that he'd slept with the young woman. But they weren't putting him on trial. His feigned ignorance when they spoke her name confirmed the affair, and that was what they had come for. Confirmation.

Lisa Jennings had also told them about his obsession with his son. How he spoke of him like he was "God's gift" even though she'd seen him and he looked like "a scrawny, self-entitled prick." She said that even though she had believed he loved her, she always knew that Jonathan would give her up in a heartbeat to keep the family name clean.

She agreed to work with an agent in New Haven. To turn over her phone records. To take a polygraph to prove she had nothing to do with the girls' disappearance—that it was an affair with

their stepfather and nothing more. Soon, she would hire an attorney and probably do none of those things without immunity.
But she would do them.

It felt like a lead. Jonathan Martin had told her things, con-
fided in her about his wife and the girls and his son. Things could
fall from her memory that seemed inconsequential but perhaps
could lead them to the Pratts, or identify the father of Emma's
baby.

Leo would focus on that, on the connection between Lisa Jennings, Jonathan Martin and a possible link to finding the Pratts'
identity.

But Abby was curious about one other thing, and that was
why Cass had given them the bread crumbs that led to this door.
Cass had lied about Emma's relationship with Lisa Jennings. That
much they believed, which meant Cass had to have known about
the affair—and wanted it exposed. Why else would she make up
a lie to send them back there? She wanted them to question Jonathan Martin, and then question her mother so she would finally
know. But to what end? Revenge for her terrible childhood? Or
something else? Abby had no doubt that Cass knew exactly what
they would find when they tracked down Lisa Jennings.

Leo was quiet for a long moment. Then he asked a question
that they had not planned on. "Did you ever refer to Emma Tanner as Lolita?"

Jonathan Martin's back straightened abruptly. He looked disgusted by the question, but it was overplayed. "That's enough," he
said, getting up from the chair.

Lisa Jennings told them how Jonathan Martin talked about
survival of the fittest, about how history had proved that the tribe
was always the strongest force. That only when a tribe was infil-
trated by outsiders was it conquered. He had numerous examples

from history and he held extreme political views about how to keep this from happening. Lisa Jennings had asked him how this applied to his blended family, and he had spoken about the girls. Cass, he'd said, was no threat. She was weak. She was a follower. But Emma, she was trouble. She wanted power and didn't know her place the way her mother did. He'd suggested that she was aware of her appeal with men and had started to use it. She said Jonathan had used that expression—Lolita.

Leo and Abby stood as well, Leo blocking Jonathan's path back to the door.

"I find this all disgusting," he said. "My daughter is missing and you're wasting all of our time on this nonsense. I think you should leave now before you upset my wife."

Leo stepped aside and let him pass. Abby waited until he was gone before letting out the breath she'd been holding.

She looked at Leo and smiled.

"What? You look surprised."

She was surprised. He was asking questions about the family.

"What are you thinking, Leo? Lolita was a young schoolgirl who seduced an older man—"

"He didn't go to Paris that summer, if that's where you're headed. Neither did the stepbrother, Hunter."

"You ran that? Why didn't you tell me?"

Leo motioned for them to walk farther from the house, down the porch steps to the driveway.

"Don't go making too much of this. I look at that guy and I don't think he cares one way or another about those girls. He came into their lives when they were both almost teenagers. Eleven and thirteen. Their half brother hated his son, and the girls adored Witt. Hunter was obsessed with Emma, which I'm sure made him blame her for being a temptation to a healthy young man with hormones—you know how that argument goes. But, believe me—when Cass said Emma was pregnant and wouldn't say who the father was, I thought about it. I thought about Jonathan Martin and I thought about his son. That would be reason to leave, to be afraid of what would happen if she stayed and one of them was the father."

"Except she'd been in France during the time she got pregnant, right? Cass said she had the baby in March. That puts conception in June, July at the latest. Emma didn't come home until mid-August."

"Right. So I made sure they weren't in Paris, that's all. Just closing the loop."

"So what now?"

Leo shrugged. "We go at Judy Martin in an hour. It's perfect—he denied it, so now we have cause to question her. Give him a narrow window to tell her himself."

"Agreed."

They walked farther up the driveway to Abby's car. She pulled out her keys.

"I read your paper, you know," Leo said.

Abby turned from the car to look at him. "When?"

"Last year. And again last night. I was lying in bed. Susan was dead asleep. She keeps a picture of the kids when they were little on her nightstand. I must look at that picture ten times a day because it's right there, you know? And I was thinking about a mother cutting her child's hair like that. Viciously. Vindictively. And to punish the other one."

Leo paused. He was shaking his head and staring at his boots.

"The sibling stuff you wrote about. How the narcissist parent chooses one sibling as the favorite, and then does everything and anything to keep that child in line. Reinforcing the alter ego . . ."

"Emma," Abby said. "That's what she did to Emma."

"And Cass, the other child, who looks to the favored one as a parent. A child raising a child when the parents are right there. It makes me sick."

"Yes," Abby agreed. She had no idea where this was headed, but having Leo understand, having him see the things she saw in this family—it meant everything in that moment.

"It makes me sick for them. And it makes me sick for you."

Abby didn't know how to respond. Cass's words were there now—how she had described the conflict—the need to love and be loved but then knowing that "everyone you could ever trust could betray you." Most people lived in blissful ignorance. But Abby's mother had taken that from her. Judy Martin had taken that from Cass. And you can never get it back, this ignorance. Was that something to be sorry about? Or did it keep them safe?

A thought rushed in then. Abby grabbed Leo by both arms.

"What is it, kiddo?"

"Everyone can betray you," she said.

Leo was confused. "What does that mean?"

"That's what Cass wants her mother to know. That's why she led us back to Lisa Jennings—to find out about the affair, to make her mother think, or know, that her husband betrayed her!"

"And then what?"

"I don't know—"

"And why didn't she just tell us? Why did she make us think it had something to do with Emma?"

"Because she has to be the one her mother can trust . . . and don't ask me why, because I don't know that yet either. I just know that she needs her mother to start trusting her, to believe her, and to stop believing in Jonathan Martin."

"Abby, I don't know what any of this has to do with finding Emma—"

Leo's thought was interrupted by his cell phone buzzing in his jacket. He pulled it out to answer.

"Yeah . . ." he said; then he listened. His eyes grew wider.

Abby waited, watching his face change expression—surprise to excitement. He hung up and smiled, his words freezing time, impossible to believe.

"They found the island."

SEVENTEEN

Cass

Everything changed when they discovered the affair between Mr. Martin and our school counselor, Lisa Jennings. Because Mr. Martin denied it, they had to ask my mother. And when they asked her if she knew, they were really telling her.

For all Mrs. Martin's cleverness, her escape from being a secretary, her seduction of my father and Mr. Martin, her control over all of us with her manipulation and hair-cutting and court maneuvers to keep us from leaving, she had not once considered that her husband was having sex with a younger, prettier woman. I think this upset her more than the fact that her husband was cheating. Not knowing, not seeing, being deceived—it makes you question everything you have come to trust. It makes you doubt your own judgment, and the truths you have come to believe in, which sometimes are so deeply embedded, you don't even know they're there, shaping your thoughts.

Mr. Martin could not deny his behavior. It was right there, in black-and-white, his cell phone number over and over and over and Lisa Jennings's tearful confession. I'm sure he regretted not being more careful, using a prepaid phone or a landline at the club.

No, he could not deny it. But that's exactly what he did.

Mrs. Martin tried to make him tell her everything. I was not able to hear the entire conversation from the hallway, but I caught enough.

"You don't find me attractive . . ."

"That's not true! You have always been very attractive. Very sexy . . ."

"Not enough, though. Not enough!"

"I did not have sex with that woman! Why can't you believe me?"

"I think you like young women!"

"No . . ."

"I think you like girls . . ."

"That's enough! I had nothing to do with what happened to the girls . . ."

"Young girls . . ."

"Stop it!"

"I saw how you looked at Emma . . . my God, am I going crazy? Am I out of my mind? Oh my God! You know him, this man. Bill! Emma is there! Emma is there! And you knew this whole time, didn't you? You did this somehow, got rid of my girls to this monster!"

"That's enough! I won't listen to this. I had nothing to do with that crazy fucking island and that is the last time I'm going to defend myself . . ."

"Nothing is real. Nothing you say is real!"

"That's it. I'm going to the city. You are losing your mind. You're losing your fucking mind!"

Mr. Martin went to New York to stay at his sports club for the night. And while he was gone that night, two things happened. The first was that Mrs. Martin went into her winter mood.

I stood outside her bedroom door. I could hear her sobbing into her pillow the way she had done when I was younger, and it took every ounce of strength not to run away, down the hall, into Emma's room. I screamed silently at myself. *Emma's not here!* And I reminded myself. *You came here for a reason.*

I went into the room and stood still for a moment to see if she would react and how she would react when she saw me. She had been able to love me again because I was crazy and no one believed me. But now it was all falling apart. Now her own husband had cheated on her and lied to her. Another woman was better, which meant she was not the greatest anything.

"Cass!" she sobbed from her bed, her body splayed out like someone had poured her onto the mattress from a cup. "Come here, Cass!"

I went to her then. I got onto the bed and I let her wrap her arms around my waist and bury her face into my lap.

"Nothing is real, Cass! Tell me what's real. Tell me you weren't in Emma's car that night. Tell me you were in your room with the door closed. . . ."

I wish I could say that I was calm then. That I smiled with satisfaction as I watched her unravel. But I am not that strong.

Instead, I fought to contain myself. I felt the blood rush from my head as my heart pounded like thunder against my ribs. It pounded so hard, it hurt. I waited for the blood to return and then I whispered to my mother.

"Shhhhh."

"Cass! Tell me!" she sobbed.

"Shhhh, Mrs. Martin. It's all right now."

I stroked her silky hair as I spoke.

Her body was writhing with agony.

Memories rushed in. Me in the corner. Emma in this bed, holding our mother.

"Shhhh, Mrs. Martin," I whispered. And then I said what Emma would always say. "You're the most wonderful mother. There's no better mother in the entire world."

I stayed with her until she calmed down. I got her a drink from downstairs and she took a white pill and drank her drink and fell asleep in my arms.

And while she slept, I prayed that this had been enough. I prayed that Mr. Martin would not use his charm and undo the work I had done. This was all I had—the affair with Lisa Jennings that I had discovered before I disappeared. Mr. Martin was very careless and he left his phone unattended almost every night. I used to fantasize about telling her. I used to lie in my bed, sometimes when Emma was there with me, and I would think about how and when I would give this gift to my sister—this weapon that would surely destroy our nemesis. But then we were gone.

The second thing that happened that night after Mr. Martin left was that they found the location of the boatman, Richard Foley. And when they found the boatman's location, they found the island.

They went there that same night. Eight FBI agents, including Agent Strauss and Dr. Winter. They stayed overnight in a small hotel and did surveillance. They got satellite imagery and land records and building permits and everything else they needed to put together a plan of attack for the morning.

I didn't sleep that night. We were not told anything about the surveillance or the satellite pictures or the details of the plan. But I knew that everything was going to happen very fast. And I knew that it was going to be dangerous because they asked me questions about guns and weapons and things the Pratts might use to make weapons. And then I became consumed with thoughts of people I loved dying.

So I lay awake that whole night wondering about death. No one who has died can tell us what it feels like. I don't think there is any kind of death that is painless, even if it is just a split second. Even if someone just cut off your head or shot you in the heart. Life feels too strong to go away without some kind of agony.

Our father was very paranoid about life leaving us, me and Emma and Witt. He got so angry when we didn't do the things he'd told us to do to stay alive. Bike helmets and seat belts were the worst. I don't know what it was like for Witt and Emma, inside their heads, when they didn't wear a helmet or put on a seat belt. Maybe they did it on purpose, because they wanted to be free of those restraints. But for me, it was just about forgetting. Our father would lecture us when it happened, about how kids feel invincible, how they don't understand that they can die. That they will actually die one day. That they are destructible. Emma would giggle and I could see that his words went through her like a ghost. She didn't care that this feeling would leave her one day. It was like being beautiful. She was going to enjoy it while she could—otherwise, what's the point?

I want to go out in a big, enormous ball of flames the minute I feel the way Daddy does. I would rather live half as long feeling alive than twice as long feeling dead already.

Emma whispered this in my ear one night as she lay in my bed. She was sixteen, and by then she didn't ride a bike and she always wore her seat belt because she was driving and she didn't want to get a ticket from the police. Still, there were so many other things like those things, rules and restraints. When she said these words to me, I could tell that she felt very grown-up. That she felt as though she had come up with something no one had thought of before. But now I know that she was just finding a way to understand what was going on inside her.

When a scream wants to come out, nothing can stop it. Not rules. Not restraints. Not even the common sense to want to stay alive.

I was more like my father. From as early as I have memories of my own thoughts and feelings, I know that I feared death and that I felt that death was going to come for me as a punishment. Every time I smoked a cigarette, I told myself I would be punished with cancer. Every time I drank alcohol, I imagined lying in the hospital with yellow skin because my liver was failing. And when I drove Emma in her car without a license or even a permit, I would resign myself to a bloody death on the side of the road.

What I have come to know about death is that it is not like that. It is not fair. It does not add up your cigarettes and drinks and irresponsible behavior and come for you when you've reached your quota. People die all the time who were very good, very responsible. And people stay alive to the bitter end of their natural lives who were very bad and who did very bad things. Mrs. Martin will probably live to be one hundred. Mr. Martin will be right beside her.

When I was young, I was undeserving of death. Even after I started drinking and smoking and thinking bad thoughts and doing bad things, I had never done anything so bad that I deserved to die. Still, I feared death as though I deserved it just because I was me, and I think I will never stop feeling that way until it finally does come.

When I chased death from my thoughts, they turned instantly to the island and what would happen in the morning when they went there. I did not sleep. Not for one minute.

How I missed Emma that night as I lay in bed—wondering what they would find on the island. And knowing what they wouldn't.

EIGHTEEN

Dr. Winter—Day Five of Cass Tanner's Return

Five miles off the coast of South Bristol, Maine, was the island of Freya. It was renamed by the current owner, a corporation named Freya Investments, LLC. The name was Scandinavian, meaning the Nordic goddess of love and fertility.

Freya Investments, LLC, was registered in the State of Delaware and owned by a man named Carl Peterson.

They found the island of Freya five days after Cass Tanner returned home. It started with a boat found drifting miles away, near Rockland. The boat belonged to the owner of a dock and small marina in South Bristol. The owner had leased the boat to Richard Conroy, who was, in fact, Richard Foley. The owner's wife eventually recognized Foley from a news broadcast showing his picture, and they alerted the authorities.

Abby, Leo and a Critical Incident Response Group, or CIRG, were moved to the closest mainland point on Christmas Cove, which adjoined South Bristol by means of a swing bridge. Satellite imagery of every island that sat at the mouth of the bay was analyzed. Cass had described three structures and one dock. The main house was on the easternmost point, facing the Atlantic.

The dock stood to the south, facing a larger island. And the two smaller structures, a greenhouse and a generator shed, were to the north of the house. On the western side were the treacherous rocks.

Only one island matched the description.

"You ready?" Leo asked as they stood on the dock. A coast guard cutter was standing by. Abby and the forensic team would wait on the boat until the island was cleared. Leo was going with the CIRG team.

"I'm nervous," Abby said.

She stared at the map she'd been given from the satellite. She could see where Freya was positioned, and the structures on the island. She could imagine Cass and Emma standing on the dock, seeing the larger island of Thrumcap and beyond that, the mainland, their freedom close but unattainable. There was no way someone could swim that distance in this water without a wetsuit. And the coast guard had confirmed that the currents were strong. Swimming across this stretch of water would be like swimming twice the distance, and that was only if the currents didn't pull you toward the rocks on the western end.

Everything had happened quickly. Too quickly for Abby to make sense of it all. The boat was found two days before Cass returned home, even though it had taken four more days for the dock owner to put the pieces together. Yet she'd said she'd come home that same night, on that boat. And it was found drifting on its own, the key turned to the on position and the gas tank empty.

"That's not like Rick," the dock owner had told them. He had always taken very good care of that boat. "We had no idea he was in trouble till we saw the news this morning. Called the local sheriff, but we didn't know his real name so no one made the connection."

The teams had come the moment they got the call. Foley's apartment was found in Damariscotta, about ten miles from South Bristol. It had also been rented under the name Conroy. A forensic team was searching the place. So far, they'd found nothing of interest. No papers, no files. Richard Foley had stayed off the grid just like the Pratts, using a different name, paying cash for everything.

And in several hours of questioning Lisa Jennings, all they'd gotten were more shocking depictions of Jonathan Martin's diminished morality, and his obsession with furthering the interests of his son. They had found no connection between either of them and the Pratts, no evidence suggesting they knew about Emma's pregnancy and had tried to help her leave. Their affair, however inappropriate, seemed to have had nothing at all to do with the girls' disappearance. But Abby already suspected this.

Lisa Jennings went back to work that morning. And Judy Martin had refused to be interviewed.

From the cutter, Abby could see the team descend on the shore and disperse into the wooded area that led up to the house. They were live on the coast guard feed and she could hear the reports as they cleared every structure. *"The house—clear. The shed—clear. The greenhouse—clear."*

Two of the CIRG team stayed at the house with Leo. The others spread out deeper into the woods. And the coast guard was given the green light to dock and escort Abby and the others on shore.

Cass's stories were playing out in Abby's head as she approached the island. The house, perched on a hill and looking out at the open ocean. The wood dock, the stairs on one side and the place where Bill Pratt had nearly drowned the baby on the other side. As the cutter landed, Abby pictured them there, terrified as

Bill kicked Emma's hands off the side, making her fingers bleed while she shivered in the frigid water.

Abby disembarked with one of the coast guard. He walked her up the long path, through sparse woods, to the entrance of the house. Leo met her there.

"It's real," she said.

Leo nodded. "I know. Wait until you see inside."

They walked through the front door, which opened into a small foyer. The stairs were directly across, and Abby could see the hallway above on the second floor. There was a large picture window at the top of the landing, the hallway then turning to the right or left. The windows were closed up tight, making the air stale. Flies buzzed against the glass panes, trying to escape.

The forensic team spread out, with two agents bounding up the stairs and the third already at work in the first-floor bedroom.

"Don't touch anything," they said to Abby, as if she didn't already know. But it was her first time at a crime scene, or a potential crime scene. All her work with the Bureau until now had involved an analysis of people—their sanity, their emotions, their motivations. Now she was in a Tyvek suit, her shoes carefully covered, her hands double-gloved. She could not ignore the nervous energy surging through her.

Leo called out to them from the bottom of the stairs. "We need to know where the hell they've gone—anything, papers, documents, computers . . ."

"The rowboat," Abby said, standing beside him. "It wasn't at the dock."

Leo nodded. "Yeah, I know. You think they could have rowed with four people? And then what—did they have a gun to Emma's head? Once she got to the mainland, I don't see how they keep her and a toddler against their will once they get off this island."

"I don't know. But I want to see every room of this house."

They started downstairs, first in the living room with the ballet barre and the television. Then the dining room, with the long, rectangular table, eight chairs with red corduroy cushions tied to the seats. A painting of a farmhouse hung over a breakfront. Salt and pepper shakers sat on top of the breakfront, askew as if they had been placed there in haste after cleaning up from a meal. The kitchen, too, was exactly as Cass described. The gas stove. The white china with small blue flowers along the rim. Four of them were neatly stacked in a drying rack next to the sink, along with a frying pan, spatula, glasses. More flies buzzed around a small metal garbage can.

"Looks like they left in the morning," Abby said. "They had dinner, washed the dishes, went to bed. They woke up to find Cass gone."

They went next to the first-floor bedroom, which was off the kitchen. It was large but informal, and the placement of it in the house indicated it was originally intended for servants and not owners. Three single beds were lined in a row, sheets and blankets sprawled on top, unmade.

"Shit," Leo said. He was looking at the bed closest to the far wall. It was stripped bare. "Why would they take the things from this bed and not the others?"

"Emma's daughter. The third bed. Everything is like she said."

They touched nothing and stepped aside as the forensic team did its work. Drawers were opened, revealing the clothing of a large man, a short but plump woman with a DD breast size. The clothes of a little girl were in the bottom drawer of a dresser—one pair of pink leggings, some flowered shirts and dresses. Several pairs of small white socks with ruffles. They were washed and neatly folded. Long gray hair came from a brush in the bathroom.

Grecian Formula boxes were found there as well, below the sink in a small wooden cupboard. Baby shampoo was on the rim of the bathtub.

"I want to see their rooms upstairs," Abby said.

To the right of the landing on the second floor were two small bedrooms and a bath. One of the bedrooms faced the front of the house, into the woods looking west. The second bedroom faced the courtyard, north. The bathroom looked out due east into the Atlantic.

The drawers in the bedrooms, and behind the mirror and under the sink—all of them were empty, some left open as if the rooms had been cleared in haste.

Thoughts rushed in as Abby walked through each space where Cass had lived for three years. *This is where she watched the lobster boats. . . . This is where she lay in bed, aching to come home. . . . This is where she showered, washing the boatman, and her guilt and her pain from her skin.*

From there, they crossed over to the two rooms on the other side of the courtyard, a large bedroom and adjoining bath. It was, or should have been, the master suite. Here, too, the drawers had all been emptied. Not even a bar of soap or a razor or a toothbrush.

Leo stood in the center, turning slowly in a circle. "Anything?" he asked one of the forensics.

The woman shook her head. "Not a lot of prints. They tried to wipe it clean. But we'll find them. Just need to keep looking."

Abby sighed, hands on hips, perplexed. "So, they wake up, find Cass gone. Can't reach Richard Foley. They pack up all of the girls' belongings, try to wipe down the entire house, then leave in the rowboat? Now we have four people and how many bags of things?"

"Dumped the bags in the ocean. Put rocks in the bags, sealed them up tight, let them sink," Leo said.

Abby walked to the bedroom window and looked out at the ocean.

"Hey!" the forensic called out. She was kneeling beside the bed. "I found something. It was taped to the frame. Someone was trying to hide it."

Abby and Leo walked to where she was and stared at the object in her hand.

Dangling from the white latex glove was a necklace. It had a thin silver chain and an angel medallion. The chain was broken, just as Cass had told them.

"Emma's necklace," Abby said in a whisper.

Leo looked at Abby, his eyes wide. "She left it behind."

"Yes. Yes, she did," Abby said.

"She hid it from the Pratts."

"Yes," Abby agreed.

Leo was confused. "Why didn't she take it with her?"

But Abby already knew. "Because she wanted us to find it."

NINETEEN

Cass

In the spring of Hunter's senior year at boarding school, something terrible happened. It started with his acceptance to Hamilton College. Both he and Mr. Martin had been very puffed up about it since the letter arrived in late March—right after we returned from St. Barts. Mr. Martin went to college at Hamilton, and he talked about it like it was Harvard. Even now I feel annoyed by this. I was in eighth grade at the time. Emma was a sophomore, and at our school you have to start thinking about college very early. Between Emma and Hunter, our house was filled with talk of SATs and ACTs and APs and the summer grid. Even when Hunter didn't come home for the weekend, Mr. Martin was obsessed with his son getting into college—Hamilton, in particular—and Mrs. Martin was then obsessed with Emma's college choices because her children were just as important as his. If Mr. Martin had talked about Hunter joining the circus, Mrs. Martin would have taken Emma to tightrope classes.

She could not admit to herself that he was better educated or more sophisticated than she was, because then he might feel more powerful and he was only allowed to feel that way in the bedroom, even though he was both those things, and even though the bedroom was the only place he lost his power. And that just proves my point about this sex power women have and how limited and flawed it is. Even Mrs. Martin's sex power paled beside Mr. Martin's status and money power, and she knew it. She knew it in her bones.

Mr. Martin had to pay a lot of money to Hamilton for Hunter to even have a chance of getting in because his grades were not good and his scores were not good. And he was not good, overall. He did not have any varsity sports and he did not belong to any clubs or do any charity work. I don't know how much money it cost to get that letter, but Mr. Martin worried and complained about it for months, so it must have been a lot. But it was worth it to him. Hunter was Mr. Martin's only child. He was named after his dead grandfather, and he had lived full-time with Mr. Martin for his entire life. Everything Mr. Martin did and everything he was began and ended with his son. His sacred progeny. His legacy.

My mother didn't go to college, but she spoke about Hamilton in a dismissive way when Mr. Martin was not around. She said it was a second-tier school and she told Emma she had better study and keep her grades up so she could do better. Our father's family had connections at Columbia. Our father went there and so did Witt, although I know Witt could have gotten in on his own because he also got into Princeton and we don't know anyone there. My mother had not known the difference between schools like Columbia and Hamilton until that year, when it became necessary for her power struggle with her husband. No one was better than she was. No child better than her child.

After the letter came, there was great relief in our house. Mr. Martin was full of pride. My mother was full of determination for Emma. I was full of annoyance. And Hunter was full of himself. He was so full, in fact, that he imagined himself invincible. He got arrogant. And careless. One weekend, he was so careless that he got caught doing cocaine on the campus of his boarding school.

Mr. Martin went on and on about how *back in the day,* such a thing would have gotten you a suspension. But not now. People had a different attitude about drugs, and schools that were not tough on drugs would not attract the best students and the parents with the most money. The school held a disciplinary hearing. It consisted of students and faculty members, who were allowed to question Hunter, hear his apologies, and watch him beg for leniency in his senior year. Mr. Martin wrote another check, this time to the boarding school. Another very big check.

None of that was enough. Hunter had not done himself any favors by being the kind of person he was, and most of the faculty and the students who were worthy of being on the disciplinary committee disliked him. Some hated him, it seems. They recommended expulsion, and after three years and seven months of paid enrollment, Hunter Martin was expelled from his fancy boarding school. Of course, Hamilton then withdrew its offer and told Mr. Martin that Hunter could apply again the following year, but that he would be "well advised" to pursue a meaningful endeavor during the year off, and turn his life around.

In May of that year, Hunter returned home. He enrolled in the public high school so he could earn a degree, which was deeply humiliating for him. He had to take exams for classes he hadn't been in all year and he got very bad grades, even worse than he was getting before. Many of the kids there he knew from town, from partying in the summer, or from years before when he was in grade school with them. Hunter did not handle humiliation well. Neither did Mr. Martin. There were many phone calls in all directions, assigning blame and plotting a way out of the mess Hunter had created for himself and his family.

I understood Mr. Martin. He had spent a lot of money for Hunter to have the name of that school on his résumé. It was something he would have for the rest of his life. Anyone can graduate from public high school. They have to take you if you live in the same town. As Mr. Martin explained it to Hunter, at some point in life, your grades and accomplishments in high school don't matter. All that matters is the name of it, and the name of the college it helped you get into. Then it would be the name of the place you worked, the company or the person or even the school if you became a professor. Names, names, names. It was no different from shopping for groceries. *Will you buy Heinz ketchup or generic? If you can afford Heinz, you will buy Heinz.* He was desperate for his son to understand.

Hunter could not defend himself, so he didn't try. And also, he knew Mr. Martin had taken those pictures of Emma, so Mr. Martin was not exactly standing on high ground when it came to being a good person. He did his best to twist things.

You had everything at stake. Everything to lose. All you had to do was hold it together for seven weeks. That's it. Seven fucking weeks! You could have come home to snort your cocaine. Did you want to get thrown out, just to spite me? But now, look what you've done. You've hurt no one but yourself!

Mr. Martin swore he wouldn't write another check to Hamilton College, but I knew he would. He could not stand for Hunter not to go there, not to collect names for his résumé.

The story we told people was that Hunter had decided to defer his enrollment so he could do community service and get some life experience. My father found him a volunteer job at an old age center for the summer. From there, he would spend three weeks building houses in Costa Rica. Then he would come home and find a job and make money, and volunteer somewhere on the weekends. He would also complete a drug- and alcohol-abuse program. It sounded bad, even to me.

There are so many pieces to our story, pieces that, if taken away, might have changed the whole course of it. And it's not just the big things, like Mrs. Martin having sex with Mr. Martin and leaving our father, or our father smoking pot again and having to give up his fight for custody, or Emma sleeping with that boy from Hunter's school. There was also Hunter calling her a whore, Emma dropping her dress for Mr. Martin, Mr. Martin giving in to his fantasies and taking a picture, Hunter posting pictures on the Internet. The suntan lotion in St. Barts, then another summer of name-calling and snuggling on the sofa. It also took this last thing—Hunter being expelled and not going to Hamilton after his senior year. And, of course, it took all of us, our flaws and our desires. My hunger for power, which I will get to next. It was all in it, in our story, like the ingredients to a complicated recipe.

I remember the day Emma found out about Hunter being expelled and his admission to Hamilton being placed on hold. She came to my room, where I was doing homework, and threw herself spread eagle on my bed, something she rarely did. I was always going to her room, barging in, begging to be let in, sneaking in. She came to my room only in the night, sometimes when she needed to say things she could not say to any other human being because they were ugly things—things that came from anger or sadness or fear. Emma could not tolerate anyone thinking she was ugly, inside or out, and she knew that I could never see her as anything less than beautiful.

Ha-ha!

She said that a few times and with total glee.

That little prick. That weenie. He thought he could get away with anything. But he was wrong.

She told me what had happened, and I could not believe it. Not because Hunter didn't do things like that but because he had seemed to me to be invincible—one of those people death would never take, no matter how many bad things he did or how much he deserved it. It seemed to defy logic that he was going to get what he deserved.

I am going to make him suffer. He thought what he did to me in St. Barts was bad. Just wait! Everyone in this town is going to know what happened. He's going to have to walk around with a bag over his head!

Emma was good for her word. She told everyone she knew—and she knew a lot of people. Hunter didn't have a chance to spin it, and when he came home the following night, social media was already buzzing about his fall.

Her next move was to be sympathetic, to be his only salvation from the emotional turmoil he was suffering. Water in his desert. But, of course, she was not trying to make him feel better. No one feels good when they need to take a sip of water from their archenemy.

You know what's like salt in a wound like this one? Being nice. It makes the person feel pitiful because you are giving them pity.

She gave Hunter a lot of pity that summer. She started hanging out with him again, at the house, and out in town. Parties and dinners and walks. She started watching movies with him again. And slowly she moved closer to him on the couch, and in every other way, really, inch by inch by inch.

I don't know if Hunter was being clever or if this thing with his expulsion and Hamilton College had broken his spirit. But he was now acting like a puppy dog, lapping that hot desert water from Emma's hands, and Emma mistook it for victory.

Mr. Martin gave him the silent treatment. I don't think he even looked at Hunter the whole summer. He and my mother went out a lot, and they even went away on trips. When they were gone, I would go to my father's house. But Emma would stay there with Hunter. This made my father very sad. And very concerned. Even Witt was worried about her.

My mother was in heaven. Mr. Martin had been weakened by the failure of his son, the failure festering on him like a large open wound. He moaned randomly throughout the day as if the thought of what had happened was pouncing upon him and taking him by surprise, causing him more pain than he could bear without some kind of verbal expression. My mother would stroke his back and look at him lovingly. And he would rest his head on her head and hold her tight and tell her how much he loved her.

Like Emma, she gave him pity. She stopped all talk of college in front of him, saving those conversations for secret meetings with Emma behind closed doors. Mrs. Martin was acting toward Mr. Martin the way Emma was acting toward Hunter, and I think they both knew it. Maybe they even talked about it and had strategy sessions in the kitchen when they closed the door or while I was away at my father's house. Their bond grew stronger as they tended to their wounded men and soaked up whatever power they could from it.

It was strange. The cold war and the hot war between Hunter and Emma had somehow become a war of subterfuge and secret agents. Emma's secret vindictive self pretending to be Hunter's friend, and Hunter's jealous, angry self pretending to have forgiven Emma for telling everyone about his expulsion and rejection. There were times when I thought the war was really over and all of this was in my imagination. But it was not. It far from being over.

My father was devastated after they found the island but did not find Emma. We had all gathered at Mrs. Martin's house to wait for the news. Mrs. Martin stayed in bed, and Mr. Martin was still in New York, so it was just me and my father in the living room when an officer from the state police came inside to tell us. He had just gotten a call from the Bureau. My father cried, but also paced the living room, pulling at his hair with both hands.

"Don't you see! He took her! He took her again!"

He got on the phone with a desk agent in New Haven, pleaded with them to step up the search, now that Bill and Lucy had been pried loose from their hiding place.

"It's just like a nest of cockroaches! They scatter and run but that's when you can find them because they don't know where to go, they have no nest to return to! This is the time to find those monsters, while they're still running in broad daylight!"

He didn't have to tell them any of this. And what he was really doing was trying to find out if they had begun to believe that Emma did not want to come home. That maybe she had gone with the Pratts of her own free will. After all, how could they move her and a two-year-old child off an island in a rowboat without her being able to alert the authorities? This thought was terrifying.

The officer sat with us for a while. He started talking to us about "kidnap" victims who really don't want to ever leave where they've gone. Not just the Patty Hearst stories, but also people who join cults or communes, things like that. Their families have it pretty bad. They never stop believing that they can reach inside their loved ones and reprogram their brains, or pull out the demon that's taken them over. Like Linda Blair in *The Exorcist*. And they are right. I believe that people never change, and so if their child or sister or brother or husband or wife was once one way, but then got sucked in by a group of psycho hippies, they could get sucked back out. People don't change. But no one is willing to help them—except for a lot of money.

I learned all this after I returned, in those countless, endless hours I spent waiting and talking to people. Grown-ups are allowed to do what they want as long as they don't break any laws, so if they want to be freaks and live on an island with other freaks, they are allowed to do that. And they are even allowed to raise their children that way.

My father grilled me relentlessly that afternoon about Emma's disposition, her beliefs, her sanity. I couldn't stand watching him unravel, so I was glad when he left. I needed to be alone with my mother. I needed to see if she was still unraveling. The Pratts were gone. Emma was still missing. I needed something to come of this. If not revenge, if not finding Emma, then what was the point? Mrs. Martin had been curled up on her bed like a baby when I finally left her room the night before. I thought that was the end of it, the end of her. I thought they would find the Pratts and find my sister and all of this would be over. *Come on!* I wanted to yell at everyone. Everything I had done was like pushing on a string—it just coiled up but didn't move. Nothing was moving! Nothing was happening!

But then I heard Mr. Martin's car pulling into the garage, which meant she had called him during the night.

I heard them fighting the moment he walked up the stairs to their bedroom. I didn't have to listen at all, because I knew what she was saying and what he was saying back about his affair with

Lisa Jennings, and what it meant for everything else that had happened between them. She was not falling into his arms and forgiving him. He was no longer someone she believed when he told her he loved her—just like what happened with me and Emma when we were little.

The switch had flipped.

I pictured that witch from *The Wizard of Oz* when they pour water over her. That was my mother. Only it wasn't water. It was reality. And although she obviously wasn't saying these words, I heard them in my head as I watched her nervously puttering around the house, chewing her nails and sneaking cigarettes on the back porch that whole day that they found the island but not my sister.

I'm melting. . . .

In September, the year before we disappeared, and after the summer of manipulating wounded men, Hunter went to Costa Rica to build houses, and Emma and I went back to school. It did not take long for Emma to find a new boyfriend, or I suppose for a new boyfriend to find her, but either way, she was with someone new by October. His name was Gil and he was twenty-six and the manager of the deli where we all gathered after school.

I will admit that Gil was very cute. He was tall and thin and had blue eyes and dark hair, and what I remember most about him was that he had an attitude like he didn't care about anything. Even in our fancy town waiting on spoiled rich kids, making their sandwiches and selling them beer if they had really good fake ID cards, he was above it all. This appealed to Emma. She was so used to everyone falling all over themselves for her, our mother being jealous of her, Mr. Martin being tortured by his conflicted feelings toward her, and Hunter being obsessed with her—this guy from the deli who didn't care less about her was intoxicating.

Emma started talking about him on the way home from school. She said he was *real*. I just listened because I did not want to spoil it. If I agreed with her, she might think less of him because she thought less of me in general. If I disagreed, she might start to see that he was really just a big loser being twenty-six and working at a deli with no plans for his future, and that he actually did care, and care very much, about the spoiled rich kids he had to make sandwiches for but that he covered it up with his attitude of not caring. Either way, I did not want Emma to lose interest in Gil. I did not want her to keep coddling Hunter like a little baby and taking all the air in our house so that I could not even breathe.

That was how I had felt—like I was not even worthy of one breath with everything being about Emma. Hunter desperate to have sex with her. Mr. Martin being so worried and angry but also so curious, and Mrs. Martin being so threatened by his curiosity and so insulted by his cruel words, like when he called Emma Lolita all the time. I wished it would all end before it ended very badly.

I got one wish but not the other.

When Hunter returned from Costa Rica, he expected things to be the way they were over the summer. Emma had not been on her social media with Gil, because she did not want Mrs. Martin to find out and Mrs. Martin had some very clever ways to infiltrate Emma's life. I also think that somewhere inside her, Emma was ashamed of her relationship with Gil the deli manager, and that the shame was part of the attraction. It was hard to understand. If I had what Emma had, I would have used it much better. I would have used it for nothing short of true love or absolute power.

When Hunter came home and found out about Gil, it destroyed him. And whether he had been sincere in his summer of kindness toward her, or just winning the war, it didn't matter, because the war was on again and it was hotter than it had ever been. Emma came right out and told him that they both needed to date people and try to be friends. She reminded him that they were technically related and that as much as they liked each other, they could never really be together, because the world would think they were monsters. Incestuous monsters. The world is very critical of incest, even though if you believe what the Bible says, we are all blood relatives and so we are all incestuous. I've never really understood that. But it doesn't matter what I understand or don't understand. It was the first time either of them admitted what was really going on between them, and it made Hunter hate Emma again. And for the rest of the year, our house was a battlefield of insults and slammed doors and cold stares. Hunter told everyone about Gil and Emma. Emma stole his pot and cocaine and flushed them down the toilet. Hunter called her nothing but "whore" again. Emma called him "loser."

It got so bad that Mrs. Martin asked Emma if she wanted to live with our father, which she refused. I didn't think I would ever see that day. That's how bad the war was.

It was so bad that when the letter came from Hamilton in March, telling Hunter he had been reaccepted, no one except Mr. Martin even seemed to care.

But Hunter pulled himself together that spring. He started seeing a very pretty senior from our high school and they acted like they were blissfully in love. He brought her to the house as much as he could so that Mrs. Martin could fawn all over her and Mr. Martin could appropriately not notice how pretty she was, and everyone could feel normal. And everyone could stick it to

Emma. When they were at the house, it was like we all stepped onto the stage and put on a play. Over and over and over. I was just in the chorus, but Emma didn't have any part at all. So by the time summer started to appear on the horizon, Emma made plans to attend a camp in Paris, which I thought was very healthy of her, and I made my own plans to attend a program in England. Sometimes you can win a war by leaving the battlefield before your army gets killed.

That was when Hunter decided to tell Mrs. Martin about the pictures. It must have been, because he executed the disclosure and the actions that followed in a way that was far too damaging to have been unplanned.

It was Memorial Day weekend, and on that weekend, Emma and I were with our father and Witt. Mr. Martin was away on a golf trip in Florida, which he did every year with his old roommates from Hamilton. That left Mrs. Martin alone with Hunter.

When we got back, Hunter told Emma that he had used his time alone with our mother very well. He told Emma that while they had breakfast on that Sunday morning, he broke down with Mrs. Martin. He could no longer keep his secret. He couldn't stand for her to have bad feelings toward him, thinking he had taken those pictures of her lovely daughter. Then he dropped the nuclear bomb and told her that it was his father who had taken the photos. He had even saved a screen shot from his father's phone proving it. Mrs. Martin confronted her husband when he got back later that evening and—just like that—the war had proliferated from Hunter and Emma to our mother and stepfather.

But that was not the end. Hunter had more bombs to drop, and as it turned out, he was just waiting patiently, his finger hovering over the biggest red button of them all.

I had the same feeling then that I had on the island, and that I had again after my return home. A force was in motion and nothing could stop it. There were so many lies. There was so much at stake. I wanted to jump out of my skin, every one of those times, and run away to a place that was calm and where things were still. After that Memorial Day weekend, I could feel the force pushing against our backs. I became that force on the island, and again when I came home. But I didn't want to be a force. I wanted to be a girl. I could never be a girl with Mrs. Martin as my mother. And it made me want to go to her room and strangle the life out of her.

TWENTY

Dr. Winter

The necklace. That was the only thing they'd found belonging to the girls. The forensics team had taken numerous samples from around the house, towels in the laundry bin, hair from furniture. It would be days before any DNA analyses could be completed, the fragments of fingerprints found on random objects and hidden surfaces analyzed.

But they knew Emma had been wearing that necklace the day she disappeared. She wore it every day, as a reminder to Cass that their mother loved her more.

Abby sat at the bar at the motel in Damariscotta, sipping on a neat glass of scotch. The team would stay there for days, canvassing the town, poring over records at the town hall, and searching the seven acres of woods on Freya Island. It was past midnight now, and they had all gone to bed after a long, emotional day. All except for Abby.

Thoughts from the day were spinning in her head. Images of the island, the house, the rooms and the woods had all brought Cass's stories to life, and they played out now as the alcohol took control. They had gone through every drawer and cupboard, finding the schoolbooks Cass had described, the ballet video, the book of lullabies. They had sifted through the garbage, finding remnants of white fish and rice pudding and an empty carton of milk. Abby could see Cass and Emma sitting at that table, suffering through a meal, pretending to be happy, obedient. She could see them, too, before they saw what was happening with the baby, feeling part of a family, feeling loved. Laughing, at ease. And in the woods, by the trail to the dock, Abby could see Cass waiting for the boatman, prepared to love him and hate him and then hate herself when she was done.

That was what Cass had described. But now, as Abby sat alone, staring out at the ocean from the small window behind the mirrored wall of bottles, she allowed herself to wonder.

There were questions about Cass's story. The boat found drifting in the harbor way up north, out of gas, two days before she returned. The answers on the psychological examination that were on the cusp of being too perfect—not to the computer that scored it, but to Abby, who had read it line by line herself, looking for the truth.

It was not easy to escape from a narcissistic mother. She knew this from her research, and she knew this from her life, and the life that had created her mother, and on and on into the past. And into the future.

Something always happened when Abby thought about her mother this way, in the context of the cycle she had studied and written about. She had been told stories about how her mother had been neglected and abused as a child. Her father had tried to make Abby and Meg understand. It's easy as a child to pass judgment: "Why can't she just stop? Why can't she just be normal?" But that was like asking the sky not to be blue or the earth to be flat. And so empathy sometimes mixed with the anger she felt at what her mother had done to her and to Meg, and it made her feel sick to her stomach. It was much easier when the anger could roam freely, without this rude interruption.

And what about Cass, then? Abby thought. Did she feel this way?

Is that what made Cass go back to her mother's house? she asked herself. *Then why is she trying to break her into pieces?* This hardly seemed like the best time for revenge, if that's what she was doing. Abby couldn't blame her for wanting this, for wanting to see her mother suffer. After all, her mother had created a home Emma had needed to leave. And it was the leaving that brought them to this island where they were forced to remain, where Cass was forced to bear years of servitude to her captors as the loyal daughter, and where Emma lost her own daughter right before her eyes.

Still, why now? Abby racked her brain. *What did we miss about Lisa Jennings? About Jonathan Martin's affair with her? About the island?*

"One more?" the bartender asked.

Abby nodded and held up her glass. She would not sleep tonight. That was a given. And the alcohol was freeing her mind.

She thought about how cautious she'd been with Leo, keeping her secret file of facts about Cass's story, afraid of what he would think. She'd been working this case with one hand tied behind her back. Maybe that was the problem.

Enough . . . she thought. She stared out at the water, shining in the moonlight. She opened the door all the way and let everything she knew, or felt, or believed in her gut, to pour in.

Judy Martin has classic narcissistic personality disorder. What she had suspected three years ago, she now knew beyond a doubt.

What are the basics? The perfect but fragile alter ego, always needing to be fed. Always so hungry. She thought about Owen Tanner and how he had fed that alter ego by giving Judy stature and money after a life of poverty and likely some kind of abuse or neglect across the river in Newark, where she was from. But then he had been too easy, too malleable, too weak. She started to see him as unworthy of her beauty and intelligence and sexual appeal. For women with this disorder, that was the kiss of death. Their male counterparts thrived with submissive women, so long as they were attractive and coveted by other men. But narcissistic women sometimes needed their men to be powerful. A woman who can seduce a powerful man is the best of the best. Holding his interest is the alter ego's perfect diet.

Jonathan Martin had fit the bill. He was a man's man, arrogant and successful. People noticed him when he walked in a room. Eyes followed him—the men's because they wanted to sidle up and ride his wave, and the women because they wanted him to notice them, even for a second, so they could go home feeling attractive in their long, weary marriages.

She had managed to keep him by her side, even as she got older. Even after she lost her girls. But now, what would shake loose from the news of his affair? She would begin to doubt not just him. She would begin to doubt herself, too. The splint would break. Her alter ego would go into a state of absolute panic as her true self, the one that was profoundly insecure, came to life again. And it would be unbearable.

There would be a battle inside her now. The two selves would fight for control of her mind. That abandoned, hurt baby would scream out that the world was going to destroy it and no one could help. No one could save that vulnerable, helpless baby. While the perfect alter ego would try to convince it that all was well. That it was under control. That it was so perfect, no one could touch it, let alone cause its demise.

But what proof could it offer to that baby after this most compelling evidence—evidence that her husband lies to her? Her husband cheats on her? Her husband no longer finds her attractive? She cannot be that special if these things have happened.

And then, what else had he lied about these many years? the baby will ask. What else has he told her, whispered in her ear in the darkness, or said to her face in the brightness of day? And her daughter—Cass? What was she lying about? There was no question Judy thought she was, or that she was crazy. But what if she wasn't? Either way, the baby was screaming again.

Abby closed her eyes, took a breath in and out. Suddenly, a vision of Cass's bedroom on the island was playing like a movie. The bed. The dresser. The books on the shelf. The window looking out into the courtyard.

And then there was that description Cass had given when she was talking about books she'd read on the island, *The French Lieutenant's Woman.*

What did she say about it? The reasons Sarah Woodruff had to lie. *Because people believe what they want to believe.*

Cass had counted everything, it was the coping mechanism she had developed as a child and which she now did almost subconsciously. Except she had not counted how long she waited in Emma's car. And how long the boat took to get to the dock where the truck was waiting. And Emma's labor—surely that kind of stress would have caused her to count. It was the counting that gave her comfort in moments exactly like these. And where had she been for two days—the time between Richard Foley's boat being found near Rockland and when she showed up on her mother's doorstep?

She saw the room again as she drew a quick breath, her hand to her chest. *Oh my God,* she thought.

She threw down a twenty and rushed out of the bar, across the lobby to the stairs, then up to the third floor. She was winded when she reached Leo's door, knocking furiously.

He answered, half asleep. "Abby . . . ?"

She pushed past him and into the room. "Close the door," she said.

He did as he was told, then walked to where she stood. "What's going on?" he asked.

"If I tell you I know something, can you just believe me?"

So many parts of her thought she knew the answer. Growing up with a parent who couldn't love you opened your eyes to the fundamental truth that most people went through life denying. It was exactly what Cass had said. No relationship was safe. No relationship could be trusted. They were all vulnerable to other forces more powerful than friendship or even love. That was the lie people told themselves—that love could make people faithful. And yet she was standing now in front of a man who had been like a father to her, asking for just that. Faithfulness.

Leo sighed and leaned against the dresser. "Oh, kiddo . . ."

His face grew more serious as he studied hers.

"Of course," he said. "I will believe you. What is it you need to tell me?"

Abby swallowed hard. She wasn't that far from being Judy Martin. From being her own mother. She knew what it was like to need protection from herself, from her fears of being betrayed.

But she couldn't do this alone. And it had to be done. Of that, she was certain.

So she just said it.

"I know how to find Emma."

TWENTY-ONE

Cass—Day Six of My Return

My father was devastated a second time when they found traces of blood on the dock, and on the bow of Richard Foley's boat.

I would have cleaned all of that up if I could have. But there had not been enough time.

It was that same day they found out who the Pratts were. The company that owned the island was registered to a man named Carl Peterson. From there it was easy. Carl Peterson was Bill Pratt's real name. His wife was named Lorna Peterson. That was Lucy Pratt's real name.

They had lived in North Carolina until seven years ago. Carl was a carpenter. Lorna worked from home as a seamstress. But I can't call them that again. To me, they are Bill and Lucy.

They lived on the Outer Banks. That's a place on the ocean in North Carolina where a lot of people have boats and know about the tides and currents. It explains why they were comfortable living on an island, apart from the rest of the world.

As I knew from my time with them on the island, they could

not have children. They had adopted a little boy, Julian, through an agency. His mother lived not far away from them, and she was very poor. She was a single mother with five children already and she did not have the money to take care of another one. They went through a legal process but this woman, the biological mother, later confessed to receiving money for choosing them as the adoptive parents. That part was not legal. It is okay to pay for medical expenses and things like that, but not cash. Still, it's done all the time. People who want children and can't have them— sometimes they don't care about what the law says. This woman needed money, and they needed a baby.

Bill's parents had died and left him what they had. It was a small fortune—enough to buy a baby. And enough to disappear after that baby died. And Lucy's mother had left her the house on the Outer Banks. Her father was estranged from her. She had one older brother who lived in Louisiana and was married with his own children. So Lucy's mother gave her the house when she died, her and Bill. Maybe it was some kind of consolation prize because she could not have children. Maybe she felt guilty that she had given Lucy a body that couldn't conceive them. I have wondered a lot about Lucy's parents because I don't think Lucy was the way she was by accident. And I don't think it was only because of what happened to the baby she'd bought from that impoverished woman.

That baby, Julian Peterson, was taken by the ocean and died a tragic death.

He had just turned two. They were out on their boat for a short excursion. He was wearing a life vest. The water was calm.

It's not exactly clear what happened, except that the bow hit a rock, making the boat stop abruptly. A stern line flew out of the boat and got pulled into the motor. Julian's leg was tangled in that line and he got pulled over, tangled in the rope and pulled overboard and into the blades. When I heard this about the accident, I wondered where Lucy was on the boat when her precious child was getting tangled up in loose lines.

I looked up the story myself as soon as I heard. I used my mother's computer. It was in the archives of the *Outer Banks Sentinel*. There were several articles. The first ones described a horrible freak accident and depicted Bill and Lucy as victims of profound loss. After finally becoming parents, God took their child in the most brutal, horrific manner. There were pictures of them leaving the funeral, crying, dressed in black clothing. The caption read COMMUNITY LENDS SUPPORT AS LOCAL COUPLE GRIEVE FOR CHILD.

But then the facts started to seep from the cracks in the story they had created there, the payment to that woman, the lies on their adoption application. Bill was a convicted felon—fraud and embezzlement while working as a bookkeeper for a small business in Boston. And Lucy had been fired from a job as a nursery school teacher for unspecified "conduct" that, when people were interviewed about it, turned out to involve obsessive attachments to some of the children. No, they were not wholesome, God-fearing people who'd lost their child. They were lying, cheating baby-stealers who had bribed a poor mother to give up her child and then allowed him to die in that boating accident with their negligence.

They were not charged with a crime for the accident. But the DA was looking into the payments made to the biological mother.

It didn't make national headlines, and the Petersons just up and left one day. They were not under arrest, so they could do what they wanted. They took over $500,000 from their accounts, in cash, and disappeared.

When I heard this story from an agent at the Bureau and then read about it on my own, I immediately pictured Lucy in our house on the island, down in the living room, staring out the window at the ocean. I believe she was looking for her child, the one she watched die. Julian. And then I pictured her the way she was with the baby, the baby she named Julia, so sure of herself as she cooed at her, bounced her on her knee, slung her over her hip while making dinner. I pictured her on that boat, her face filled with satisfaction at being a parent. Feeling vindicated for the wrong done to her by God or her mother or the Universe. Meanwhile, she had not secured the stern line. She had not had a hand on that little boy. She had not been looking at the map for rocks. I could see her. So confident. Feeling so worthy to have this child in her care. Thinking she was doing everything right. Believing she was perfect. All the while being so careless.

I thought about those cards I used to make for my mother. *Number One Mother! Greatest Mother in the World!*

I think there was a reason Lucy Pratt could not have children.

Just like there are lawyers who should not be entrusted with guarding over children.

I did not have time to consider philosophical implications of this story about God and fate and whether there was any divine justice in the Universe, because my father was devastated by the blood and thinking Emma was dead.

"He killed Emma! I know it! I know she's dead! He killed her and then they went and escaped with her little girl!"

He went on like this all afternoon, until they ran a test that confirmed that the blood found on the boat and dock was a man's.

But before that test came back—hours, it seemed—his despair was like an opening into his soul, and I was able to look into that opening and see that for my father, hope is just a word. Even after my return and after the search for Emma began, he could not feel joy at seeing me or hope of finding Emma, because there was always too much fear of losing us again, or seeing that we'd been damaged, or the world was coming to an end in a fiery apocalypse. He could not allow himself to ever be happy. I don't know if this thing about my father was created because my mother had sex with Mr. Martin and left him, or if it was this thing about him that drove her to do it.

Witt saw into the opening as well. We gathered at our father's house after we heard the news. Witt is very strong and he held our father tight while he cried. We were sitting in the kitchen, and Witt just kneeled down in front of his chair and pulled him in. When my father was done crying, he went to his room to lie down. I'm sure he smoked some pot first or maybe took a pill, because he was very eager to leave and I know from experience that when someone is that upset, they can't just go and rest without taking some kind of drug. I did not judge him. I had taken Dr. Nichols's pills.

When he was gone, Witt sat with me at the table. He asked me straight out about the night I escaped from the island and whether I was lying about how it happened.

What I had told him was all true. During the time I was getting power over Rick, I had also been working on the other part of my plan inside the house. Lucy had her pills for sleeping and she kept them in her bathroom. I knew I would need to get to them. So I had been a very good girl. Happy to be with the Pratts. Happy that I had seen the mistake I had made in trying to leave.

Eventually, they stopped watching me. They stopped worrying about me. They got distracted.

It's hard to even remember how crazy I felt the night I managed to get to Lucy's pills. Endless days of fear. Endless days of dreaming. Endless days of pretending and hating myself for any real feelings I had for anyone or anything in that wretched place, of looking out at the land so close but impossible to reach. And endless days having sex with a man I pretended to love but then had to shower off me.

The thought of being free overwhelmed me with happiness. The thought of getting caught overwhelmed me with fear. Waves of elation and dread rolled through my body like the ocean, each one crashing against a wall and giving way to the next.

Heart exploding, sweat dripping down my face from the fear and heat of that summer night, I sat on the couch with Bill, watching a movie. Lucy had gone to bed and we hadn't seen or heard from her for half an hour. She had taken her pill. I brought Bill his glass of wine. I had dissolved the pill inside it. After a while, Bill said he didn't feel so good. You aren't supposed to mix the pills with alcohol. I told him maybe it was the heat. I told him I would get him some water and I went to the bathroom.

I waited a few minutes there. I waited until it was quiet. And as I opened the door, my mind was racing with horrible thoughts of Bill standing on the other side, his hands reaching for my bare throat to kill me because he'd tasted the pill and realized what I was doing. I almost cried out when I pulled that handle and could see behind the door, Bill on the couch, unconscious.

I let out a gasp, but then forced myself to move. Bill kept a cheap old cell phone in his pants pocket. He used it to message Rick when he needed the boat. I reached into his pocket and grabbed the phone. I sent the message and I knew Rick would come. Rick always came, day or night. So I took all the cash I could find from his wallet and the bedroom drawers where they kept it, and I went to the dock and waited until I could see the lights from inside the harbor.

TWENTY-TWO

Dr. Winter—Day Seven of Cass Tanner's Return

They found the body of Richard Foley the next morning. It was lodged in the rocks on the westernmost point of the island of Freya. The cause of death appeared to be drowning because there was salt water in his lungs, but he also had contusions on his upper torso and a large gash on the back of his head. Wood splinters were found embedded in his skin.

They had not determined the exact time of death, but the extent of the decomposition was consistent with the time period between finding the boat and finding the body.

Abby and Leo did not change their plan to return to Connecticut. They took calls from the field office as they drove.

Theories were being spun about Cass and whether she had killed Richard Foley to escape: "It would explain why she lied about the timing . . . the two-day gap. . . . She killed him and then had to figure out what to do, how to get home. . . . She was never on a truck. . . ."

But others were willing to pin the death on the Pratts, who had now been identified as the Petersons: "They panicked, confronted him. Maybe he threatened to turn them in. A heated argument turned violent."

Abby wanted to believe this as well, but Cass's stories were impossible to ignore.

"What was it she said, Abby? About that first night when she got on the boat?"

Abby was thinking the same thing. "She said she knew it was dangerous to fall in the water between the boat and the dock. She said her father had told her years before how the boat can get pushed back and crush you against the dock."

Leo hung his head. "Jesus."

"Are you still okay with this?" Abby asked as they pulled into the Martins' driveway.

Abby had a plan, a way to find Emma. But they would have to lie, both of them, and very well.

Leo didn't hesitate. "Let's do it."

Cass

Day seven was the last day I kept track of my days back home. It was the day Dr. Winter told us that Emma had been found.

She told us as soon as she and Agent Strauss returned from Maine and the island of Freya, where they found my sister's necklace but no sign of Emma or the Pratts.

I have such a clear picture of Dr. Winter from that afternoon. She was wearing jeans and a light blue T-shirt that matched the color of her eyes. The sun was shining through the window of the living room and through her blond hair, making it glow. But it also made her face appear dark and full of shadows from her nose and her cheekbones, and I had to remind myself that it was the backlighting from the sun that was causing this. Not me. Not the trust in me that was driving her disclosure of this news about

Emma. I felt responsible for those things, and the weight of them nearly crushed me.

Dr. Winter said that they'd found the brother of Lucy Pratt, or Lorna Peterson, and he had been very cooperative. He told them his family had owned another piece of property, a small cabin farther north, near Acadia. They confirmed it with the will of their mother and tracked the conveyance deed. They had an address, and surveillance teams had made a positive ID. Dr. Winter and Agent Strauss told us that Emma and her daughter were inside that house. The Pratts as well.

I nearly burst open. I don't even know what it was—joy, relief, nerves. They were surging together in a toxic potion, through my veins, through my body.

Agent Strauss was with Dr. Winter when she told us these things, and he said that we could not tell anyone, not even my father, because they did not want to spook the Pratts. They were going to do more surveillance to assess the situation, maybe for a day or two. They wanted to make sure there were no weapons in the house and observe where Emma and her daughter were sleeping at night. They had time. There didn't appear to be any immediate danger, and the worst thing would be to rush in and have someone get hurt. They were telling me because they needed my help—they wanted me to interpret the things they were seeing, the behaviors and schedules, especially of her daughter. When did she nap? When did she bathe? They told Mr. and Mrs. Martin because that's where I was staying and they wanted me to have emotional support. They told us we could not tell anyone else.

My mother had been upset when she heard about the necklace being found, so you can imagine her reaction now. She did not want to believe Emma had really been with me on the island. She wanted to believe I was crazy, even though I was the only person in her life who could still tell her she was beautiful and smart and perfect.

I started to wonder if I was out of my mind. But then, finally, after all these days of waiting, she went out of hers.

She waited for them to leave, and then she ran upstairs to her bedroom and slammed the door. Mr. Martin told me that she was angry because if this story was true, then Emma was avoiding coming home, and that was very hard for my mother to accept.

That was all a lie. But I pretended it wasn't. I pretended to believe him. And I held my breath.

Dr. Winter

It was the view from the window that gave Cass away. She had been so careful with her stories, with the details and descriptions. Every emotion, every reaction and interaction that she described was exactly as it would have been if her story had been true.

But the view from the window—that had been Cass's only mistake.

She told them about that first night on the island with precision. The fight over the necklace. Hiding in Emma's car. The headlights shining on Emma, lighting up her face as she stood in the sand under the moonlight.

Then the long car ride, the music playing. Parking by a small dock in the woods. Feeling powerful and clean like they could start over. And then Rick, the boatman, and the ride to the island. Lucy being so kind, but keeping her apart from Emma. She said she could see Emma through the window, across the courtyard. The same window Abby had looked out after they'd found the island.

She described what she saw on Emma's face: *She looked like she knew exactly what she was doing and like she was certain that what she was doing was the best thing anyone could ever do.*

The problem was, Emma's room was at the end of the second hallway. And all the windows faced east to the ocean. The window that faced the courtyard came from the hallway.

Cass could not have seen her sister from her bedroom window.

When Abby told this to Leo, he nodded silently and let her continue.

"There were other things, little things." She explained about the counting, how Cass had not been in Emma's car that night—if she had, she would have counted the time, she would have told them the minutes that passed while she waited. And the same was true of the birth. And the boat ride to meet the truck.

Then there was the affair between Jonathan Martin and the school counselor. She needed them to help rattle her mother. Because she knew what Abby had realized in that bar as she pictured the layout of the upstairs bedrooms.

Emma had never been on that island.

Cass

Hunter left for Hamilton College in the late summer. He left five weeks before Emma and I disappeared. He'd broken up with that pretty girl and apparently was enjoying his freedom, and the access he now had to women wanting sex. We heard all this through Mr. Martin, who spoke about his son with pride again. This made Mrs. Martin very angry.

Something had shifted in our mother after the incident in St. Barts with the suntan lotion that one spring over two years before. It wasn't that she was suddenly attracted to Hunter, but rather that she became attached to the thought of him being attracted to her. This thought must have eased her mind when she

felt jealous of Emma for being so beautiful and for just being
Emma, the girl every man hungered for. I think her need to think
of Hunter this way grew into an unruly monster after Hunter
confessed that Mr. Martin had taken those pictures of Emma.

It was very subtle, but I saw it. I saw everything. When Emma
and I came back from Europe that July before we disappeared,
me from England and Emma from Paris, Hunter and Mrs. Martin had become very close. They had inside jokes and they watched
TV shows together. Mrs. Martin was always waiting on him,
getting him food and doing his laundry, and he was thanking her
politely and she was saying things like *Oh, it's no trouble!* As annoying as this was to watch, and as angry as it made Emma, it
was otherwise harmless. It felt like one of those movie relationships where an older grandma blushes when a young man notices
her as a sexy woman. People usually think that's cute, but if the
grandmother were Mrs. Martin, they would also find it annoying. Emma talked to me about it one night in my room.

*It's pathetic, Cass. She can't even see that he's just being nice to her
to make me angry and to piss off Jonathan. You know she says things to
him like "Why can't you be as nice to me as your own son!" Hunter is an
asshole, but he's a smart asshole. He's making us hate her and he's making his father hate her and she can't even see it! When he leaves and
doesn't give her the time of day anymore, she'll have nothing.*

Hunter had started college that August, but he came home one
weekend in late September. It was starting to get cold; the leaves
were beginning to change. I remember it very well because it was
the weekend before we disappeared.

My mother was beside herself to see him, but he was doing
what Emma predicted and not giving her any attention. You
could see the confusion and disappointment swirling around like
a cyclone when it hits the plains and gathers power. Dishes were

slammed on the counter. Huffing and puffing came from her mouth. And she sat with her legs crossed and her arms folded so her chin could rest in one palm and she could look away with pouty lips and indifference as he told us all about college.

On Saturday night, Emma went out in her car to meet her friends at the teen center. Mrs. Martin made her take me with her, which Emma was not happy about. Mr. Martin had gone to play poker at the club. That left Hunter and Mrs. Martin alone downstairs.

He'd said he had plans to meet friends from high school around ten, so he could stay and help her with the dishes from dinner. Before we left, Hunter whispered to Emma, *How many deli managers will you fuck tonight, whore?* Emma whispered back, *As many as I want, loser.* Emma had stopped dating Gil months before, but she would never live it down, how she'd been with the deli manager.

The teen center was crowded. I found some friends and pretended to enjoy hanging out, talking about our teachers and movies and boys. But my mind was stuck on Hunter and Mrs. Martin. Hunter and Emma. I felt extremely irritated.

I walked up to Emma and pulled her away from a boy she was flirting with. I told her she needed to take me home or I would make our mother come, and then she would be in big trouble for causing such an inconvenience. She was furious, but I think she secretly wanted to go home to see Hunter, to see if he really went out to meet friends or if she could engage in more warfare with him, even if it was just pulling his attention further away from Mrs. Martin.

We did not go inside the house. We were done screaming at each other and we both needed to calm down. Emma said she was going to the basement from the back door because that was

where we hid our vodka and cigarettes. Emma was hoping
Hunter had also left some pot there. The light was on in the
kitchen, so we stopped before we got to the window. Emma
peeked her head around just enough to see. I did the same from
beneath her. If Mrs. Martin was in there, we would crawl past
the window.

Dr. Winter

They left the Martins in a state of disbelief. Judy had come to
trust Abby, which had been Abby's plan. She had been kind to
her, flattering to her. It was not hard to earn her trust this way.
Abby knew what to do and what to say. And so Judy believed her.
She had no reason not to.

She had tried to feign elation that her daughter had been
found, but she was not able to pull it off with conviction. They
could hear the commotion from outside the house as they walked
to Abby's car. Judy yelling at her husband. A door slamming.

They stood by the car, looking up at the master bedroom. The
shades were drawn.

"Here we go," Leo said.

Abby was light-headed. Her breaths were quick and short. She
leaned against the door and hung her head.

"Hey"—Leo's voice was concerned now—"it's going to be
okay."

Abby looked up again, exhaling slowly as the wave of panic
subsided. "What if I'm wrong?" she asked.

Leo shrugged; then he smiled. "What if you're not?"

Cass

Emma and I looked in that kitchen window at the same time.
And we saw the things we saw at the same time. Mrs. Martin

leaned over the counter, her pants around her ankles. Hunter having sex with her from behind, his hands on her bare hips. It was indescribable, the horror we both felt, and yet we could not stop watching. Our mother was holding on to the edge of the counter with both hands. Her mouth was making a narrow, closed smile like a Cheshire cat as her body thrust back and forth into Hunter. Her eyes were wide open and staring right at us, though seeing only the darkness of night reflected from the window. As for our stepbrother, his eyes were closed. His mouth was gaping wide. He looked satisfied with himself, and I understood why he'd come home. Why he'd been treating our mother with the one thing she couldn't stand. Indifference. He knew she would do whatever was necessary to get back the attention she had become so addicted to over the summer.

And once she did what was necessary, he would have something that would kill my sister inside—he would have Emma's kryptonite in his arsenal.

We sat on the ground when we couldn't watch anymore. I stared at Emma's face, not sure what she was going to do. Cry, laugh, scream. She just sat there staring into the darkness and shaking her head. Then she took my hand and pulled me toward the basement door so we could drink and smoke and try to erase what we had just seen.

Dr. Winter

They waited in Abby's car down the street from the top of the driveway, toward the end of the cul-de-sac, which had no outlet. A row of wild shrubs protruding from the woods hid the car from view.

They had supplies—sandwiches, chips, coffee. They were prepared to wait out the night, and the next night and the next.

Talk of the investigation got them through the first few hours. The blood found on the dock and the bow of the boat matched that of Richard Foley. Agents were interviewing employees at the major train and bus stations, and a plea had been made to the public to help find the missing couple, Emma Tanner and her daughter.

After that, the silence set in. There were many things Abby wanted to say, things about the past, her rush to judgment, how she'd shut out Leo and his family, who had been so good to her. It made sense in her heart, but when the words began to form in her head—words that could explain what she had felt when he hadn't backed her up before, and what she felt now as he put his own career on the line for this crazy hunch—they sounded absurd and she could not bring herself to say them.

And so they sat in the darkness. Watching. Waiting.

Cass

On the night they told us Emma had been found, my mother finally lost control of herself. It had been building the whole time I had been home.

Emma would have been proud of me.

When Emma came to me in the night, she would tell me about the future. *One day when we're older, we will tell her the truth. We will tell her that she's not that pretty and that she's not that smart, and that she is not a good mother. We will tell her that she's old and ugly and stupid and horrible and mean. And she will not believe us at first, but our words will eat at her like acid until there is nothing left.*

When she said these things, I could feel her heart pounding so fast against me and I could feel the heat of her breath like it was coming from a fire. I could feel her scream in the night when she came to my room. And then I would feel my own heart break because nothing I could do or say could ever make it better.

On this night when my mother broke apart, I heard her and Mr. Martin fighting again. I could not make out their words except for *fucking idiot!* Mr. Martin yelled that a few times before their voices grew hushed, and then finally stopped. I peeked my head out and saw them as they disappeared into the mudroom, Mr. Martin pulling my mother by the elbow.

When I heard the garage door open, I ran down to the mudroom and found my mother's keys hanging on the rack. I waited for Mr. Martin's car to disappear down the driveway and then I took her car and followed them. I kept the lights off until we were on North Ave. Then I just stayed far enough behind so they wouldn't notice me, although I don't think they would have noticed an alien spaceship hovering over them that night. They were lost in their anger. Lost in their fear. Lost in the past.

Dr. Winter

"Here we go," Leo said quietly when they saw the car pull out of the driveway. Abby started the engine and began to pull away from the brush, but then they saw the second car.

"Cass?" she said.

Leo was watching the cars begin to disappear down the road in front of them. "Just go."

Cass

They parked at the river gorge and got out of the car. Mr. Martin was carrying a shovel in one hand and dragging my mother by the arm with the other hand. She was screaming, *I don't believe you! You're lying to me! You've been lying all this time!* And he was seething with anger. *You'll ruin us both! You fucking idiot!*

I parked down the street and then had to run to catch them. But then when I hit the woods where there was no trail, I had to stop because my feet were making the ground crackle. I walked a few yards, then hid behind a tree, listening for the sound of their voices and my mother sobbing. They were not being careful about the crackling, so it was not hard to follow them.

The river gorge is a seventy-acre park belonging to the neighboring town. It has a lot of wetlands and walking trails. Our father used to drag us there when we were young because he thought we should be in nature. But we hated the bugs and the soft ground that sucked in our sneakers and covered them in mud. We hadn't been there since we were little girls.

When Mr. and Mrs. Martin stopped, I stopped also and crouched behind some prickly bushes. They were whispering now and Mr. Martin was digging with his shovel in the soft ground near the wetlands. Mrs. Martin was crying even harder.

That's when I felt the hand cover my mouth and pull me to the ground. I thought then that this was how I would die, that somehow Mrs. Martin was not standing in the distance with Mr. Martin, or maybe Richard Foley wasn't really dead, and instead he was here and he was going to kill me for doing this. I thought, *So . . . this is how it ends.*

The night Emma and I disappeared was just over one week after Mrs. Martin had sex with Hunter. Hunter had gone back to Hamilton, all puffed up by his victory over all of us, but especially over Emma. He didn't even know that we knew, but inside he had the kryptonite and I could see that he would get great pleasure plotting out how and when he would use it on my sister.

Emma came to my room after dinner. She had not been able to calm down since that night. Not the vodka or the cigarettes or even the pot she stole from Hunter's stash had helped her. She was losing her mind.

I'm gonna tell her tonight. I'm gonna tell her what we saw.

I begged her, *No!* I told her that we could use the information in a better way to get something, like maybe being able to live with our father finally. But Emma didn't want to live with our father. She had become just as addicted to the war with Hunter and the competition with Mrs. Martin as they were addicted to their wars and their jealousies.

Tell her something else, Emma. Tell her you're pregnant! Tell her it's Hunter's baby!

Emma shrieked. *You're a genius, Cass! Oh my God! This will kill her. It will actually make her die inside!* She left my room laughing even though she was not happy. I did not follow her. I went to the edge of my room, right by the door. A few moments later, I heard the murmur of talking from down the hall, inside Mrs. Martin's bedroom. The talking began to escalate until it turned to yelling. It was then I could hear the words.

You're going to ruin this family! You stupid whore!

Me? What about you? You were fucking Jonathan while you were still married to Daddy! You brought them into our house, and now look what they've done!

Look what you've done, Emma! YOU!

Lights came down the driveway and shone into the window from the upstairs balcony. Mr. Martin was home. The screaming stopped for a second, so I peeked out from behind the door. The light had shone into Mrs. Martin's room as well—I could see it lighting up Mrs. Martin's angry face. Emma ran out but Mrs. Martin grabbed her by the hair and she screamed again, first from pain and then from rage.

Get off me, you bitch! I'm telling him! I'm telling him! I'm telling him what his son did to me, how he raped me and got me pregnant!

Mrs. Martin pulled harder. Emma swung out her arm like she was about to slap her face, but her hand caught the edge of a framed portrait hanging on the wall and it crashed to the ground. Mrs. Martin grabbed both her arms before she could try again. Emma squirmed and spun her around, and they both fell against the railing of the balcony, Emma's back to the railing and Mrs. Martin's body pushing against her from the momentum of their struggle. Emma screamed one last time as she felt herself hovering over the top of the railing. I know what that feels like, when you are about to fall unexpectedly, when your body sends you an alarm to grab hold of something or adjust your feet or brace yourself with an open palm. Her back arched. Her arms reached out for our mother. But Mrs. Martin swatted her away like a pesky fly and then stepped back so she had nothing to hold on to. Nothing to save her.

I was lying on the ground in those woods, the hand over my mouth, staring into the eyes of Dr. Winter as I remembered the sound my sister made when she fell over that railing, over that balcony, and hit the ground below, as I remembered the sight of my mother staring at her still body, hands covering her mouth and finally silent.

Dr. Winter

When Cass saw who was holding her, she stopped fighting. Abby put a finger to her lips to tell her that they needed to be quiet and she nodded. She sat up then, beside Abby, and they both watched as Jonathan Martin dug into the ground with his shovel with Judy standing beside him sobbing like a small child.

Agent Strauss was on the hill, crouched behind a wall of bushes, watching them dig.

Cass

I scurried like a quiet little mouse back into my room that night. I was shaking. I couldn't think. I heard Mr. Martin come inside, and I peeked out the door enough to see him. He cried out in shock when he saw Emma lying on the ground, not moving. I did not see her with my own eyes, but I know she must have been still. I know there was no blood because they tested for blood all over our house when we disappeared and found none. But from the urgency in their voices, I knew it was bad.

Mrs. Martin screamed from up above that it was an accident. That they'd been fighting and Emma pushed her and she pushed back and then she just fell!

Mr. Martin sat beside Emma. *Call 911, for Christ's sake! Why are you just standing there? Oh, God!*

Mrs. Martin rushed down the stairs. Emma had told our mother that Hunter had raped her and that she was now pregnant. She said she was going to have the baby and that Hunter's life would be ruined because he would go to jail and be a sex offender for the rest of his life. She said she was going to tell everyone whose baby it was so the world would know what kind of house this had become.

I heard this explanation come from my mother's mouth in a panicked voice after Mr. Martin asked, *What happened, Judy! In the name of God, what happened here!* Then they went back and forth with things like *What do we do? What will happen to my son? They'll find the baby inside her! They'll find out who the father is! What will happen to him? What will happen to me? Dear God! What do we do?* I was too scared to cry and could barely see through the haze of fear that covered my eyes like a white blanket. But I was able to see enough to notice the necklace that lay against the wall where my mother hung her treasured photos of us. It had broken from Emma's neck and fallen into a little tangled ball between the wall and the edge of the carpet runner.

I grabbed the necklace, then ran back into my room. I could only hear whispering because they had calmed down and were deciding about what to do. And then I heard shuffling and huffing and moaning coming from my mother and Mr. Martin and then walking and then the mudroom door and then the garage door and then a car leaving from the driveway. Emma's car. Then I heard the mudroom door again, and my mother's crying and babbling to herself as she stood in the foyer where Emma had landed.

At some moment, she realized that she had not seen or heard me all afternoon. She walked up the stairs and down the hall and she came into my room. The light was off.

Cass? Cass, where are you?

I did not answer. I was hiding beneath my bed.

When she left to look for me in the rest of the house, I lay there for several minutes letting this new realization sink in. Of all the things I had come to understand and regardless of how grown-up and clever I thought I was, I had never, ever considered this before. I had never imagined that my mother might actually kill me.

Dr. Winter

Jonathan Martin dug for close to an hour. The earth moved easily because it was more like silt, but he was digging in very deep. By the time he stopped, Judy was no longer crying but instead shining a light from her phone into the hole of soft dirt. She was staring into that hole with a blank expression. Jonathan reached down and pulled at something. It looked like some kind of bright green landscaping or lawn tarp. He used his hands to move the dirt away from it. He seemed frantic, like he wanted to get it over with, like he was desperate to move that earth and find what he was looking for.

Abby held Cass tighter because she already knew.

Cass

Something green came from the ground. Then there was more digging. I could not see well, but I could see enough. He dug and dug, on his knees, until finally he pulled something else from the hole he'd made. He held it in the air and then looked at Mrs. Martin long enough for her to understand that what he was holding were the bones of my sister's hand.

When he drove away that night in Emma's car, I had prayed that he was driving her to the hospital. Even though I had feared my mother might kill me that night when she came looking for me, I still would not believe Emma was dead. And even as I climbed from my bedroom window, without a coat or a purse or anything, climbed down from the roof and ran from that house, into the night, I did not believe it. Mr. Martin carried Emma to her car. That was the last thing I heard. And it was very possible he was taking her to get help.

I walked four miles to the train station. I hid on a train to New York and then I walked to Penn Station. I remembered going there once with our father and he said you can get a train anywhere from there. I saw an ad pinned to a wall along one of the passageways. It said to call if you were a teenager and if you needed help. I called the number collect the way it said to. A man answered. His name was Bill. He talked to me for a while and said he could help, but I said I wasn't sure and I hung up. I did not know where I should go. I considered calling Witt. I considered calling my father. I fell asleep before I made a decision.

When I woke up, a man named Bill was sitting beside me. He had a cup of hot chocolate and a doughnut and a kind smile. There was a woman with him, and she looked nice. They asked if I was hungry. And I was. So very hungry.

Dr. Winter

When Cass saw Emma's bones, she broke free of Abby's hold and started to run toward the grave. Agent Strauss was barreling down the hill, gun drawn. He got to them first and got them to their knees. They were in shock, but Judy managed to start her defense right then and there, crying about how she had no idea her daughter was dead.

She would later claim that she also had no idea how Emma died. She would testify that she came home to find Emma at the bottom of the stairs, already dead, and that her husband insisted they hide the body because she was pregnant with his son's baby and he did not want his son's life to be destroyed. He drove Emma's car to the woods and buried her, then left the car at the beach so everyone would believe she had drowned in the ocean. She would turn on him viciously to save herself, disclosing his obsession with his son, his emotional abuse of Judy herself, and his attraction to her daughter.

Jonathan Martin told a different story after conferring with his lawyers, the story that would eventually be believed by prosecutors and become the basis for a plea bargain. He told how he arrived home to find his stepdaughter dead. He admitted to being scared for his wife, who had killed her own daughter, and also for his son because of what Emma had said about being pregnant. He claimed he was overwrought with fear about what it would do to his son, so he hid the body and left the car at the beach to stage a drowning. He begged for understanding, for the compassion of fellow parents who do stupid things to protect their children.

Jonathan Martin passed a polygraph. Judy refused to take one.

An autopsy of Emma Tanner's skeletal remains could not determine if she had ever been pregnant.

Cass

For days and weeks after I ran away, I watched any television show I could find as they reported about me and Emma and how we had disappeared. I talked to the Pratts about it, but I did not tell them the truth about Emma. I told them she had run away after fighting with our mother and that I couldn't stay there without her.

At first, I prayed that Mr. Martin had driven her to the hospital and that I would wake up to see news of that—of an accident in a home and the girl recovering nicely. When I heard about the car being left at the beach, I knew they had staged her disappearance and used my own running away to give it credibility. And even then, I hoped beyond reason that I was wrong—that she was safe somewhere. That Mr. Martin had paid her to go away and never come back and that it was enough money for Emma to do it. Maybe she thought she could always come back for more and more and torture them all forever. Or maybe she had moved somewhere exotic and was living with a handsome native, or worshipped by an entire island of natives, and finally being happy. It was crazy to think this, but it was enough to keep me from going home, to hide in the train station so I could think of what to do. It was there that I met Bill and Lucy. I got in Bill's

car and rode all the way to Maine. And then got on Rick's boat
and felt free and powerful as we crossed the harbor to the most
beautiful place I had ever seen.

I returned after my escape to find my sister. I was still holding
hope that she was alive somewhere—I gambled that I could make
them bring her out of hiding. Or that the press would make her
surface. I didn't know the outcome. But I knew if I could make
my mother doubt her husband, make her believe he had lied to
her all this time because he had also cheated on her and because
everyone was believing me that Emma was on the island, that she
would break. Summer would become winter inside her mind and
she would threaten to reveal what they had done that night, whatever it was, and that Mr. Martin would be forced to show her
proof. That is what happens when we lose faith in a person. We
have to see the evidence. Words and promises are no longer
enough.

I knew if I could do that, if I could break her, the truth would
be set free.

I ran to my sister's grave, to my mother and my stepfather. I
ran to Emma, finally, after all those years.

Mr. Martin and my mother were on their knees with Agent
Strauss holding a gun to them. They looked up when they heard
me, and Mrs. Martin started pleading even harder for everyone
to believe her about that night. Mr. Martin was silent. He had
the good sense to wait for his lawyer.

And with all this going on, all I could really see were the lifeless bones of my sister's hand coming out from the ground. And
all I could really hear was the scream inside me, echoing into the
darkness.

TWENTY-THREE

Dr. Winter

Finding Emma Tanner was not the end of the story. It was only the beginning.

The investigation was taken over by local authorities. Detectives and prosecutors descended upon Cass, the Martin family and the Bureau as they attempted to piece together the events of the past three years.

On the other side were two teams of defense attorneys, one for Judy Martin and one for Jonathan Martin. They aligned briefly for an offensive strike, going after the Bureau, Agent Leo Strauss and Dr. Abigail Winter. They made a motion to dismiss the charges on the grounds of entrapment, seeking to dismiss the evidence and testimony from that night when the Martins led them to the body of the dead teenager. It was a frivolous legal argument because the Martins had not been coerced into committing any crime, but rather leading authorities to evidence of a prior crime. But the claim had to be defended.

Leo was steadfast in his testimony at deposition. "We do it all the time. We lie to suspects about things we know and things we've found. We had a hunch and we went with it."

He did more than that. When pressed about where this hunch had come from, he mentioned the inconsistency with the location of the bedrooms. "Abby figured out that Emma had not been on that island, and she knew that Cass was saying things that didn't add up. No—we did not know what had happened to Emma Tanner. We just knew that she had not been on that island and that someone in that house could have the answer." He did not elaborate. But he took full responsibility for their tactics. He said it had been his idea. This was his case. He was the lead investigator and he made the call to run this lead without involving anyone else on the team—except, of course, for Dr. Winter. "Why? Because she knew that family better than anyone. Because I needed her."

Abby had weighed in on the reasons Cass had told them things that were not true with a theory that made it impossible for them to charge her. "I believe Cass Tanner was in a state of profound emotional stress, which caused her to have short-term dissociative disorder. It's common in cases of severe stress like this. It is my opinion that the trauma of her escape and the return home, where she relived the death of her sister and faced the extreme conflict of being home with her mother but also knowing what her mother had done, were too much for her to handle. She created a false reality to cope. A reality where her mother was not responsible for her sister's death and was therefore a safe place for her to be. She needed to feel safe again."

She went on from there, on the pathology of short-term dissociative disorder and her opinion that Cass was now well—that she had a full recollection of what happened to her sister and understood now that her sister was dead. She had insisted that the other stories about the island were true, that they had happened to her, and that she had no idea how Richard Foley died. She had come to remember meeting Bill and Lucy Pratt at Penn Station, how they offered her hot chocolate and then, after learning she'd run away, a place to stay.

And the story about the beach, the one described with meticulous detail right down to the moonlight and the sand groomer—well, that was all just part of the delusion. Her mind could not dismiss the facts of Emma's disappearance, so it incorporated them into the fantasy.

Of course, none of this was true. Cass knew exactly what she was doing when she told that story. She had crafted it perfectly—fitting the details to the factual findings so the Bureau would believe her, letting her mother spin theories about what had really happened that night after her husband drove off with Emma's body.

No charges were brought against Cass. Her attorney used public sympathy and Dr. Winter's testimony to weigh on the prosecutor and block every effort to have Cass evaluated again. Other than one visit to her pediatrician, Cass evaded physical examinations as well.

In the end, they rolled Jonathan Martin with a plea deal for obstructing justice in exchange for his testimony. A forensic autopsy confirmed a broken neck—Emma had been dead on impact. They used Abby's theory to explain Cass's behavior and convince the jury that she was sane. Both testified against Judy Martin, who was, in the end, convicted of federal obstruction charges. But without more of a motive, without the truth about what had gone on in that house, and with two possible theories about how Emma fell—at the hand of Judy Martin or the hand of Jonathan Martin—the jury was hung on the charge of manslaughter.

Abby and Leo had not been in the same room until the day of

sentencing nearly seven months after finding Emma's body in the woods. They had to be careful about appearances. But Abby had met with Cass to help with the evaluation of her mental state. And Leo had written reports, given depositions, and met with the higher-ups at the New Haven field office to walk them through everything that had happened.

The investigation had not ended, even after the conviction of Judy Martin. There was the death of the boatman, Richard Foley, which was being investigated by the Maine state police in conjunction with the Bureau. The working theory had it pinned on the Petersons. Their rowboat was found in a wooded area near the water's edge in nearby Christmas Cove, confirming their hasty departure from the island. The couple had not been found. The Bureau was heading up the search for them—Carl and Lorna Peterson, a.k.a Bill and Lucy Pratt—and possibly one unidentified child whose clothes were found in the dresser drawers.

There were two pieces of the puzzle that had fallen through the cracks. The first was the child.

Other than one book of lullabies, some clothing in a drawer and a crib found in the basement of the house on the island, there was no evidence of a child. Dishes, drains, linens were initially examined for biological evidence, but the search came to a screeching halt after Emma's body was found. With Abby's guidance, Cass was able to process what had transpired and soon reported that the child had, in fact, been part of her delusion. The working theory was now that the clothing and crib and the book were keepsakes from the child the Petersons had lost years before—although that child had been a two-year-old boy, and the clothes belonged to a two-year-old girl. Still, there was no reason to expend additional resources on forensic evaluations until they found the Petersons and had some kind of crime to prove.

The second piece was composed of the family dynamics that preceded the fatal incident on the balcony of the Martins' home. They had some idea that Emma and her mother had a volatile relationship. Owen Tanner testified about the fighting between them. So did Witt. But Owen could not bring himself to accept that Judy had killed their daughter. He bent his testimony to cast the doubt on Jonathan and Hunter. The defense introduced evidence about the nude photos, which gave Jonathan Martin a motive, undermining his credibility. Hunter Martin, likewise, was offered as a witness by the prosecution to support his father's testimony and cast the doubt back on Judy. He told of Emma's promiscuity and Judy's jealousy of her—things he observed merely as an innocent bystander. He denied getting Emma pregnant. And while Cass recounted the story about Emma's hair and, of course, what she recalled about the night her sister fell to her death, her testimony came under fierce scrutiny. After all, she had been delusional. She had told everyone, in great detail, about her sister's being alive and having given birth to a child that was never born.

Wasn't there anything else? The prosecutors had begged her for more stories about her childhood with Judy Martin—anything that would help the jury leap the hurdles they were asking them to clear to find Judy guilty over her husband. But Cass insisted she had nothing. And so the jury remained uncertain and unable to convict her of more than the obstruction charge, and a panoply of smaller crimes related to the removal and burial of the body.

"There's more. I know there is."

Abby sat beside Leo on a park bench outside the small courthouse. The media had dispersed. The lawyers had gone back to their offices. And Judy Martin had just been sentenced and was on her way to the women's federal correctional facility in Aliceville, Alabama.

Cass had chosen not to attend the sentencing.

"She doesn't care. This wasn't about justice," Leo said.

Abby sighed and shook her head. The system had failed Emma Tanner. And Cass had been a part of it. Her stories could have tipped the scales. But she did not want the truth about what went on in that house to see the light of day.

"She just wanted to find her sister, Abby. That's all."

Abby knew he was right. Watching Cass testify against her mother had been infuriating, so much so that Abby had struggled with the decision to continue protecting her, lying for her. And, in turn, asking Leo to lie as well.

"No one is looking into the past, into how bad things were in that house, and so no one is looking for the child. Those two pieces—they go hand in hand," Leo reminded her. "Remember what Cass said? People believe what they want to believe, and no one wants to believe that a mother could kill her own daughter. It's so much easier to swallow an evil, controlling stepfather protecting his son than a ruthless mother. No one wants to see a mother like that. A mother that evil, even if it does come from an illness. It shakes us to the core."

Abby looked at him. "And no one did see. Not Owen Tanner. Not the court. Not the school. Not even the girls, until it was too late."

"Do you understand now? Why I didn't want you to go after this three years ago? You would have been destroyed, Abby."

That was a hard one for Abby to swallow. Even after the truth had come out and the remains were found, the prosecution had chosen not to use any expert testimony or pursue any psychiatric evaluations of Judy Martin on the theory of narcissistic personality disorder. They didn't have enough to back it up. It was too subjective. Too rare. And because of Abby's past and the paper she'd written on the subject, it would turn the light back on the trap they had set for Judy and her husband. And no one at the Bureau wanted that.

"I don't know how to feel about any of this. I don't feel relieved. I don't feel vindicated about being right."

Abby stared at the courthouse. It was a beautiful but cold winter day. Blue skies. Puffy clouds. The air was crisp and cut right through her wool coat. She shivered and Leo put his arm around her.

He had saved her from what could have been a disastrous outcome. If he had told the truth about the decision to lie to the Martins—that it was Abby who had wanted to set the trap—the case and her career could have come undone.

But that was not his only deception.

Somewhere in the Tanner file was a piece of paper with a name and a number, buried deep now, just in case he ever needed it. It was a witness from the train station in Portland. Leo would say he never called her back because the case was solved before he had the chance. He would say he forgot about it, or that she sounded like one of the other nutjobs who had phoned in tips on the case. After all, she'd said that a woman who looked just like Cass Tanner was riding a train for New York and had asked to use her phone to look up an address. And she was not alone. Beside her, curled up and fast asleep, was a little girl.

Abby and Leo both believed that Cass had spent those missing two days delivering her daughter to safety before she returned home. And they had bets on Witt being an accomplice. They had said nothing, and done nothing about any of it.

"What do you think she'll do now?" Leo asked.

"I don't know, exactly. But I do know she'll do whatever is best for her daughter."

"And the father? Hunter? God forbid, Jonathan?"

"Jesus . . . my money's on Hunter. It's what Emma told her mother that got her so enraged, she pushed her over the balcony. The best lies are the ones closest to the truth."

"If she had told us what really happened in that house, it would have been enough. All the charges would have stuck. She helped her mother get away with murder to protect her child."

"Yes, she did."

"And you know what that means?" Leo reached in his bag and pulled out a weathered bundle of paper clipped together in one corner. It was a copy of a paper titled "Daughters of Mothers with Narcissism: Can the Cycle Be Broken?"

Abby smiled and nodded. She felt the tears wanting to come, but she held them back. Leo studied her face. He squeezed her shoulder and pulled her closer.

It was ironic how she could know so much and still be so afflicted by the past. The cycle was a force that kept pulling her back in. But then she thought about Cass and this ability she still had to love selflessly. She had escaped the cycle. Love for her own child had been more important than revenge against her mother.

Cass was not completely free. No one ever was after growing up that way. Maybe she would forever number things like Meg. And maybe she had an invisible shield that would make it hard to be loved, like the one Abby could feel starting to break under the weight of the evidence that was now before her. For the first time in her life, she felt hopeful.

"You look tired, kiddo," Leo said.

Abby laughed, but then the tears broke through. "I don't think I've slept for nearly four years."

Leo nodded slowly. "I know. Those damned ghosts always come at night, don't they."

A moment passed.

Then Leo stood and took Abby's hand. "Come for dinner tonight. Susan wants to make you a cake."

"But it's not my birthday," Abby answered.

Leo smiled then, his head tilted, one eyebrow raised. "Yes, it is."

TWENTY-FOUR

Cass

It was very hot the summer before I ran away. Records were broken. Everyone was complaining. People started talking about global warming again, even though the prior winter had also broken records for snow and cold. I think sometimes that having too much information can be a very bad thing. It pulls our attention this way and that way, that way and this way, until our heads are just spinning around and we are never able to see what's right in front of us. We are not owls and our heads were not built to spin.

When I see and hear exploding news stories, like that summer with the heat wave, and when it makes me get worried about things, I make myself remember something I learned in the sixth grade. We were studying the solar system and we learned about how the earth began 4.5 billion years ago and how the sun will die in about the same amount of time. It's so easy to think that we are important and that the things that happen to us are important. But the truth is, we are so small, so insignificant in the scope of even just our solar system, which is itself meaningless in the scope of the Universe. The truth is, nothing really matters unless we decide it matters. We could set off every nuclear bomb we've ever made and kill all life on the planet, and the Universe would just shrug and yawn because within the next five billion years while the sun is still shining, some kind of new life would come and we would be talked about by them the way we talk about dinosaurs.

After my escape, I could have taken that train anywhere in the world. Or at least anywhere that train was stopping all the way down to Florida. I could have stayed gone forever. My father was sad, but it was three years old, his sadness, and it had become more of a scar than an open wound. The same was true for Witt. He'd gone to law school and gotten married. I'm sure he missed me, but his life had filled in whatever hole my leaving had caused, like when you make footprints in the sand and then the water comes in bringing more sand and more sand until they disappear.

It was not necessary that I come home. It was not necessary that I find Emma. It caused a lot of upheaval to everyone, including myself, and in the scope of the Universe, it was irrelevant and unimportant. But in my years on the island, I made a theory for myself about the meaning of life. I decided that life would be about choosing things to make important even though they are not, and cannot ever be. I took this theory and I started to make a list of the things I would choose to be important and that I would honor. I decided that I would measure myself against my list and whether I had been true to that list of important things.

Finding Emma was on that list.

The summer before we disappeared, Emma had left for Paris in early June. I did not leave for my program in England until two weeks later. I had not been alone in the house with Hunter, Mr. Martin and my mother before. Not ever. I always went to my father's house when Emma was away.

The truth is, I could have gone to my father's house. My father wanted me to stay with him, and with the war going on at the Martins' house, I was like a bird on the battlefield. I knew I would be fine if I just flew off when the soldiers returned. I also knew that no one sees a bird on the battlefield when they're always on the lookout for the enemy soldiers. It was hard to be that bird that no one saw and that would be crushed if it didn't fly away when the fighting began again.

I was fifteen that July. But that is no excuse. I felt invisible and powerless in my family and in my life. But that is no excuse. There is no excuse for what I did that July.

The idea came to me one night at dinner. Mrs. Martin had wanted to go to the club, so we all got dressed up and went—me, Hunter, Mrs. Martin and Mr. Martin and Hunter's girlfriend. Hunter was still being annoyingly flirtatious with my mother, so she wore a sexy dress and put on extra makeup. I saw Hunter's eyes run up and down her when he knew his father was looking at him. He was relentless in his efforts to keep them estranged until Emma got back from France. It was part of his plan to destroy her. Or maybe to win her back. To this day, I don't know which it was, with love always turning to hate, hate turning back to love.

I got dressed in Emma's room. I wore one of Emma's dresses and I used her special flat iron and I put on her makeup. I knew what I was trying to do. None of this was subconscious. I did not want to be invisible and powerless anymore.

Hunter's girlfriend was very talkative at dinner and she was also very nice to me, which was almost as annoying as my mother and Hunter's flirting.

Nothing really happened at that dinner, except for one small look. Emma had talked to me about how you know if someone likes you and how you can tell someone you like them, and I had trouble believing her because I had never done it or had it done to me.

It's hard to explain, Cass, she said one night in my room, her arms around me.

It's a look that comes in a different way or that you send out in a different way. It's just a tiny bit longer than a normal look. And it's completely still, it's not moving with a smile or talking or even eyes squinting or your eyebrows lifting up or anything at all. It's totally frozen, like a deer in the headlights. It's frozen by a thought that has just hijacked your brain for that second and that's why it lasts too long, because you have to rescue your brain from the hijacker.

I asked her what that thought was that could hijack your brain and freeze your face like that.

It's the thought that you want that person.

That night at dinner, I finally understood what she meant. My mother had noticed the dress I was wearing and the makeup and my hair, and she did not like it one bit. She did not like that I was trying to be like Emma and take attention away from her. She had made a few comments to me as we were leaving the house and I ignored them, but inside I was smiling because my plan was working. I was reappearing from my state of invisibility. I was finding some power of my own.

When we were at the table at the club, Hunter's girlfriend said how pretty I looked. How grown-up I was becoming. My mother smiled at me and said, *Isn't that Emma's dress?* I said it was but that Emma didn't want it anymore. I lied and said that Emma told me I could have it. My mother smiled again and said, *Well, remind me on Monday and I'll take you to the tailor. It really needs to be brought in around the bust. You definitely got your father's side in that department. All the women are flat as boards.*

I felt my face flush as the blood rushed in. I felt adrenaline seething through me. Hunter's girlfriend looked horrified but that was because she did not know the kind of mother Mrs. Martin was and that I had incited her fury by trying to take some of her attention for myself. She wiped the horror from her face and said again that she thought I looked beautiful.

It was at that moment, in the chaos of blood and adrenaline and horror, that I saw that look come my way, the look Emma had told me about. It was coming from across the table. It was coming from Hunter.

I looked away as fast as I could, but I would soon learn that I had not been quick enough. I had not rescued my own brain from the hijacker in time, and now I had seen Hunter's hijacked brain and he had seen mine.

I knew that our hijackers were different types of criminals. I won't pretend that I came to see this after I was older and wiser. I knew it then, right then, at that dinner. Hunter saw that I was no longer irrelevant to the war. With one dress and some makeup, I had made myself a weapon he could use against my mother, and then against Emma when she returned from Europe. And I saw that Hunter could make me a weapon and I wanted to be a weapon because a weapon is, at the very least, seen by everyone on that battlefield. I was tired of being a bird.

Three days later, after more hijacked looks had passed between us, Hunter came to my room. I was asleep. It was past 2 A.M. He got into my bed. He got under the covers. He didn't say anything and I didn't say anything. He started to touch me and not only did I not say anything but I didn't do anything either. Not one thing to help him as he struggled with my pajama bottoms and the covers and then his pajama bottoms. And not one thing to stop him as he climbed on top of me. I lay still, very still, for as long as I could. Denying that I was letting this happen. Lying to myself that I wanted it to stop. Because I didn't. I hated Hunter Martin. But there were things about my life that I hated even more. When he was done, he fell asleep beside me. I could smell the alcohol on his breath. I did not sleep the rest of the night. I just lay there, staring at the ceiling. Thinking.

It happened only three more times while Emma was gone. That was all he needed. And that was all I needed. I did not care that he kept seeing his girlfriend. I did not care that there were no more hijacked looks. And I did not care that when Emma returned, they still treated me like the bird. I did not care, because I knew I was not the bird anymore. I knew I was the weapon and that I had power, and knowing was enough for me.

I also knew I was pregnant by the time school started. I ignored it at first, but then we saw our mother with Hunter, and Emma was wanting to confront her about it. This was my chance to see what would happen if she knew what he had done. This was my chance to see if she would help me if I told her I was the one pregnant with Hunter's baby. If she would help Emma, then maybe (maybe) she would help me.

I got my answer.

I had the baby on the island. It was horrible and I won't pretend it wasn't. I thought I was going to die. I wanted to die. But then I had my baby, my little girl, and she became the first thing on my list of things I decided to make important.

They took her from me slowly after the first three months, not the way I told them it happened to Emma. But the rest was true. When I resisted and cried, they let me see her only once a day. We had been inseparable before that. She slept in my bed. She stayed in my arms all day. We took long walks in the woods. And I sang her lullabies from a book Lucy bought us. From my heart and out through my hands, love gushed out of me and into my baby. All the love I had felt for Emma. All the love I had felt for my father and Witt. And all the love that I had wanted from my mother when I was a little girl.

When they took my daughter, I hid that book under my bed and I held it in my arms every night and cried myself to sleep. I waited outside their door at night and listened for the sounds of sleep. And on the nights I could be sure of it, I would crawl across the floor and sit by my daughter's bed. I would sometimes reach my hand onto her back and let it rise and fall with her breath.

When I finally woke up from their spell, I added to my list escaping from the island with my daughter.

I am afraid now. I am afraid of myself and what I am capable of. I am afraid of my own mind.

The Pratts were sick people. I know now why they became psychotic about having a baby and how their isolation on the island made it worse, so they could no longer make sense of reality and understand that what they were doing was wrong. Dr. Winter explained this to me before she learned that I had told so many lies. They had been turned down for adoptions for fifteen years, then lost the one child they were given. They took me in so they could mother me. But then came my baby. She was the gift from God they had been praying for. And I was just an evil force trying to get in the way of God's will.

But Dr. Winter told me something else after that night in the woods. She wanted me to be prepared. She told me that when they find the Pratts, or the Petersons, if they ever do, they will tell a different story. They will tell the story of a scared teenager who showed up at their home, asking for help. Asking to be saved from a wretched family. They will explain that I was always able to leave. They will use the things I did in my moments of weakness, laughing with them, eating with them, letting them hug me and kiss my forehead and tell me they loved me. I have been such a liar. And they will use that against me.

But it won't matter. Because I will find a way to make them pay.

It was not easy to wait those last two years to escape. Being nothing more than a sister to my own baby, yearning to come home so I could find the sister who had disappeared—I would binge on their kindness until it made me sick. I was so hungry for it, and my hunger disgusted me. I told myself I was just working at my plan, to make them trust me. But that would also be a lie.

It was even harder to make Rick see me and want me and make me his lover. And when I was pretending to love him, I feasted as well on his love, what I thought was love, what I pretended was love. I feasted until I was sick from that, too.

The night I gave Bill the pills, I signaled Rick with the phone. I collected my daughter from the small bed in Lucy's bedroom while Lucy snored, her fat belly rising and falling beneath the covers. I got all the money I could find from Bill's wallet and Lucy's dresser. I carried my daughter down to the dock and put her in the rowboat under a blanket. I told her to wait there, under the blanket, and if she could be very good and very quiet and stay hidden, I would take her to a very special, magical place. I watched for the boat. And when I saw it come closer, I called out to him.

Help me! Please. Take me away from this place!

He maneuvered the boat to the dock. He saw the blanket in the rowboat, and my daughter squirming beneath it, and he called out again. *What's under there? Is that the child?*

I did not answer him but he knew. I could tell by the anger I saw on his face. I had been planting seeds in his head for months and I had become convinced that I had destroyed his trust in the

Pratts and replaced it with my love. I knew he believed that they had told me about Alaska, what he had done there. And I made him believe that they thought he was an immoral man.

I thought I had read him. I thought I had given it enough time. He would see how desperate I was and take us to shore. But I was wrong. When I jumped onto that boat, he did not agree to help my daughter and me escape. Instead, he did exactly what he had done before. *You're gonna take that child back to the house*, he said.

The shock of it flooded my brain and I felt dizzy. I thought I had been a good student of Emma and Mrs. Martin. I had done everything right. I had figured out what he desired and I had become that. I had deciphered his relationship with the Pratts and I had unraveled it, slowly and with patience and what I thought was devious cunning. And in those stolen moments in the woods or on the boat when his body was on my body, when our skin was touching and our arms and legs were wrapped together like a knot that will never come undone, I thought I was being calculating. Every sigh. Every moan. Every kiss. Every touch. It was all calculated to be that thing he desired. The woman who needed to be rescued. I felt so clever that I could feel his love in the way he devoured me with such force but then held me with such tenderness. That was what I thought.

I was stupid. I was weak. I did not have the same appeal that Mrs. Martin and Emma had. Whatever Rick needed from me was easily undone by the weight of his debt to Bill and Lucy. I had not destroyed it. Not with my cunning and not with my sex power. Not even with my love, which had become real, mixing with the hate.

I will say this quickly and not say it ever again. Rage took control of my mind. It was bigger than my reason and more powerful than the currents that were always trying to bring me back. My daughter was waiting for me in the rowboat. And this man was going to keep me from saving her. From saving us. I was filled with an army of rage, with soldiers from every corner of my life heeding the battle cry. Soldiers from the times I reached for my mother and she pushed me away. Soldiers from the times my father failed to protect us. Soldiers from Hunter and Emma and that woman from the court. And soldiers from the joy I allowed myself in the arms of these monsters, Bill and Lucy and Rick. One by one, the soldiers of rage formed an army that was unstoppable.

I picked up a metal gas container and I hit Rick in the head, knocking him over the side. I threw the container in the water and I didn't wait for a second to pass before I got behind the steering wheel and back on the throttle and then up. I steered the hull right over his body, crushing it into the dock. I reversed and did it again. Twice and then a third time. The soldiers fueled each strike, the final one leaving him still, floating facedown in the cruel, cold water that had shown me no mercy.

I took my daughter from the rowboat and we drove in *The Lucky Lady*—so fast, we were both holding on with all our strength—into darkness and far up the coast. I was not thinking that this would make it harder to find out the location of the island. I was only thinking about getting far, far away. When we ran out of gas, we got pulled into a harbor by the current. I let the boat run up against the brush and then I just let that boat go, into the harbor, with the ignition still turned on but the motor stalled. I carried my daughter to a gas station and called a taxi to take us to Portland. I had four hundred dollars of the Pratts' money and I would use it to get home. I noted the name of the town so I could send someone back to find the Pratts. Rockland. But that had not been enough, and my stupidity gave them the time they needed to escape.

I rode the train with my daughter. We rode from Portland to Yonkers. Then we took a commuter train to Rye. We walked to Witt's house. He did not know we were coming. He did not know I had found him with the help of a stranger's phone on the train and that I had memorized his address so that I could bring my daughter to him and keep her safe while I tended to my list. While I tended to finding Emma. It was Saturday afternoon. Witt was in his yard pulling weeds and I started to laugh. I can't describe that feeling. Even after I saw Rick die, even as I was watching the landscape roll by from the train window, my daughter asleep on my lap, and even as I walked down the street, totally free, I did not feel free. Not yet. It was not until I saw my brother in his yard, and until he saw me and wrapped me in his arms and lifted me into the air, tears rolling down his face, that I felt it, my life coming back to me.

He listened to me but did not agree at first. His wife wanted to call the police and have my mother and Mr. Martin arrested. They both said they would find Emma. Somehow, they would find her. Wouldn't they? It was Witt who finally understood. It was Witt who could see that Emma would never be found and my mother and Mr. Martin would never be punished for what they did to her. Mrs. Martin had never been punished for anything she had ever done. She was a master illusionist. Even people trained to see, even people looking for exactly what was there to be seen, could still not see. Instead, I would be the crazy one, the one with the daughter fathered by her stepbrother. Hunter would try to take my baby and I would lose everything—my sweet child, my freedom, and my sister all over again. So they kept my daughter for me and they lied and pretended and swallowed their guilt.

I went to my mother then. I made her wonder if Mr. Martin had lied to her, if Emma had been alive and if he had conspired with me to hide her. It took time to do this. It took the FBI investigation. It took the small pieces of evidence they found. It took the necklace. It took Lisa Jennings and the affair she had with Mr. Martin. But it also took the gift from Dr. Winter—the lie that Emma had been found—to turn that switch for the last time.

The local district attorney considered bringing charges against me because I had obstructed justice and lied to the authorities. But there was too much sympathy for me in our community and they thought it would fuel Mrs. Martin's defense of entrapment.

He wasn't wrong to want to charge me. I had lied to everyone, including my own father, my poor father who will never get over the death of his eldest daughter and the guilt he carries for leaving us in that house where she was killed. I lied to my mother and Hunter and Mr. Martin. I lied to Dr. Winter and Agent Strauss and the other agents—about Emma and the baby and, finally, about not knowing who had killed Richard Foley. And about my daughter. I lied I lied I lied.

But telling the truth is not on my list.

When the case was over, I left my father's house, where I had been staying since the night we found Emma in her grave. I told my father I wanted to live with Witt and his wife and take some classes in New York. I told him I needed not to be in this town where my sister died. I told him I would see him all the time, anytime he wanted. And someday soon, I will tell him about my daughter. I will have to tell everyone because she cannot live in the shadows. I will tell them she is the daughter of a stranger, some man I met in New York after I ran away. It doesn't matter. She will not be the child of Hunter Martin.

Witt gave me a huge hug when I walked in the door. He

started to cry and he told me we would only look forward from now on. No looking back. I nodded and told him how grateful I was to him for keeping my secret and for taking care of my baby while I was tricking my mother. He laughed and said that his wife now wanted a child after having one all these months and so I owed him "big-time" because he had planned on a few more years of being free.

I heard a different kind of cry come from up the stairs. Then I heard little feet running and then I saw little blond curls flopping on a little round face that was smiling.

I took my daughter in my arms and I squeezed her so tight. I kissed her face and I pressed my cheek against her cheek and felt her skin and smelled her smell and let her fill me again with hope.

I knew I would have to learn to live with it—the hope and the fear always together.

The hope is easy. I believe children do that to us. They make us have it because without it, my God, can you imagine? Looking at your child without hope for the future would be like feeling the sun on your face five billion years from now.

It's the fear that is hard. It's hard because I know what's inside me. The scream my mother put inside me, which got bigger and bigger. The scream her parents put inside her. The scream I fear is inside my daughter after all that she's been through, that maybe I put inside her.

It has also been explained to me that my mother is a pathological narcissist, which means the scream inside her got so big, she had to become someone else, the prettiest girl in the world, the smartest woman in the world, and the best mother in the world. And she had to make everyone love her that way by using every weapon she had. Sex. Cruelty. Fear. This makes sense to me and I understand it. But it does not give me any comfort.

They say sociopaths are created in early childhood. They say we are all formed by age three. I like to think that I got my daughter away in time. I know what I did to my sister by thirsting for power and escalating the war that led to her death. I know what I did to Rick, the boatman. I know what I did to my mother and Jonathan Martin. And I know what I did to Dr. Winter, making her lie and live with that lie forever, risking her career. I have added to my list making amends with her because she saw me, understood me and knew what to do to find Emma. This is a gift I can never repay.

I know all these things I've done and so I know what's inside me and how it got there. And so when I look at my daughter, this beautiful child, I have hope but also fear.

"Mommy," she said. And I looked at my brother, surprised. For her entire life, she has only known me as Cass.

"I've been showing her your picture," he said with a big smile. "I've been telling her your name, your real name, is *Mommy*."

I kissed her again. My face was drenched in tears.

My list is very long now. It is filled with the things I will do and will not do to protect her from what might be inside her and to protect her from what I know is inside me. I will dedicate my life to this list. I will do that for my child and to honor my dead sister.

"And what should I call you?" I asked her. She had been named Julia and I had called her that because it felt cruel not to.

But then she answered, "Emma!"

"I taught her that as well," Witt said.

"Emma!" I cried back to her. "That's right. Your name is Emma. And my name is Mommy. We were just playing a game before. But now the game is over. Now we've come home."

My heart was, all at once, full.

"I love you!" I said. And I knew that I mean it in the purest, most perfect way. When I hold her, I feel my sister, my first Emma, when she would come to me in the night, when we felt safe and love felt possible.

I will cling to that now, like the boat that finally brought me home.

Acknowledgments

It is a precarious endeavor to write a novel about a psychologically disturbed family, as the most obvious question that arises is whether it is based on my own life. So it must be said, first and foremost, that I have a selfless and loving mother who bears no resemblance to Judy Martin. Not only is Terrilynne Walker my biggest fan, she is a frequent visitor to local bookstores where my novels often (and mysteriously) find themselves on the front displays well after their publication dates. If anything from my life shaped *Emma in the Night*, it is the bond between the Walker siblings that our mother helped forge and which became the inspiration for the relationship between Cass and Emma. As always, I am eternally grateful to my family.

I have been so fortunate to have had such incredible guidance and support in the writing and rewriting (and rewriting!) of *Emma in the Night*. My brilliant editor at St. Martin's Press, Jennifer Enderlin, worked tirelessly to reshape and refine the story—reading draft after draft—until I finally got it right. Beside me the whole way, also reading multiple drafts and assuaging the inevitable doubt that creeps in when a story is being written, was my agent, Wendy

Sherman. Without these two talented (and patient) women, this book would not have come to fruition.

To the entire team at St. Martin's Press, including Lisa Senz, Dori Weintraub, Brant Janeway, Erica Martirano and Anne Marie Tallberg, thank you for your enthusiasm and tireless work publishing and promoting my work.

Thanks also to Jenny Meyer for bringing the novel into countries around the globe, and to Michelle Weiner at CAA, who always has a vision to bring my work to film and television.

On the technical front, I was so fortunate to have experts educate me about narcissistic personality disorder and FBI forensics. As always, I took some liberties to make the story work, but all of you helped keep me in the ballpark! So, many thanks to Dr. Felicia Rozek, Ph.D., Dr. Daniel Shaw, and Special Agents Robert and Beth Iorio, NCIS (Retired).

It has been such a pleasure to be on the road promoting my work with other authors and industry professionals. In particular, Carol Fitzgerald at Bookreporter.com—thank you for your boundless energy and expert advice about navigating social media and the retail world. Barbara Shapiro—thank you for your generosity and friendship as you travel the globe promoting your beautiful novels. I feel blessed to be a part of this industry.

To Andrew, Ben and Christopher—my beloved boys—thank you for filling my life with joy each and every day.